Tender Misdemeanors

by

Alana Lorens

Tender Misdemeanors

Cover Art by *Kim Mendoza*

The Wild Rose Press, Inc.
PO Box 708
Adams Basin, NY 14410-0708
Visit us at www.thewildrosepress.com

Publishing History
First Crimson Rose Edition, 2020
Print ISBN 978-1-5092-2939-0
Digital ISBN 978-1-5092-2940-6

Published in the United States of America

Levi leaned back in the chair, eyed closed. He took a deep, slow breath. "The group is splintering over the level of violence which they're willing to use. As I said, we began with the idea we could do some minor monkeywrenching and leave it at that. But there's an element of the group that wants to go farther." He gestured to the pictures. "I have consistently advised against such action and made it clear that if it were to occur, that I would disassociate myself from the group."

"How convenient." Mike's tone was dry and disbelieving.

Levi tensed so fast Caryn didn't even notice until his fist crashed onto the tabletop. "Convenient? It's not at all convenient. Look at this mess. A couple of troublemakers destroy the possibilities of saving the forests and kill innocents in the process! It's a travesty."

"What troublemakers?" Caryn asked. "Who are they? Help us get them off the land so these murders stop now."

"Murder?" Levi blinked at her.

"If someone dies during the commission of a felony—which these ecoterrorist acts are—then they can be charged with murder," Caryn explained. "Even if there was no intent to kill."

Mike sat up straight, then angled his tall body a little closer to Levi. "So are you willing to be an accessory to murder? Or are you going to come clean and let us know who's behind this?"

Mike was coming on a little heavy-handed, but Caryn was glad he had taken on the role of inquisitor. If she were to be true to her oath, she had to prosecute this case to the fullest extent. *No matter what I think about Levi Bradshaw as a man.*

Praise for Alana Lorens

Alana Lorens' most recent awards include a fourth-place win in the annual *Carolina Woman* magazine 2019 contest. She has also received multiple wins in the Pennwriters' annual contests, as well as first place wins in flash fiction contests across the country since her first story acceptance at age eighteen.

~~

Acknowledgments

Thanks to my editor Ally Robertson for her support of this book and the others she's done for me and the Wild Rose Press. Always a pleasure working with you!

A special thanks to Jay Zimmerman, of Meadville, Pennsylvania, who invited me to meet his pet iguana and shared all sorts of good information so I could make Niabi the treat she was.

Thank you as always to the Fellowship of the Quill writers group in Erie, PA, who shepherded me through the first half of this book, always with respect and loving support—Terry Dawley, Christy Reuling, Kathy Otten, Todd Main, Judy Bosley, Amy Bovaird, David Szymanowski, Chuck Becker, Rebecca Frank, and the others. You are the best critique group ever!

A special, special gratitude to Eleanor Yarboro, who singlehandedly helped relight the spark in my creative soul so I could get this story finished. She pushed and prodded and encouraged until I finished birthing it. I'm proud of her work and mine in delivering this love story to you, the reader.

Dedication

For everyone who follows their heart,
even when it crosses forbidden lines

"Love is friendship that has caught fire. It is quiet understanding, mutual confidence, sharing and forgiving. It is loyalty through good and bad times. It settles for less than perfection and makes allowances for human weaknesses."

~*Ann Landers*

"A wolf pack: the first three are the old or sick; they give the pace to the entire pack. If it was the other way round, they would be left behind, losing contact with the pack. In case of an ambush, they would be sacrificed. Then come five strong ones, the front line. In the center are the rest of the pack members, then the five strongest following. Last is alone, the alpha. He controls everything from the rear. In that position he can see everything, decide the direction. He sees all of the pack. The pack moves according to the elders' pace and help each other, watch each other."

Chapter One

Nerves on edge, Caryn Orlane inched forward, angling off the path to track the repetitive hollow metal clang of heavy hammers on steel ahead. Rumor had it that the terrorists were working nearby, but she hadn't expected to find them on her day off. The telltale sound told her exactly what was going on.

Ecotage.

Her mid-afternoon hike through the thick old-growth Montana south of the dam started out peaceful. She'd noted the location of an eagles' nest for the naturalists back at the ranger's office. Stretching legs cramped from a few days of desk duty at the Bureau of Land Management, she'd let loose and run along the hard dirt paths. Everything was fine, until she'd found this.

She respected the ecotagers' goals, which mirrored her own—to protect and save the old forests from reckless commercial exploitation. But these radicals rose to terrorist level in the eyes of the FBI and the BLM. The actions of eco-saboteurs cost millions in property damage, and worse, the lives of innocent people. They had to be stopped.

Carefully avoiding the myriad pinecones on the trail, she paused behind a large Douglas fir, then leaned out to spy ahead. Movement caught her eye. Fifty feet away, a dozen people dressed in camouflage, faces covered by ski masks, stood at varying heights on ladders propped against trees, tools in hand, pounding against the trunks.

She knew what she'd find after they'd gone: six-inch steel pins buried in the wood, heads removed, hidden there to be discovered only when loggers took a saw to them. When taking the trees down, if the logger's saw hit a spike, the blade could crack and break, usually causing costly delays, but sometimes bloody injuries. Those spiking the trees at a significant height would intend to target the log mill workers, where high speed blades could shatter, maiming

Wanting an exact count on the perps, she moved closer and ducked behind a tree. Still too far away. Another thick trunk stood some fifteen feet closer to the activity. She took a deep breath, then ducking down low, she tread as lightly as she could, negotiating the viny undergrowth, until she'd achieved her objective.

Hidden behind the tree, she dared to peek out again. Even though she thought she'd made an ungodly amount of noise, no one seemed to notice. *Probably couldn't hear with all that pounding going on.* A small clearing lay before her filled with buckets, tools, paint cans and brushes, either spiking the trees or painting them with large orange Xs.

That was the thing. At least the monkeywrenchers played fair. The markings warned the loggers which trees might be spiked, to avoid as much injury as possible. Hence the name "monkeywrenchers"—their acts threw a wrench into the works. Often anonymous calls would be made to law enforcement, alerting them that a particular stand of trees had been targeted, likely one that had been set for harvest. At some point, the potential cost of working around the damage rose above the estimated profit, and the harvest was abandoned. Trees saved. A righteous goal.

Caryn had to respect that. She understood the majesty of these forests that had seen so many seasons come and go, generations of Native Americans, settlers, all the wildlife that existed here. It pained her heart as well.

Even before Logan Pass had opened this year in Glacier National Park, some twenty miles north, reports of new ecotage had begun to filter in ahead of a planned sale of land just south of the Hungry Horse Dam to a logging concern. The forest might be precious, but these acts were still against the law.

She popped the tab on her Glock's holster. This was the kind of evidence her office had been looking for since the snow started melting in May. She had to bust them. Counting again, she realized there was no way she could arrest this group by herself. At the same time, she didn't want to spook them. Better to catch them in the act.

She pulled back and texted the BLM a terse message with her GPS coordinates.

—Monkeywrenching in process. Get here ASAP with backup—

Despite the difficulty of identifying masked perps, documentation never hurt. Clothing, even body shapes could be recognized in the investigative process. She used her cell phone to snap pictures of the scene. At least she'd have something to show the federal prosecutor.

After she had a complete record, she leaned against the rough tree bark, its thick striations rough even through her fleece vest. That alone told her the tree was old, perhaps two hundred years or more. Her father had taught both Caryn and her sister Trescha a deep respect for nature and lives that long surpassed humans' time on the planet.

Of course, I carry a gun, defending natural rights, and my wacky sister worships trees in pagan ceremonies and burns sage to combat potential enemies...

Her cell vibrated, drawing her attention away from her dysfunctional family and back to the scene. She checked the message.

—-*On our way with sheriff deputies. Sit tight. Don't you let them escape.*—-

Robert Novio's terse admonition came across as smugly as if he'd spoken aloud. Where did he get off bossing her around? They'd been hired the same week by the law enforcement branch of the BLM in Kalispell. Just because he went everywhere in spit-and-polish, and she preferred to dress down to blend into the local populace...it didn't make him her superior by any means.

Trying to ignore the irritation that burned up through her, she checked the time. Ten minutes since her original call. Adrenaline coursing through her veins made the wait awfully difficult. Her very skin twitched with a need for activity. She breathed slowly, in, out, in, out, the sounds of illegal activity continuing behind her.

Where the hell were Robert and his team?

Frustrated, she stood up, trying to get the adrenaline jitters out of her legs. A red-tailed hawk dove into the trees from above, then when it spotted her, wheeled about and took off upward. The distraction mesmerized her, then slowly she noticed a decrease in the noise level behind her. She leaned around the tree again to check on everyone's whereabouts so she could report to Robert when he finally showed up. The ecotagers seemed to be winding down, collecting the paintbrushes in a bucket, folding up the ladders.

No! We're going to lose them!

Thinking only of the missed opportunity about to take place, she stepped forward. A dog barked, and she froze. She spotted the animal across the clearing, at least three feet tall, short russet hair with a brown nose and amber eyes. It appeared to be mostly muscle, except for the whorled ridge of hair along its midback. No question the dog had seen her as well. Still barking, it bolted toward her at an alarming rate of speed.

Instinct drove her into retreat; she wouldn't shoot the dog unless she had to. Quick flashes of the scene as she ran showed the men snatching their equipment, scattering into the woods.

Damn, damn, damn!

Watching over her shoulder, she missed a thick fallen log in her path and tripped over it, falling hard on the ground, her breath snatched away for a few moments. The impact knocked the gun from her hand, and she struggled to retrieve it as the dog came crashing through the brush. It landed squarely on her, still barking, its nails driving into her back, its hot breath in her ear. She expected to feel the sharp bite of teeth at any moment. Desperate, her fingers quested forward for the gun.

A shrill whistle sounded off to her right. "Rosie, what have you got there?"

The dog bounded off her. Caryn lurched for the

gun, then shoved herself up into a seated position, holding her weapon in both hands. The person who had spoken appeared in her sights. Aware of the panting animal not three feet away, she couldn't spare a look, her attention focused on the man.

Nearly six feet tall (or was it just her perspective from the ground?), he stared down at her, seemingly in shock. Thick dark hair lay tousled across his brow, as though he'd just removed one of those ski masks. He wore a simple red plaid flannel shirt and denim jeans, with heavy nut-colored work boots. His build was athletic, and she guessed there was plenty of muscle under the fabric of his shirt and his padded black ski vest. He could have been a model in one of those outdoorsy catalogs, a perfect example of a rugged, handsome western mountain man.

At first, his warm brown eyes captured her interest. But second, his quick movement brought a handgun of his own from behind him, perhaps tucked into his belt, and he pointed it directly at her.

They remained frozen for several long moments. Caryn felt at an enormous disadvantage on the ground but couldn't move. He'd drawn down on her, so she could justify shooting him. But with so many others he could provide evidence on, she'd be better off with a live suspect. She didn't trust him, though, so she didn't dare put her own gun down. She was stuck.

He studied her, not moving. "So is this where you tell me I'm under arrest for violating any one of a hundred federal laws and clap the handcuffs on?"

His question had an underlayer of humor, almost mocking. It annoyed her. She started to her feet, but the dog growled in a most unpleasant way and she hesitated. "You know this is illegal. What else do you think will come of it?"

"Hopefully, justice. No one has the right to rape the forests."

His voice, full and rich, resonated with righteousness. He tucked the gun away. In the distance, car doors slammed and engines roared to life. They were getting away. All of them. Except this one. At least she might have this one. She gauged the distance between herself and the man. Could she launch herself quickly enough to subdue him before the dog got her?

Her muscles tensed in preparation. He must have noticed, because he took a step back, and whistled again, something sharp and pointed. The dog jumped at her, and she raised an arm to protect her face. Knocking her to her stomach again, the dog hesitated, then suddenly snapped its head up like it was listening before it bounded away to the east.

Caryn was alone.

Ribs aching, she stood, then moved into the clearing. She caught a glimpse of dust on the far side, and a black Avalanche disappearing into it. Nothing else. Just the trees and the painted Xs. At least she had her pictures. Not that they identified much other than the activity.

But it's more than you had before.

Disappointed, she waited for ten more minutes, fumbling for an explanation to give Robert when he arrived. She hadn't meant to alarm the monkeywrenchers. If it hadn't been for that dog...

Or your impatience...

She growled at her inner nag. *No, it was the dog. Rosie. And the dog's owner, the one with the thick hair.*

And those eyes…

Before she could help it, she imagined running her fingers through that hair, touching those full lips, hearing that rumbly baritone voice close to her ear.

Stop that. He's on the other side of the law. Your job is to take him in and let him face his charges.

Don't tell me my damned job.

No matter what she told herself, she couldn't get his face, that intent look, that hint of a smile in his eyes out of her mind. Not even when Robert showed up five minutes later, out of breath from running the distance from the road. He'd brought with him half a dozen cars from the Flathead County Sheriff's office and three guys from the BLM.

"Where are they?" he demanded, face red and eyes blazing.

She took a deep breath, dusting herself off. "Gone."

Chapter Two

Hours later, when they'd run the photos through analysis, they found they didn't have much. Fellow agents Robert Novio, Jessalyn Brown and their boss, Samuel Evans, seemed unconvinced that her actions didn't scrap the bust.

"Look, you know what we do here," Evans growled. "Exactly what our name implies. We manage natural resources. We issue cutting permits to logging concerns. Sometimes it's for the money, but sometimes, Orlane, it does the forest good to clear out the upper canopy."

She avoided his gaze, not wanting even a glimpse of his pot belly, his bald head, his squishy gray pig eyes, his rumpled shirt. During the whole conversation, he'd ignored the blood on her pants leg, her short breaths from her rib area and her scraped face, never once asking if she needed treatment or if she was all right. *All business with him.* Something snapped in her and she opened her mouth to just let him have it.

Jessalyn, her brown hair braided into a bun, wearing a jacket too big for her, stood behind Evans where he couldn't see her. She waved her arms and shook her head. The gesture was easily translated: *Don't.*

Caryn chewed her lip a moment, the sharp edge of her teeth drawing tears to her eyes. *There. Control.*

"Yes, I—"

"But these eco-terrorists, the Earth Liberation Front and Earth First! just muck up the works. I don't care how often they say they marked the trees they spiked—you know as well as I do they're a bunch of lying lawbreakers."

Caryn's foot tapped anxiously against the bare office floor. She prayed her frustration would leak down through that surface into the underworld, where it could power some other nefarious scheme instead of blowing up in her boss's face.

When her tongue seemed to be under her control, she looked up from the floor. "I'm sure I know exactly what we're up against. Thank you so much for the reminder."

Her chin came up, and his expression told her he read exactly how she felt. *Not like it was the first time they'd had this exchange.*

"Orlane…"

She didn't move.

Sam rumbled, "Right. Enough for today. I've already got a headache. Get out of here. But this isn't over."

Caryn didn't wait for a second invitation. "You bet it isn't. Sir." She took a breath, let it out, glanced at Evans, then beelined for the door before her frustration exploded.

Seated in her silver Toyota Tundra, she cranked up the CD player, some classic Kansas, *Dust in the Wind*, letting the sound surround and fill her. After several moments soaking in the vibrations, she set the truck into gear and left the parking lot, taking Route 2 east to the Mountain View campground where her motor home was parked, just outside the tiny town of Hungry Horse.

As the music swirled around her in the closed cab, she focused her attention on the scenery outside. Montana held some of the most beautiful terrain she'd ever seen in her traveling life, deep green forests along crystal blue waters, and along every horizon, the mountains for which the state was named laid a counterpoint to the lowlands. Even this late in the year, the tops of the huge granite crags were frosted with a dollop of snow. Caryn had come to terms with the annual seven months of winter each of the three years she'd been stationed there. She just got used to wearing layers of clothing year-round. One of these days, she'd promised herself she would take up winter sports, skiing and ice fishing. But for now, work kept her pretty busy.

Not like she had a love life, either.

"I hardly need one," she muttered as she pulled off the main road onto the dirt path that led back to her home.

But scarcely had she thought of the subject of romance when the face of her drawdown opponent clicked into her mind. She remembered every detail of his countenance, right down to the faint scar on his left cheek. She knew she'd never seen him before; why did he seem so completely familiar?

Maybe he's part of the FBI most wanted posters in the back room of the office. Now there's a great place to snag your next boyfriend...

A growl escaping her, she pulled the truck behind the twenty-seven-foot motor home she'd named *Serenity,* her home since she'd left Humboldt State University in northern California. That piece of paper she received at the conclusion of her degreed education was supposed to open the door to the job of her dreams: Special Agent for the Federal Bureau of Investigation. But it hadn't. So she'd taken her graduation money, bought a house on wheels and headed out for anywhere that would have her. She was in the best shape of her life—well, except for those few weeks before she applied for the FBI slot—and she'd take on anyone in a fight, fair or otherwise. Her quick temper made that happen more often than not. She was ready for these criminals.

She unlocked the door, her eyes scanning for anything out of place. As the last camper parked in the row, closest to the foot of the mountain, deepest in the trees, she had a good deal of privacy. No one really came back here. That suited her just fine.

Carefully opening the door just enough to squeeze through, she tossed her bag onto the fold-out sofa. She closed the door tight behind her, her eyes flicking up to the shelf in the front over the cab, then to the rear of the camper, where her double bed lay unmade, blankets twisted and tangled. The windows on both sides were open, a cool breeze coming through the screens as dusk approached. She clicked her tongue a couple of times and flipped on the light over the tiny sink set into the kitchen counter.

A light thud came from the bedroom, followed by the scritch of nails against the linoleum floor. A three-foot green scaled iguana shimmied up the bench seat at the table and jumped across to the sink, head cocked, eyes blinking in her direction.

"At least you're glad to see me." Caryn scratched the lizard along the spikes at the top of its back. "You don't think I'm a major screw-up, do you?"

She studied her companion, who just closed her eyes, basking in the attention. *Not like Niabi would point out her owner's flaws, now would she? Inside* Serenity*, she had everything she needed—her cage, her favorite pine branch, her 'swimming pool', her—*

Caryn yelped as Niabi's ridged jaw clamped down on her finger. Startled, she jerked back. The bite hadn't broken the skin—iguanas didn't have teeth, per se, but they could still do a lot of damage, and it had happened once or twice. Clearly her pet was not happy. "What?"

She glanced behind her to the five-foot cage that sat over the driver's seat in the cab and noted the hollow emptiness of the feeding dish. "Ah-ha. Mystery solved." Watching the hungry iguana to avoid a further attack, she skirted the narrow counter, reaching into the cupboard over the sink for a box of dates. She set one on the counter near Niabi. "This should hold you."

Another skitter of nails and Niabi was across the room, perched on the back rim of the sofa, busily chewing the dried fruit, one eye fixed on Caryn.

"All right, I'm getting it, I'm getting it." Okay, so maybe Niabi had jumped on the "Caryn's a major screw-up" bandwagon with the rest of the people Caryn knew. The more the merrier, huh?

She opened the small refrigerator, taking out a clump of swiss chard and collard greens, slicing them into bite-size pieces. Adding an apple wedge and a handful of frozen mixed vegetables, she put the meal into Niabi's dish in the cage, checking to make sure the overhead lights focused enough heat into the cage area to keep the cold-blooded creature warm. One disadvantage of living in the camper was the volatility

13

of daytime temperatures, particularly if she was away.

Also the smell of the undercage tray. Her nose twitched at the sharp odor. When had she cleaned it last? She tended to that next.

With Niabi happy, Caryn took care of her own needs in the tiny bathroom, then got herself some icy green tea with ginger, its sharp bite satisfying her thirst. She scooted into one of the bench seats at the table, looking through the mail she'd picked up at the post office box in town. Two magazines she'd never have time to read, her lot rent bill from the campground. Alumni organizations asking for money. Charities asking for money. Political campaigns asking for money.

Disappointed, she tossed them aside. Everything was about money, right? Those who had, and those who didn't. Whether the number was one percent or forty-seven percent or ninety-nine percent, everything hinged on the desires of those who had enough money to throw around. Like the logging concern that had purchased the rights to those trees in the Hungry Horse district. Despite Sam's rationalization that cutting some old growth would promote strong new growth of the younger trees coming along, Caryn regretted the loss of these towering wonders of nature.

But just because she felt sad didn't spur her to try to kill people.

The thought brought her back to her mystery opponent, the one she couldn't seem to forget. In those few seconds they'd faced off against each other, she'd sensed a strength in him and a solidity that many of the other monkeywrenchers didn't have. She wondered who he was. Her contact with the breed as a whole showed that while they came from a true cross-section of people, a lot were skinny, self-sacrificing, educated types without much in the way of roots. They firmly believed in what they were doing, just as Thoreau had a hundred and fifty years earlier, when urging his readers to civil disobedience when they found a government overreaching its bounds. Thoreau would have loved the Patriot Act, huh?

With a wry grin, Caryn looked again in the refrigerator for something to feed herself with. The search didn't take long; beyond Niabi's leafy greens, the shelves were mostly empty. She grabbed an organic yogurt and an orange, taking them outside to eat at the picnic table provided by the park, letting her gaze move on to the mountains that surrounded her on three sides. Deep breaths of pine-scented air calmed her and let her know that she could release the day for now. Work could be left till tomorrow—along with some grocery shopping, if she intended to eat.

But one last plan still haunted her. Definitely one of the first priorities in the morning included a full search through the BLM and other federal resources to nail down the identity of the monkeywrencher with the dog. Why they hadn't shot each other, she didn't know. She'd fully expected it when he'd first pulled out the gun. But he didn't seem to take her presence personally. His attitude seemed to be more something like, *Hey, you're doing your job, and I'm doing mine.* Very different from most of them.

Maybe he was just a minor player, a dilettante along to play protester for a week or two, and he didn't matter to the movement. He'd almost challenged her to arrest him.

And you didn't get the job done.

After the debacle that afternoon, she didn't expect to encounter the stranger. The ecotagers had been discovered and they'd find a new area to terrorize. That should have been the end of it.

But her mind kept returning to him. *Why does it feel like such a great loss if you never saw him again?*

Annoyed, she tossed her empty container and orange peels into the bear-proofed trash can at the end of the *Serenity*.

Time for Niabi's walk. She headed inside to find the iguana's harness and leash. A good half-mile stroll would clear her mind and let her return with a fresh outlook. Maybe she'd even have time to read one of those magazines. Maybe…

Chapter Three

"So who was she, Levi? Homeland Security? FBI? BLM?"

A rumble of voices followed that first question, and everyone turned to Levi Bradshaw for answers. Unfortunately, he had none. Stalling, he glanced at the fire, checking that his dog Rosencrantz was resting somewhere warm and appropriate. The encounter with the gun-toting woman in the forest had wound the dog up, and with a Rhodesian Ridgeback, once that hunting instinct was activated, it took time to dissipate all that adrenaline.

Good thing I only had Rosie and not Guildenstern, too. That poor woman would have been shredded.

After their aborted operation, the monkeywrenchers had reassembled at the log cabin vacation home belonging to one of their junior members' parents. Crowded in, eleven of them in the small space, their sweat-soaked clothing reeking, their faces demanded explanation.

Levi cleared his throat. "I didn't wait around to ask. She wasn't wearing a uniform, and she didn't have a police vest, so maybe none of those."

Alex Sullivan spoke up from where he leaned against a support pole in the back. "Right, because tourists always carry heavy-duty handguns while they're strolling through the woods."

17

Privately, Levi might have agreed, but he hated being called out in front of the group. The rest, especially the new guys, looked up to Levi as the alpha male of this wolf pack. Even though Alex and a couple of the others were strong contenders, they were beta males, and always would be.

"Well, I didn't see you sticking around to check her out, Alex. Looked to me like you grabbed your brushes and ran like hell."

Several of the guys snickered. Alex squirmed, then scowled.

Levi continued, "The important thing is that we all got out without being pinched. We're mostly done with that sector, anyway. If she was establishment, she can bring her people all over that ground. We didn't leave anything. It's a sign we should move on to the job in Billings."

"Yeah, when are we going to do that?" asked a pock-faced, skinny college dropout named Sage. Waiting by the coffeepot, he scratched idly at his torn jeans.

"First team should head out the end of this week. Alex, who are you and Ron taking?"

Recovered from his small smackdown and ready for the limelight, Alex picked up the conversation, nominating five men to travel to Billings with him. As he gave orders and laid out details, Levi took the opportunity to rifle through the refrigerator. It had been a long time since he'd left home in the dark that morning.

Poking through plastic-wrapped packs of lunchmeat and cheese, Levi found his attention wandering from his grumbling stomach, and even from the litany of equipment Alex requisitioned. His thoughts traveled back to that woman. Their encounter had lasted less than five minutes, but her face stuck in his mind.

He hadn't noticed much about her clothes beyond the lack of uniform. That face, though, he remembered. A tanned complexion showed that she spent time outdoors, her cheeks a healthy pink. Her eyes were a peculiar shade of hazel green that hardened into the color of a peridot gem when she was agitated. Hair streaked like a California girl, blonde and loose around her shoulders.

The way she held her gun whispered that she was a professional. But she hadn't shot him when she'd had the opportunity. What were the chances they'd meet again? *None, if you head off to Billings with Alex.*

He couldn't do that, though. Responsibilities at home called him. His pile of environmental consulting requests filled a basket on his desk. These long day trips strained his resources. He'd need to head home today. He could return to Hungry Horse in a few weeks to check on the site. The compelling stranger would have to wait.

"Right, Levi?"

The sound of his name grabbed his wandering attention. "Hmm?"

Alex sounded annoyed. "We're still committed to the final goal, right? Do you have any points I missed in the briefing?"

"I'm sure you've covered it." To justify standing there with the refrigerator door open, he grabbed a package of ham and some rye bread. *What do you think you're doing, mooning over someone whose likely*

19

mission is to lock you up? Are you insane?

He made a show of building a sandwich, adding a slice of tomato and a smear of dark mustard. When he looked up, all eyes were on him. "Anyone else want something to eat?"

Rosie looked up from his place at the fire and barked.

The sound broke the tension in the room, and faces relaxed into smiles. A couple of the guys lit cigarettes, opening a window to let the smoke out. Levi tossed Rosie a thin slice of ham, and he caught it in midair. Sage and some others gathered up their packs, ready to head home.

But the dark cloud on Alex's brow and also on that of Alex's friend Ron Ranning set off a warning buzzer inside Levi's head. While Levi was the ostensible head of this group, Alex and Ron were both members of the local militia, too, and often had more direct solutions in mind than painting warning markers on spiked trees. They had an extensive knowledge of explosives, and an incredible arsenal in their underground bunker outside Missoula. Some days it was all Levi could do to ride herd and keep them from taking matters into their own hands.

"Look, Alex, I'll handle this. Take the team on to the next site, and I'll scope out this woman, find out if we should be worried. It *is* possible she just packs because of wild mountain men and kidnappers. Ever since that movie came out—"

Ron growled a dissent. "Yeah, but she's not Kristy whats-her-name."

He looked fully ready to restart the argument, the others tuning in to watch the battle.

"I said I'd handle it," Levi said, in a tone he hoped meant the end of the conversation. He took a bite of his sandwich and stared the others down. His hunger had faded by the end of the conversation, but he kept eating, forcing himself to appear unconcerned. His gaze fell on Alex, who crossed his arms and stared back a long moment before he shrugged it off.

"You heard Levi. Let's get the gear packed."

Once orders were given, those undecided snapped into action. Within five minutes, the team heading to Billings was out the door, and Levi was left to lock up.

A long sigh was the only sound other than the crackling of the dying fire. Levi cleaned up the mess from his sandwich, then checked the whole cabin for any detritus of the group's passing. Bobby's parents would probably put up a fuss about them using the place if it wasn't kept in decent condition. Having a getaway hideout so close was certainly a blessing. And better than Levi's place.

He put out the fire. "Come on, Rosie. Let's go home."

The dog snapped to his feet, bounding to the door. Levi opened it and let him out. He started barking as soon as he cleared the door and headed down the driveway.

What now?

Wondering if thirty-five years old was too old for this game, Levi shoved his arm through the strap of his backpack and hurried after Rosie.

He didn't have to go far. Ron leaned against the left front fender of Levi's black Avalanche. His boots were fine-tooled cowboy style, not work boots, and the denim jeans he wore came from a high-priced specialty store, not the local Big-Mart. His square-jawed face was set in disapproval.

"Did you forget something, Ron?"

Ron's beady dark eyes focused on him like laser sights. "Not me, Leev. But I'm really wondering about you. I remember a time that you would have put up a fight when someone stood in the way of the group's mission."

Where was Ron going with this? "'Stand in the way'? Who's standing in our way, Ron? We did exactly what we set out to do out by the dam. That logging company won't dare harvest those trees—not as many as we spiked and marked."

"What about the woman?"

Again with the woman. He tried not to roll his eyes. "What about her?"

"Oh, come on, Leev. She was clearly law enforcement. We could have buried her out there. Who would have known?"

Levi's throat closed up. *Murder? Cold-blooded murder? Not on his watch.* He'd never killed as part of his eco-activities, and he didn't intend to start. All he could do was shake his head.

"You getting soft?"

The question raised the hackles on his neck. He cleared his throat. "You getting ridiculous? We aren't in this to kill people. We're here to save the planet."

Rosie came up and sniffed at his hand, looking between him and Ron, eyes troubled. Levi patted the dog, scratching behind his ears for reassurance.

"We're committed to working in non-violent protest, aren't we? We've purposely separated ourselves from ELF and the others, their attacks on buildings and businesses, the bombings and the fires." He studied Ron's impassive expression. "Haven't we?"

"And big corporations are still cutting the trees down. The animals are losing their habitat faster than they can even breed. The rain forests are nearly gone. Climate change guts the landscape, and no one cares as long as the profits keep coming in."

This was Ron's standard rhetoric, nothing new to Levi's ears. *Also not something that would make him hang behind to confront me...after the others had gone. Might this be a veiled challenge to my leadership?*

Over a woman?

It couldn't be. It had to be some kind of red herring. Ron had grabbed whatever excuse he could to pound his chest a little. The fact he hadn't done it while Alex was still present showed he hadn't lost his sense of place in the universe altogether. Levi just needed to set him straight. He clapped Ron on the shoulder, a smile on his face.

"We're still on the same path, friend. It's good that you shared this with me. I'll handle this intruder. I've got something in mind. You go on now."

Ron opened his mouth, but Levi turned his back on his companion, opening the truck door for Rosie to jump in. He followed the dog inside and shut the door, its window still open. "Go on. I'll be in touch." He slipped the key in the ignition and turned it, the engine roaring to life.

He pulled away, leaving Ron standing in the middle of the driveway, brooding. That wasn't the end of that argument. But it was all he was having today.

He swung out onto Route 93, heading north. Whitefish was a good thirty-minute drive, and he had to cross over the bridge on the far side before he'd be home. Home. If you could call it that.

The house was located halfway up Big Mountain, a failed dream known by the locals as the Candy Cane house. The huge red and black Victorian had appealed to his parents some fifteen years before, and they'd sunk both their retirement accounts into buying the place at a foreclosure sale, with the hope of turning it into a bed and breakfast or other guest house, intending to cater to all the skiers and other winter sports enthusiasts who frequented the northwestern Montana area.

But within six months, Levi's father had been diagnosed with cancer, absorbing his mother's spare time and certainly all the family's spare money. Levi and his older brother Zane had been left to watch each other.

Zane, being Zane, bailed as soon as he could legally escape the house of sadness, working his way through a state law school, then moved to the California coast. Their father died before he left for college, leaving just enough money to pay Levi's tuition. By the time he'd finished his Masters in Environmental Studies at age 30, his broken-hearted mother passed away, too, leaving this empty monster house for Levi to manage.

"We manage, don't we, Rosie?" He caressed the dog's head, the rough edge of that ridge of hair that ran down his back rubbing against his hand. The dog licked his fingers and seemed to wink. It was enough of an encouragement for Levi. "You love me, as long as I feed you, right? You're not going anywhere."

He turned on the radio to distract himself, just in

time to catch a rant on National Public Radio by one of the Patriot movement leaders, complaining about pressure local governments put on the pro-white organization Pioneer Little Europe. He listened until his blood pressure started to climb, then flipped it off with a muttered curse.

"Exactly what we need here. Not enough problems with the environment and the Native American tribes asserting their rights. Let's sprinkle in a couple communities of white supremacists and set the fuse alight, right, boys?"

Rosie cocked his head like Levi was talking nonsense, and he had to laugh. He opened the heavy wrought iron gate with the remote attached to his sun visor, and pulled into his driveway, which, while fifty feet long, was a clear shot from the gate so passersby could admire the gingerbread trim and fancy touches his mother thought would bring in the guests by the hundreds each winter.

Two more dogs came running from the back: Rosie's brother Guildenstern, a red-colored Ridgeback, and Ophelia, a German short-haired pointer, her short, bristly coat also in the red shades, with a mottling of white down over her hindquarters and onto her legs. She came a little slower, victim of a perpetual limp after she'd been hit on the road outside the house, but was twice as affectionate, seeking Levi's attention as he climbed out of the cab.

"Hey, there! Hey, there." Levi barely got out of Rosie's way as he bounded out of the truck to rendezvous with his brother, both of them barking merrily as they connected and sniffed each other. Levi scratched Ophelia down her neck and back, noting she'd been out mud-rolling somewhere. She'd need a bath tonight.

What else did he have planned for the evening anyway, hmm? Some reading by the fire. A whole pile of Freedom Of Information Act releases awaited him on his desk, all requested over the last six months, trying to figure out where the BLM was going to try to pull a fast one next, wiping out a whole stand of old growth before anyone could catch them. Billings might be the next target, but it surely wouldn't be the last.

He let the dogs inside, the echoing tap-tap-tap of their nails scattering against the unfinished wooden floors. Even in June, a damp chill filled the interior of the house, probably because so much of it wasn't finished. No insulation or storm windows in some of the upstairs rooms let in cool night air. He closed and locked the doors, then took the left side hallway, walking to the great room to light a fire.

Stacking the logs with the ease of years of experience, he tucked in bits of newspaper and old survey maps around the twigs at the bottom, then lit it. While waiting for the room to warm, he went to the kitchen and filled the dogs' water and food bowls, their enthusiasm expressed in loud yips and staunchly wagging tails, their toes tapping with excitement in their little "food dance." He wished he could be as excited about his own meal, but there was little that appealed to him in the refrigerator beyond some Black Star, the specialty beer of the local microbrewery. He grabbed two bottles and headed back to the great room, to begin reading at his desk, near the fire.

Two hours later, he took off his reading glasses, his eyes burning. All three dogs lay on the rug before the fire, coiled in various poses of sleep. Yeah, not such a bad idea. They'd started pretty early in the woods today.

He glanced across at the antique sofa, its bronze flowered brocade flickering as it reflected the firelight. He remembered his mother sitting there, covered in a knitted blanket she'd made with her own hands, reading, or listening to his father read aloud in the evening. They were big on education, his parents. Probably why his poor pets got stuck with those Shakespearean names. The family never had a television while Levi and Zane were growing up, though Levi had a small LCD set in his bedroom now, mostly just to catch the news and weather. He could almost see her sitting there now, her blonde hair—

Hang on a minute.

He realized belatedly that it wasn't his mother he was picturing there at all, but the woman from the forest. Could someone from the other side ever be a friend? He didn't see how. Certainly he wouldn't imagine that she'd lounge on his couch, sharing the fading embers of his evening fire.

There are more things in heaven and earth, Horatio, than are dreamt of in your philosophy...

He grinned. He couldn't explain it either. So he'd just let that picture lie. No one ever really knew what might happen on the next day of their life, right?

"Come on, dogs. Let's hit the hay."

The three canines joyously bounding around him, they headed up the open stairway to call it a night.

Chapter Four

The BLM team went out to the spiked site first thing the next morning, but after two hours of pacing through the area, none of them could find a trace of evidence to identify the monkeywrenchers that had attacked the forest, not even an abandoned paintbrush or bucket handle that might have fingerprints. A metal detector sweep showed dozens of steel pins in the trees at varying heights. It would take hours to dig them all out before the wood could be harvested, more work-intensive hours than perhaps this particular logger might want to invest when there were more attractive sites elsewhere.

Robert surveyed the scene, pinpointing the place where Caryn had taken a header. "Huh. Pretty large dog prints. Sure it wasn't Bigfoot?"

Caryn eyed him, wishing her anger could physically scar him. Just a little. "Could have been, I suppose. Why don't you check my report?"

Jessalyn pointedly turned away, focusing her attention elsewhere to hide her grin.

Caryn silently decried Jessalyn's lack of support and changed the subject. "Nothing more to be found here. I suggest we split up and follow the tracks from their parking area over on the north side of the clearing." She studied the CSI report. "Tire tracks show some heavy vehicles, trucks, SUVs likely. I know I spotted a black Chevy Avalanche."

Robert blew air between his lips, just missing a whistle. "Imagine that. A whole fleet of rugged four-wheel drivers out here in the mountain lands. Who'd have thought?"

"Bite me, Bob."

Caryn turned away and marched back to her truck. Sure, it was a long shot. But they had at least a chance that the group traveled in a pack. Maybe they were sitting down at the Huckleberry House right now, having some coffee and pie, making new plans. *Beat the hell out of walking around in the woods without a clue left behind.*

She headed into the tiny town of Hungry Horse, where its population of under a thousand built their lives close to the edges of the state highway, clinging to the thoroughfare like a shy child. Her sharp eyes caught nothing out of the ordinary, just the usual parade of carved red folk-art horses that seemed to decorate everything from the post office to the café's front yard. Plenty of SUVs parked at the supermarket, like Robert had said, but none of them set off her internal radar.

She drove ten minutes northeast to the next small city, Columbia Falls, five times the size of Hungry Horse, with a lot more to pull in visitors and locals alike. Known as the Gateway to Glacier National Park, the city also housed a genuine tourist attraction, the Montana Vortex, which demonstrated the effects of earth energies moving up from the earth, with twisted tree trunks and odd magnetic properties. Rafting companies and fishing excursions flourished in the summer, and skiing and other winter sports after the snow fell. Caryn liked the place. A couple of bars hosted local bands who helped her waste some lonely nights away, and the fresh produce all through the summer at Wild Rose kept both her and Niabi eating healthy.

Route 2 was busy for a Thursday morning. Vacationers by the hundreds would cut through town, probably not even giving its many restored Victorians a second look on their way to the park. Caryn was just about to quit when she spotted a black Avalanche parked outside Montana Coffee Traders. She noted the Sierra Club sticker on the right side of the back window and realized she recognized it. Her gut pinged.

Got you, you bastard.

A smile creeping onto her lips, she pulled in around the corner from the other vehicle, checking to see if it was occupied before she left her own truck. *Now let's see who might be here, ready to take a fall for that bad action yesterday...*

The interior of the café was dim after the bright sunlight outside. When her eyes adjusted, she admired the place built to appear rustic, with redwood paneling, its tables rough-hewn out of thick cut wood. Busy serving staff scooted through the crowded tables, heavy trays loaded with steaming food and cups. The clatter of dishes came from the back, occasionally punctuating the buzz of breakfast conversation.

Caryn couldn't resist the smell of fresh-ground coffee that permeated the place, so she slipped onto the last stool at the counter, making sure she could see most of the tables. Northwestern Montana was a mecca for fresh ground, high-quality coffee, as evidenced by the myriad coffee shops, even those that seemed to pop up on street corners in small, brightly painted sheds where those in need of a caffeine fix could just drive up to be served. Hard to pass up the goodness.

The thin, blonde waitress behind the counter stopped her multi-tasking long enough to smile at Caryn. Something about those too-blue eyes screamed contact lenses, and Caryn recognized her from prior visits to the restaurant.

"What'll it be, hon?"

"What's the flavor today?"

The waitress glanced over her shoulder. "Organic Mexican dark roast."

"Perfect. Large, cream. No sugar."

"You got it." She scribbled a note just as the cook yelled out, "Judy!"

"I'm coming, I'm coming," she muttered, with a wink at Caryn. "Men. No damn patience, you know?" She pocketed her notepad and disappeared into the back.

Yeah, sister, I know.

Caryn let her gaze lightly frisk the restaurant's patrons, a little more intent than a sweeping glance. She wanted to get a good feel for each and every person there. It was, of course, entirely possible that the Avalanche outside belonged to someone who wasn't even at the tainted site yesterday. Could have been a borrowed car. Could have been a rental, even. But her gut told her that she'd learn something before she left this room...

There, in the back corner. Seated at a two-top, alone, reading the morning paper.

Unbelievable.

It was the man with the dog. Well, not *with* the dog, since animals weren't allowed in here. But no question it was him. The face that had even appeared in her dream last night. Somehow in that moment when they stared each other down, ready to shoot, it had burned that visage onto her memory engrams forever.

Judy came out, pausing to unload a cup of coffee from her full tray for Caryn before continuing on to deliver the orders she carried. She came back for some ketchup and a stack of jelly, then paused behind the counter.

"Nice to look at, isn't he?" Judy said, a smirk on her face. She jerked her head in the man's direction.

Glad once again she wore plain clothes, Caryn grinned. "Sure is. Who is he?"

"Levi Bradshaw. Lives up on Big Mountain outside Whitefish."

She asked, "He looks pretty tough. Is he with one of the logging companies?"

Judy snorted. "Levi, a lumberjack? Ha, that's rare! Pretty much the opposite of that, honey." The customers waiting for their condiments waved impatiently, and she excused herself to deliver them.

Caryn pulled out her cell, running a quick criminal record check for Levi Bradshaw of Big Mountain, Montana through NCIC and the state CJIS. While she waited for results, she sipped her cooling coffee, which was top of the line.

Nothing significant came up on her search. Not even an arrest for suspected terrorism. Just a single DUI some seven years before that had been routed into the alternative resolution track and expunged. Her boy was clean.

So far.

The restaurant was packed. Surely someone known

to the community wouldn't start a scene in here. Especially anything that involved shooting. A quiet confrontation might be all that was needed. Caryn left three dollars on the counter, picked up her coffee and traveled the long way around the room, looking as though she was heading to the ladies'. She noticed as she approached that he was eating one of the best plates Coffee Traders offered, the Big Sky breakfast, grilled potatoes, black beans, avocado, topped with eggs, bacon, cheese, salsa and toast. It looked delicious. She willed her stomach not to growl in envy as she slipped into the chair across from him.

"Seat's taken," he mumbled. When she didn't move, he glanced over the top of his paper and his eyes widened, then flicked side to side. Was he checking the aisles for escape routes? Apparently satisfied, he folded the newspaper and laid it on the table beside his plate. Then he picked up his fork and started eating his breakfast.

"It is now," she said, the smug smile coming to her lips even without her bidding. She toasted him with her coffee cup. "I've got to say, you've got good breakfast taste anyway, even if your usual choice of companions just doesn't measure up."

"No doubt." He speared a forkful of avocado and beans. "What brings you here? Live nearby?"

His lack of concern after that initial look of surprise seemed odd. Why wouldn't he be worried that she had located him? Perhaps buddies of his in the restaurant, too, prepared to protect him? A mirror caught her eye, from which she could see a good portion of the restaurant. No one seemed to be paying particular attention to the two of them at all.

"Just needed some joe."

She studied his actions, even his manners. The way he held his fork, used a napkin, even the timing of his bites showed her he'd been raised at a table where dining etiquette had been clearly enforced. Not what she'd pictured at all, after dealing with some of those supremacist roughnecks.

"Who'd have believed we'd find each other twice in two days? Seems like Fate, right?" His initial shock faded and color returned to his cheeks, along with a mischievous grin.

Ignoring the appeal of that bad-boy smile, Caryn leaned forward and set her cup down. "Not fate at all, Mr. Bradshaw. Justice. I remember how important that sounded to you yesterday."

His fork hung in midair just a moment, then he set it on the edge of his plate. "I'm sorry, I don't think we've been properly introduced." He held out his right hand. "I'm Levi Bradshaw. Which you apparently know. And you are…?"

She took his hand, debating whether she could slap handcuffs on him right here, while she had a grip on him. *No, too many people. I can get him outside.* "Caryn Orlane," she said, taking back her hand as soon as it was polite.

"Caryn. I like that name." He winked and went back to his meal.

She'd been prepared for a number of different outcomes to this encounter, but somehow a calm meal together hadn't been one of them.

He said nothing else while he ate his wheat toast. Conversation continued around them about day care snafus, vacation plans, dog grooming and other personal crises. Caryn heard them like the drone of a beehive on the outside periphery of her conscious listening. Instead, she watched Levi Bradshaw, wondering just what was going on inside his head. He'd obviously recognized her. Did she seem that much less threatening without a weapon in hand? He couldn't just ignore her; she wouldn't allow that.

"What kind of dog is Rosie?" she asked at last.

His chin snapped up so he stared right into her eyes. "My dog? A Rhodesian Ridgeback. The breed originated in Africa, bred to catch lions. They're work dogs." He nodded and took a long sip of coffee, then pushed his empty plate aside. "You know, we're done here."

The statement caught her off guard. So many potential meanings. "I'm sorry?"

"Our work protecting the environment. We'll be gone by the weekend."

She bit her lip, debating her next step. Should she nail him before he could get out of town? Would he turn on the others, so they could all be arrested before more damage was done?

"Who are you, anyway? Not cold enough for Homeland Security, I don't think." He studied her, looking her up and down in a most possessive way that nearly made her blush. "Not uptight enough for FBI. Guess that makes you BLM."

"You're a regular Alex Trebek, aren't you?" She stared him down. "Doesn't really matter what agency I'm with, though. It's your behavior in question, not mine—"

"No!" He leaned closer, his voice wound tight, quiet and intense. "It's not my behavior that's an issue at all. I think you understand that. It's these damned logging companies and the government that lets them come through and destroy our natural heritage. Thousands of animals and people from all walks of life depend on these forests for their daily lives, now and a hundred years from now. Why should anyone own the right to take that away from them? Especially for the almighty buck? That's the outrage, Caryn Orlane. That's the outrage."

Startled at his outburst, she leaned back, almost worried he'd come across the table at her. But he just leaned back in his own chair. The waitress came by with a pot of coffee and offered to refill both their cups in the silence that ensued, then took his plates away.

She wanted to argue with him but couldn't come up with anything off the top of her head. *It shouldn't matter why. You know it shouldn't. The law is the law. You've got to bust him. You have no choice.*

But she still couldn't make words come out of her mouth, or reach in her pocket for her cuffs. A weary look on his face, he watched her, those expressive brown eyes seeming to look right inside her. Finally, he sat up straight, putting his elbows on the table. "Can I tell you something? The honest truth?"

The way his voice softened, she was nearly taken in. He'd confide in her, a woman he'd just established as his enemy? How stupid did he think she was? *Why not let him roll?*

"Sure. Please do."

"Whatever you think of the movement in general, you know there are extremists in every group. You don't know me, so you might believe this and you might not, but I have done my very best to keep that element in check in this group. Some want to pick up where ELF and the others have left off and create open demonstrations of force against these companies, but I've tried to be the voice of reason here. You don't preserve lives through use of bombs, arson and other overt attacks. What might have been done in the woods yesterday was a little warning, nothing more. The company is well aware of what trees are spiked, and can avoid trouble by leaving them alone."

He almost sounded rational. "Oh, really. And you think hammering giant metal spikes into your sacred trees really does them a lot of good?"

"It's a far sight better than having them cut down and sent back east to be sliced into boards." He scowled, adding a very different character to his rugged face. She found it appealed to her almost as much as his smile.

Knock it off, Orlane. This is business. Remember?
"That's not my call."

He nodded. "I know it isn't. All I'm asking is for you to bend a little. You try to keep an open mind. I know you do, because you didn't shoot me yesterday. Not even in the kneecap." A faint smile. "I guarantee you that if you leave this alone, right here, right now, that you won't see us again in this area. And no one will get hurt."

Now wait a minute. Was he dissing her lack of action? That jab about the kneecap. She could have winged him, sure, but he had his own gun. He might have shot her dead. Then what enforcement action would she have been able to take, hmm? None.

Indecision tore at her. Did he really expect her to believe his so-called 'guarantee'? He'd violated a host of state and federal laws that she was duty-bound to uphold. So why didn't she?

He leaned forward, studying her intently. "Look, I think my guys know who you are. Not like BLM and our groups are best friends, you know? Could be dangerous for us to be seen together, for both of us." He reached for her hand, but she pulled back. He chuckled. "On the other hand, there's just too few beautiful, intelligent women here on the mountain to let you just walk away. I want to see you again."

And there she had her answer. As he kept talking, her insides melted like expensive chocolate in a fondue pot. Something drew her to this man, and until she could sort out her feelings, she wanted to believe what he said about this being the end of the violence here.

She knew she couldn't be dissuaded by his fancy talk, though. He had pointed a gun at her. He had to face consequences. She dug in her pocket for her cuffs, but he didn't wait. He suddenly stood up, gathered his paper and his check. "I know where to find you," he said, then he walked up to the counter, dropping the check and some paper money by the register. He was out the door before Caryn recovered her composure.

She jumped up, catching the edge of the narrow table with her hip, knocking the glassware sideways with a loud clatter. Everyone turned to look at her. Embarrassed, her face a flush of heat, she maneuvered her way out of the crowded restaurant, even those waiting in line at the door to be seated blocking her, until she could get outside.

He was gone. Again.

I know where to find you, he'd said. Was it fair that those words filled her with anticipation? And it had nothing to do with her job. Nothing at all.

"That's it. I'm going straight to hell," she muttered. She climbed into her truck and headed back to her office.

Chapter Five

His errands in town taken care of, Levi was halfway home before he realized the blunder he'd just made.

When he'd told Caryn it wasn't wise for them to be seen together, he'd not meant avoiding his own arrest, but rather the attitudes of men like Alex and Ron. Neither one of them would have hesitated to shoot her if they felt it would propel the movement forward. He had no intention to be a party to murder. But his tenuous connection with Caryn seemed to be more than just the potential lawlessness of his monkeywrencher companions.

What he'd said to her had been no lie. He was lonely. She did appeal to him. He could discern in the struggle of her facial expression that she shared his belief about the environment. The place they'd been marking the day before was a spectacular hike, one of his particular favorites. He tended to believe that she was, in fact, just out for a walk when she came upon his group at work. Even if she was in the law enforcement end of the BLM, the job by its nature meant spending a large amount of time out under the open sky. *And Montana has the biggest sky of all...*

He replayed the scene in the café in his mind, the suspicion in her eyes, the tight set to her jaw. She believed he was a criminal. That certainly wasn't the impression he wanted her to have, not at all. He had to do something to change her opinion. But what?

The dogs came barking to greet him when he pulled into the driveway of his home. He parked and got out, letting them jump on him, their tails wagging joyfully as he roughed each of them behind the ears. Once they'd welcomed him, they bounded away again, having done their duty. He scooped up the mail he'd retrieved from the post office, then carried it and a small bag of groceries up the red-stoned path to the double door, its etched glass windows slightly frosted.

His heavy boots' footsteps echoed in the empty foyer. He kicked them off, his hands too full to remove them gracefully, then continued through the back hall to the oak paneled kitchen, where he tossed the mail on the table and put the groceries away in his well-stocked walk-in pantry.

Family members always expressed surprise that, as a bachelor, Levi had more in his cupboards than beer and stale potato chips. But he knew it was a matter of survival. These shelves stayed full year-round, with a complete array of canned goods and other non-perishables. This far up on the mountain, he'd experienced many weeks in a year where the plows couldn't get up the hill to clear the roads, or the electric would go out because of heavily iced power lines. He and the dogs were well equipped to remain at home for as long as it took for normalcy to be restored. *Thanks, all you Boy Scout leaders who drilled that need to be prepared into my head. You saved me a lot of hungry evenings over the years.*

Reluctantly eyeing the mail that awaited his attention, he debated cracking open a lager, but decided against it. Too easy to get started with one beer and then let the ones that followed take his loneliness and this big empty house and toss them together, letting that barrenness that was his life reverberate deep into his soul.

Instead, he put on a pot of coffee, inhaling the aroma of the fresh-ground beans to set him in the direction of a more positive outlook. While the coffee brewed, he washed up the dishes he'd left in the sink the night before, then took his coffee and the mail out the sliding glass doors to the broad deck that overlooked Whitefish Lake. A cool breeze blew out of the northwest, carrying with it the sound of birdsong. He stood still a moment, surveying the land around him, feeling much less alone outside than he'd been in the house. This was his real home.

He settled into one of the padded Adirondack chairs made from recycled materials and began sorting the envelopes, accumulated over a week or more between trips into town.

Unfortunately, nearly half the mail wasn't even worth opening. Most of the environmental groups he belonged to promised that they didn't sell their mailing list to anyone, but somehow advertisers latched onto him. Today's collection wasn't any different. He set the junk mail aside under a granite paperweight to help light the fire later.

One particular letter caught his attention: an invitation by the Friends of the Pines to host a fund-raising event. He perused it quickly, his imagination catching ablaze. He wasn't all Dark Knight, doing his "good deeds" on the wrong side of the law. Here he could throw a party at his spacious home, raise some money for a good cause, and have the opportunity to impress Caryn Orlane with his dedication to the moral "right" at the same time.

Win, win, win.

He stashed the bills and a few offers to bid on a consulting job in his pocket to put on his desk when he went back inside, then took the last of his coffee to the railing around the deck. From there, he could see almost all the way to Whitefish, though the thick evergreens blocked a view of the city itself. The hill below had several well-worn paths that led to the main road. After his father's death, Levi had devoted his broken heart to work in the woods, a volunteer with the Park Service, the Sierra Club, anyone who needed a pair of hands to invest in the wild. He built hiking paths, laying stone by stone, handrails and fences, and many other tasks he'd never formally learned. Two paths ran up the mountain, one leading to the road, and another spiraled out around the girth of the granite to a clearing where Levi had once encountered a family of wolves.

The panorama re-centered him and reminded him why he had joined the monkeywrenching squad in the first place: to save this little bit of nature in its present state for the years to come.

He hadn't intended to become the man in charge of the group, not by any means. Alex and his older brother had been the backbone of the movement, according to Alex. The brother had been arrested and sent to jail for a third charge of DUI, and Alex really didn't have the skills to motivate others as a true leader. Once Levi discovered the group's existence and started meeting with them, he naturally gravitated to the top of that heap. The others were satisfied to let him give orders, and he found it easy enough.

But the natives were beginning to get restless. If Ron's earlier conversation was any indication, his place as #1 could be in jeopardy. How much longer would they take orders without protest or even open rebellion?

The thing was, he didn't really need that group. He'd found it stimulating to take physical action and truly fight the destruction of the forests. The hours he spent on petitions and campaigns, reading government documents and exchanging emails with like-minded folk had some effect, he knew that. But it wasn't the same as *doing* something.

The risk now, however, might outweigh the benefit, particularly if the Bureau of Land Management was onto them. Better to take their activities out of the area altogether for now; the Billings maneuver was a good idea. If the heat got too great there, Montana wasn't the only state where monkeywrenching had made some breakthrough. California's redwoods needed protection. Oregon had plenty of logging operations that needed to be stopped from taking down cherished old tree stands.

Which brought him back to the Friends of the Pines fundraiser.

A guest list was already coming together in his mind. He'd start sending emails in the morning. For now, he had to get back to his lists. Whatever the government was up to, he'd have to find a way to block anything that impacted his land, and the resources that fed it. If legal routes wouldn't be effective, then he'd have to examine his other options. Who knows, maybe the lovely, intelligent Ms. Orlane would come around to the right side and help him find a way to do what he needed to do. They certainly thought alike about the state of the environment. Why shouldn't she come to see his point of view?

The thought giving him a little rush of adrenaline, he picked up the rest of the mail and took it inside. Time to get to work.

****

When Caryn pulled up to the BLM office, she noted that Robert and Jessalyn hadn't returned yet, but an inordinate amount of vehicles filled the front lot. She pulled up her own truck and went to the side door where the employees keyed themselves in. Her eye fell on a familiar silver sedan.

Oh, crap.

She turned around to get back in her truck, but it was too late. Sam Evans spotted her through the door and beckoned her to come in. A sigh escaping her, she complied. The lobby echoed with women and men loudly shouting and chanting. Someone kept rhythm on a desk or a counter—the sound was not hollow enough to be an actual drum.

As she approached, Sam took her arm and guided her right into the middle of the mess, bringing her face to face with a woman in a hand-embroidered green dress that dropped all the way to the floor, her strawberry blonde hair in braids, a woven wreath of summer leaves on her head, and eyes the exact green of Caryn's own that flashed as she chanted, "Keep the forests free! Keep the forests free! Keep the forests free!"

Sam rolled his eyes. "You fix this. Now."

He retreated to his office and closed the door with

a bang.

Her ears ringing from the noise, Caryn crossed her arms and surveyed the nearly twenty hippie-clothed throwbacks to the 1970s, chanting, drumming and dancing in the BLM anteroom. Wasn't the first time this had happened; she was pretty sure it wouldn't be the last time, either.

After Sam disappeared, the strawberry blonde waved her hand in the air, and silence shortly ensued.

"I hope you don't think you can stop us from practicing our chosen religion. It's one of the most fundamental of American rights."

"So is the right to assemble," chimed in a long-haired boy in Native American leather tunic and dungarees.

Caryn didn't move. Of all the people in the world she didn't want to fight with, it was her baby sister. They didn't share that many other living relatives. They ought to quit causing each other trouble—or at least stay out of each other's orbits when they misbehaved.

She eyed her sister. "Apparently, so is the right to act like an idiot. What were you doing?"

"We had a solstice ritual at dawn out west of the dam at the Little Glacier turn in the river. You know, the place where we—"

"Yes, I know," Caryn interrupted. No need to share that particular youthful escapade with this group.

"Tribal cops sent us here to get a permit. But your boss won't give us one."

Of course he wouldn't. And Tresch couldn't see that the tribal council was just trying to divert the real trouble from landing on Earthenkrafte Circle.

"So what was it, the battle of the two halves of the

cycle, fire and ice fighting it out for the right to rule the faithful, blah, blah, blah?"

Discontent rumbled through the group at Caryn's mockery of their ceremony.

She spoke a little louder. "Knock it off."

She grabbed her sister's arm and pulled her aside. "Trescha, what the hell?" she scolded. "You know the Kootenai claim that whole area around the bend. You can't desecrate Native American ground."

Trescha shot back, just as intently, "We weren't desecrating it! We were welcoming the longest day of the year and allowing our internal calendars to be adjusted to reflect the long journey into the darkness."

Caryn was all for natural rhythms, but this seemed like a crock. A double-edged, cut-your-own-throat kind of crock.

"Since they've complained, you're going to have to move your little ceremony somewhere else. I'm sure the only reason tribal law enforcement hasn't busted you before now is they know we're related. But I can't protect you forever."

A voluptuous woman with short curly auburn hair and gold-rimmed glasses came to join them in her handmade sandals, her wrists wrapped in strips of leather fringe, and a wreath of holly on her head. No one knew what name this leader of the Earthenkrafte Circle had on her birth certificate, but for pagan business she went by Cynthia Fallingstar.

"Perhaps I can provide some input?"

Caryn tried to avoid looking at the woman's loud-colored beaded muumuu, thinking sunglasses might be a great help.

"No, thanks, Cynthia. I understand all too well

where you stand on the use of public and non-public lands."

Cynthia glared at her through narrowed eyes. "And I understand how you fascist government types will do anything to prevent people from worshiping the beauty of the earth."

"That's correct. We at the BLM hate nature. That's why we come to work every day." Caryn groaned. "So are you being charged with the violation?"

"Who knows?" Trescha said. "They made us pick up all our sacred items and bring them along."

Cynthia's voice rose to resonate with the very walls. "Is that what America has come to now? That we can be jailed for our faith? I don't see anyone trying to lock up Christians for sunrise Easter services."

The clamor of protest that rose from the group rattled the windows, and Caryn glared at her. "Who said anything about jail? Don't you dare cause that kind of a scene, or I'll call the sheriff's office and have every single one of you locked up for obstructing justice *in here.*"

Trescha's face paled. "Come on, Cyn. I don't want to go to jail. I've got a date tomorrow night." She turned to Caryn. "With that bartender at the Mike."

Caryn's mouth dropped open. "Shut the door. I thought you were seeing Arik."

Both sisters turned to single out a lanky, well-dressed man in the midst of the noisy group. Caryn had never liked the guy, but Trescha had always defended him as a charming prince. Until now.

"I am. I mean, I was. But Arik decided we should 'see other people.'" She pouted, then her eyes took on a twinkle. "Then I met Tommy. He's so sexy."

Caryn just shook her head. No point in trying to keep up.

Trescha looked at the pagan leader. "So we're not going to jail, right? We're going to work this out?"

"My dear," Cynthia said, wrapping an arm around Trescha's shoulders to draw her aside. "You need to be serious about the cause…"

Left alone for a moment, Caryn decided to escape from the din. She scurried along the hall to Sam's office, walking in without knocking. "That was cold."

He looked over from his computer screen, left hand pausing as it leafed through an open file on his desk. "She's your sister. Why is it my mess?"

Not like I'm my sister's keeper. The girl is twenty-two and out of college. Not my problem anymore. I hope.

Sam shrugged. "Look, the chief was hot under the collar about them trespassing again. Just tell them to stay off that land. Threaten them with citations. Then get them out of here."

"This is the last time. Next time, do your own damned dirty work."

She left the office, closing the door just about as hard as he had when he went in, then ignored the yell from inside. Marching back to the lobby, she cornered her sister again. *If I have to deal with this, then at least I can be the hero.*

"I'm not sure how much longer I can keep you out of trouble, Tresch. The Kootenai have federal and state jurisdiction covered. They'll go to court and get a restraining order, and then you *will* go to jail when you pull these stunts."

"They're not stunts. We're worshiping the earth.

Paganism is a religion with a long, long tradition of celebration, even back before the druids, and into the Mesopotamian cultures—"

"Shush! I don't need to hear all that." She pulled her sister aside. Her voice dropped so only Trescha could hear. "Nana would roll over in her grave to hear you carry on about this tree hugging crap, after all those years she dragged us to Methodist Sunday school."

"Don't you dare bring up Nana! After you called off your engagement to—"

Another piece of history we don't need to revisit. Her love life had never been any more successful than her application to the FBI. Bust all the way around.

"Fine. We're even. But as long as I have a badge and you don't, on this point I win. They're not pressing charges. Today. This is the last time." She eyed her sister intently. "I mean it."

Trescha gave her a warm hug. "Thanks, Sis. You're the best." She turned to go, then peeked over her shoulder. "I'll let you know about the bartender."

Caryn rolled her eyes. "You do that."

She stood there trying to look stern as Trescha, Cynthia and the rest slowly trudged out, carrying their paraphernalia and muttering about how terrible it was to deal with "The Man."

Yeah, you have no idea. Short-sighted dabblers, playing at being Indians, stealing their centuries-old traditions... Just because you open every day with a nod to the wind in each compass direction, that doesn't mean you'll have good fortune.

No such thing.

After the last of them cleared the door, she retreated to her office, conscience nagging her. She'd had a bit of good fortune today; she didn't have any business putting down the possibilities.

And you didn't get shot yesterday. Another plus, hmm?

She plopped into her so-called 'manager's chair," a hulking black leather seat with wheels, pulled herself up to her desk, and flipped on her computer. Each day the thing took a little longer to load. She'd asked when the IT department would get some new equipment, but the answer was always the same: when the budget allowed.

A pass-the-buck way of saying never, right?

Her half of the office was neat, hardly anything out of place. Over the years she'd learned to travel lean. There wasn't much to become cluttered. She kept a couple of genuine souvenirs of her time with the BLM, things the Native Americans had given her, a few pictures touring schoolchildren had drawn for her after presentations, a picture of her father in his hunting garb, posing with an elk he'd shot.

A police officer retired in his prime due to an injury he'd received in a high-speed chase accident, Richard "Duke" Orlane had always kept his spirits up— and Caryn's too, a lot of the time. Her little sister had always been the screw up, the wild child who didn't have to act responsible. Duke had babied Trescha, leaving Caryn at the age of twelve to act like the house matriarch after their mother died. Now her dad was gone, too.

She pulled up her web browser and checked her email, finding another irksome reminder from her boss that she was due for weapons requalification within the next thirty days. *Get off my back, Sam, or I'll come redecorate your office…*

While she wouldn't actually do it, the thought of all the damage she could cause if she really let her frustration loose was fairly satisfactory.

Nothing else of note in her email, she let the computer go into sleep mode, preferring to retreat into her earlier success. She took out a yellow pad of paper and wrote down everything she could remember about her earlier encounter with Levi Bradshaw.

After she reviewed her notes about his confession of his involvement with the group and their alleged plans for the future, she went back over the conversation one more time. This time, to her irritation, she found that what she most remembered was the spark of life in his eyes and the little smile that played frequently around his lips. She admired the strength of confidence and conviction he seemed to project, even when caught completely off guard.

Why did he stick in her mind so? She had been on her own for five years now. She wasn't the kind of clinging vine that Trescha was. Perfectly happy without a man by her side, Caryn was content to do her job and enjoy her time in the wilderness. That had always been enough.

Until now.

Damn him.

Chapter Six

Alex checked in with Levi the next morning, reporting that he'd made contact with the local monkeywrenchers near Billings, and they'd chosen the area of woods to be marked and spiked in the Custer National Forest.

"What group did you say it was again?" Levi asked.

"I don't think I did say," Alex replied. Something in his tone set Levi's teeth on edge. After a long pause, he went on, "It's some guys loosely associated with Ed Abbey's group."

"But not ELF?" Levi persisted.

"No, Levi, not ELF. Jesus." Alex huffed and puffed. "You've got to get your head out of your ass about this. If we want to make a real statement, we've got to take some strong measures. Quit playing it safe, you know?"

Levi gave up at that point, not wanting to fight.

"It's important work. I get it."

They finished their conversation with Alex promising to keep Levi in the loop as their project proceeded. Once he hung up, the phone kept ringing, with those who'd remained at home growing antsy, wanting Levi to come up with some stirring action for them to do in the interim.

Ron seemed to be the most persistent. "What seems

53

to be the problem, Leev? Last month you were all talk about how we were going to shove it back in the face of the Man and how loggers weren't going to rule these woods. Ain't the loggers you got to worry about, you know, it's the government. Damned feds think they want to tell all of us how we need to breathe, eat and live our daily lives, in the good socialist manner."

Levi's blood pressure crept up a few points; he could feel the rushing in his ears. When Alex had offered to bring the guys in from the militia groups, Levi had been pleased at first. Most of them had ready skills and had trained so they were able to be observant and made great lookouts. But then they wanted to expand and experiment with the other skills they knew as well. Like bombs.

In more dramatic and publicized events, ELF had reportedly caused nearly fifty million dollars' damage in the United States, and were high on the FBI list of domestic terrorists. From the arsons at the Vail resorts, Boise Cascades, and a Pennsylvania Forest Service station to countless smaller spikings and sabotage, they were thoroughly dangerous, and growing more so each year. Lesser groups had moved beyond the passive aggressive method of spiking trees. They'd laid whole dirt roads with twisted nail devices called caltrops to flatten tires in a heartbeat, regardless of the possibilities that herds of deer and other wildlife in the area could lose a foot or get a broken leg in these ambushes.

But ELF had made a name for themselves. Levi's guys were champing at the bit to see if they could get their own fifteen minutes of fame.

It wasn't the fifteen minutes of fame Levi worried about, exactly. More the fifteen years behind bars.

Sure, what he and the others had done in the glade up at Hungry Horse could get them arrested by an agency like the BLM. It wasn't just the arrest they'd have to worry about, but all those nasty federal conspiracy laws, probably RICO, too. Severe consequences applied. That was one of the reasons he'd never allowed the group to meet at his house, because if that could be proved, he could lose the Candy Cane house to forfeiture. *And that consequence is just not in my plans.*

"I'm not building my workload around what the feds do, Ron."

"Well, you should. They're gunning for us every day. They'd like nothing better than to take our guns and all our rights. We're not gordamned sheep, Levi. We have to be able to express ourselves. The constitution gives us the right to free speech and to bear arms and to defend ourselves against a government that becomes too damned overbearing."

Levi brought the phone and his coffee to his small desk and sat down. The fire crackled in front of him, and he smiled at the two dogs lying on the rug in front of it. Rosie had bailed out the back door earlier after something he'd seen in the woods. Levi hadn't seen anything, but the dog's eyes were better geared for such things.

"You know, Ronnie, I don't think you have anything to worry about. You seem to express yourself real well."

He swallowed as much of his sarcasm as he could. A lot of the militia members' advantages were also their disadvantages. They were just as much on the radar of the feds as the monkeywrenchers, maybe more so now that the Pioneer Little Europe white supremacist group had begun their small community outside Kalispell, inviting others of like mind to join them. Any time this group of volatile people got together, it seemed their fuse burned shorter and shorter. How long would it be before real trouble exploded?

"Yeah? Well you'd best watch yourself, Leev. Now that the Fed's onto us, they'll all be out here stalking our guys. You mess with shit, you get splattered. There's bound to be accidents."

Levi knew what he meant had nothing to do with accidental action at all. *And a lot to do with a certain Fed I'm interested in.* He scowled at the thought.

"I'll do that, Ron. I'll watch myself. You'd better do the same. All of you. Any of us rats the others out, I expect there will be trouble, right?"

"You're damned straight there will."

"Then we need to work together." *Or we'll certainly hang together, won't we?*

Levi finished that call as quickly as he could, the emotions engendered by it disturbing him. He returned to his plans for his Friends of the Pines fundraiser. The caterer had already signed the agreements, and she'd taken pity on him, agreeing also to order some floral pieces for decoration so Levi wouldn't have to. He didn't play the poor single man with no clue about social events card often, but he wasn't above using it when it came to his advantage.

He sent out written invitations to many local environmentalists, particularly those who had a bit of money. Perhaps e-invitations were all the rage, and perhaps some of his most rabid brethren would argue that he'd killed a tree to make the point. His mother, though, had always taught that invitations and thank yous had to be in writing, personal and concrete. She'd been a lady of impeccable etiquette; how could he ignore her advice?

His fingers moved across the desk to the single envelope sitting alone, and he picked it up, his fingertips assessing its smooth texture. This one he wasn't going to mail. He'd hand deliver it. He wanted to make that point in person.

But where could he find Caryn?

Sure, he could march into the BLM office, bold as brass, and see her at her desk. But after their woodland encounter the week before, there was a strong risk that he could be pinched by Caryn and her comrades- in - arms. Even he wasn't keen on moves that were blatantly stupid.

No, better to discreetly trace her, the same way she'd found him at the coffee shop, and surprise her when she was alone. Nothing threatening, just safer for him. And for her, too, actually. With hotheads like Ron about, who's to say they wouldn't let impulse get the better of them and do something Levi would definitely regret?

He tapped the invitation on the desk, trying to guess what her expression would be when he gave it to her. Would those lightly freckled cheeks blush? Was it possible he'd see that brilliant white smile? Or would her green eyes flash like a faceted emerald, cold and hard, cutting him with her disdain?

I'll hope for the smile.

He tucked the invitation in the pocket of his vest, so he'd be prepared to give it to her the next time they met. Hopefully soon.

His imaginings were interrupted by the sharp barking of a dog outside. Guildy and Ophelia stumbled up off their comfy rug, wide alert, baying at the ceiling before they took off for the dog door, claws tap-tapping on the tiled hallway.

Now what?

He had forty-three wooded acres, most of it not visible from the house at all. These dogs earned their keep, acting as an early warning system for intruders.

He grabbed a rifle from the gun case in the study, then made a beeline for the deck, wanting to see what had disturbed the dogs. The two had cornered a couple of young men in flannel shirts, also carrying rifles, near the southwest tree line. As he watched, Rosie came out of the woods behind them. Fortunately for them, they didn't try to shoot the dogs.

"This is private property," he called to them. "There's no hunting here."

The one on the right raised his hand and waved. "Sorry, man. We were heading along the lake edge and just got drawn off course. We'll be on our way."

"You do that." He waved in the same friendly way, taking the man at his word. Usually it was on the upper hill that people got lost, not knowing it was owned and managed by someone. Most of the lake edge had been bought up years before. People knew that.

Maybe they're from out of town. They should know better, yes. But ignorance is...ignorance.

The two men started east, but Levi waited several seconds before he whistled to Rosie and the others, calling them back to the house. He wanted to make sure the intruders really moved on.

Once the men were out of his sight, he went inside

and locked the doors. Perhaps it was time to install that security system he'd been contemplating. Cameras both inside and out would let him know if he and the dogs were safe. Considering the way this fight with Ron and the others was heating up, it certainly seemed worth whatever it might cost.

In the kitchen, where he pulled out several big butcher bones he'd been saving for a special reward. This certainly deserved a little reinforcement. As each shimmied through the flap on the back door, tails wagging furiously with pride, he handed it a meaty bone. The dogs took the bones onto a nearby rug and settled down, gnawing at them with delight.

Pleased with them and with himself, he watched for a long moment, wondering what he could use to train his rowdy rebels just as well.

Chapter Seven

Caryn inched her way into a long corridor lined with doors on all sides, clutching the butt of her gun like it was a lifeline, ears straining to detect the voices she needed to hear. Instead, rock music blasted from the first two closed doors she passed, distracting her.

Her orders were to capture the terrorists, distinguishing between a building full of civilians and half a dozen bad guys. She'd gotten separated from the rest of her squad, but she was so sure she was on the right track that she'd continued on. Just a few steps more...

When the small round object landed on the floor in front of her, it took her several seconds to register that it was some kind of grenade. By that time, the flash-bang went off, and she stumbled back into the wall, her senses reeling. Someone grabbed her from behind, and she knew it was over.

It's over...

She woke with a start, scrambling aside from the remnants of her dream, her recurring nightmare, the replay of her 'audition' for the FBI. The tense three days that came before that oh- so- polite letter telling her she hadn't been accepted. Wishing her the very best in the future. When all she'd ever wanted was to be an FBI agent.

The position might have been her father's

aspiration for her, but it was *her* dreams haunted by what might have been. She'd missed the chance to be FBI. Her grades had been proficient, even advanced, her application ripe with recommendation. But she hadn't measured up.

So this job she had with the BLM had to be enough. She was determined to hold onto it with both hands.

And yet, in the face of another set of terrorists, she found her resolve slipping as the result of her unexpected attraction for their leader.

She dragged herself out of bed, wiped the sweat from her face. She squeezed along the edge of the bed and ducked into the tiny bathroom. A quick peek in the mirror showed dark circles under her red eyes, and skin that looked worn and dry. She wasn't one to be obsessed with her looks, but she'd always appeared pretty healthy, at least. *I've really got to pull myself together.*

A clatter sounded in the front of the camper. She peeked out of the bathroom just in time to see Niabi dump her food dish, scattering seeds and fruit peels on the shelf over the cab.

"Really?" Caryn asked. "*Et tu*, Niabi?"

The iguana climbed up the pine branch Caryn had wedged across the front quarter of the cab, where she eyed her mistress, something accusing in the cock of her head.

Caryn, muttering, ignored the mess and put on some coffee instead, the aroma of the brew filling the small interior space of the camper. She opened the outer door, leaving the screen door in place to contain the iguana, and finally got the broom to sweep up the detritus of her pet's meal.

"I've got to train you to clean up after yourself. Damn straight."

Niabi came down the branch, close enough to jump to Caryn's shoulder. Caryn grabbed a rag towel from the cupboard, draping it over her arm before she extended it. Niabi scrambled into her usual place, nibbling on the bottom of Caryn's ear. Who needed a man when she had this lizard to keep her amused?

But Niabi's claws were sharp against her nearly-bare shoulder, and she could feel the trickle of blood on the top of her arm.

"Honey, I've got to get a shirt on before you get to ride."

She gently cradled the lizard as she removed it from her arm and returned it to the tree. A napkin on the table served to wipe off the blood and she tossed the stained paper into the garbage. It wasn't the first time blood had been shed in her home, and it likely wouldn't be the last.

She ducked back into the bedroom, snatching up her summer bathrobe, a light floral rayon thing with a worn belt, something she'd had since before college. Living by herself she just didn't see the need to have anything sexy or new. Once she put it on, she returned to the narrow counter, pouring herself a cup of coffee. She added a splash of creamer and sat in the chair just inside the door, letting her bare feet dangle over the steps while she admired the view of the Bitterroot Mountains beyond. Just the barest hint of snow on the mountain tops now, even this late in June.

She'd been up to the summit of Big Mountain just north of Whitefish the week before, riding the chair lift to the top, starting at 70 degrees at the bottom and arriving in a 37-degree chill, walking in snow in her sandaled feet. Fortunately, the return trip didn't take long, and within five minutes she was warm again. Up there, though, it felt like walking on top of the world, at eye level with the crests of the other mountain peaks around. Certainly it was one of the most beautiful views in this area of Montana—and there were so many incredible vistas with which to compare it.

Her cell buzzed, vibrating on the table, and she moved to intercept it. The office number on the screen. *Early for them. Curious.* "Orlane," she said.

"Yeah, Orlane, it's Novio. You need to get down here right away. There's been an accident."

Caryn didn't like the way Robert had phrased that. *Not Trescha and her pagan wackos again, please?* "What accident? Involving who?"

"Ecotagers. One logger down, another holding on for dear life. Your buddies from the other day, most likely. Sam says get here now." Novio clicked off.

Caryn drained her coffee, then stepped into the shower, allowing the briefest scrub and rinse. She hopped out, grabbing the nearest clean clothing she could find, not worried if she would look pressed and professional. She slipped on her heavy boots, and combed her hair, not bothering to dry it. The rest of the coffee went into a take along thermos. On the way out, she poured a cup of iguana feed into Niabi's dish and left her some carrots and half an orange.

"Hold the fort, babe. I'm counting on you to keep the place safe." She scratched behind the lizard's ears just a little, then took her keys and headed out.

She skidded to a stop upon arrival in the BLM lot

and bailed out, hurrying inside. The switchboard operator waved her toward the conference room, and she didn't slow down, her boots clunking across the floor.

The faces of the dozen or so gathered in the room turned as one, like those desert radar dishes, to stare at her. Their expressions let her know she must look a little rough. She paused to run fingers through her hair and straighten her jersey shirt. "What? You said come right away."

Novio nodded. "So I did."

Sam Evans cleared his throat. "If you don't mind, Orlane, I'll continue with the briefing."

"Hey, sure. Go right ahead." She gave him her best smile and took a seat at the table. The others' faces were grim. Bad news indeed.

"As I was saying," Sam went on, his eyebrows knotted together in consternation. "This morning a team of loggers began their scheduled tree harvest just east of Martin City. After they pulled in, the road was sabotaged with homemade caltrops. When the team started to set up, they were attacked with smoke bombs. The smoke triggered an asthma attack in one of the loggers. When they tried to get him carried out to one of their trucks, they were pelted with paint pellets, rapid-fire style. I don't know why these poor bastards didn't have a security detail with them, since we know monkeywrenchers have been sabotaging trees in the area, but they didn't."

He scratched his belly and took a long drink from his cup. "Bottom line is, they couldn't get out of the parking area because their tires went flat, and the rescue vehicle carrying the victim skidded sidelong into a big pine, injuring the driver." He took a deep breath. "The asthmatic died before he could get to the hospital."

Her stomach roiling, Caryn slumped in her chair.

What the hell? Levi Bradshaw had told her his group was moving on. Now they'd killed someone? Surely he didn't think that would be overlooked.

"So we're out to pick up as many of that group as we can. Orlane, you reported you'd found the man in the Avalanche, didn't you? Bradshaw? I want him brought in for questioning. Today."

Sam fixed his pointed gaze right on her like a burning laser. All she could do was nod.

"The others, any we've got a bead on, we'll bring them too. Novio, you and Brown head out to the scene and see what you can find by way of evidence. There's got to be a fingerprint on something. The local team will beat the brush, see what we can flush out of these criminals. We had some intel on their vehicles. Can't be that hard to find in an area like this. Not that many people around."

He wiped a hammy hand across his forehead. "We've got to stop this before it gets any more out of control. Last time these ecoterrorist assholes got rolling, they blew up half a new condo development in Idaho. We're not going through that again."

He paused, then snapped. "Well, go on! Time's a-wasting!"

Caryn was one of the first out the door, stopping by her office to pick up a clean uniform shirt, which she changed into in the restroom. The crisp folds of it made her feel more official. She grabbed a Kevlar vest for body protection, wishing there was a similar device to protect her heart. She had her gun and her badge in the truck, as she always did.

Headed your way, Levi Bradshaw. You'd best not make me hurt you.

"Sure you can handle the man?" one of the Flathead County sheriff's deputies called to her as he walked out to his car. He paused by the front fender, adjusting his brimmed brown hat in the way that a man does when he knows women find him attractive. "He's got some clout."

"What do you mean?"

"Bradshaw owns a pricey spread on Big Mountain. Town council cut him some breaks on zoning after the place got dumped on him when his parents passed. He's on a first-name basis with most of the legislators and council members in the northwest end of the state."

Really? What would someone like that be doing, mixed up with these ecoterrorist lowlifes? The concept boggled her mind.

"Huh," was all she could make come out of her stunned mouth.

The deputy stopped and walked over to her. His nametag read 'Thompson' and that jogged her memory. His first name was Mike. He stood nearly six feet, but she didn't feel he looked down on her, even though he was taller.

"You want back-up?" he asked.

Back-up was a way of police life, she knew that. For just a fleeting second, she remembered staring down the barrel of Bradshaw's gun. What would she find if she cornered him at his home?

At the same time, she juggled her reputation. Pretty-boy Mike had plenty of gals who'd be pleased to be on his arm at a party. Caryn wasn't *that* kind of girl.

She had to maintain a professional distance if she wanted to keep that respect he clearly seemed to give her as a fellow officer.

"I don't mind, Caryn." A smile crossed the deputy's broad face, the relaxed curve of his lips showing genuine pleasure, not a duty-driven polite expression.

His friendliness made her feel a little more appreciated. "Thanks." She took a step back, casting a glance toward the window, where she spotted Sam staring at her with a bemused expression. His surveillance made her anxious. She took another step back. "Sure. Why not? Better safe than sorry, right?"

He saluted her and headed for his car.

She got into her truck, and once behind the wheel, gunned the engine with sincere authority, loving the way it roared, then made her way out to the main road. Her brain still puzzled over what interest Levi could have in working with a bunch of hooligans.

But you know he is working with them.

Still doesn't make sense.

It didn't make sense at all. If he was sincere about his love of the forests, there were better ways to help, especially if he had the kind of contacts the sheriff said he did.

Maybe this was a different group of monkeywrenchers.

Maybe it was. Maybe he had nothing to do with the gang that attacked the Martin City crew.

If so, then he should have no problem justifying where he'd been, proving an alibi, and maybe finding some way to distance himself from these killers.

Hell of a lot of maybe's. She sighed and settled in

for the half-hour ride, debating how she'd get Levi Bradshaw to open the door, and once she and Mike were in, how to get Levi in the car to bring him in for questioning without any of them ending up on the wrong end of a gun.

Chapter Eight

Levi dropped his mail at the Whitefish post office, including the invitations to his fundraiser, then stopped in front of the Buffalo Café, intending to go in for some blueberry pancakes. Someone called his name from the corner of the building.

An invisible man apparently, because he saw no one.

Curious, he walked toward the parking lot on Third, peering around the corner. A dark blur moved quickly to drag him aside, yanking him nearly off his feet. Ready to swing on his attacker, Levi caught his balance and looked into the face of one of the 'kids' of the group, a twenty-year-old college dropout named Greg.

The young man's face was covered in black grime, the left sleeve and front of his flannel shirt charred, black threads hanging from the edges of burnt holes. Panting, he clung to Levi's arm and wouldn't let go.

"Greg, what the hell happened?"

Levi checked the injured arm, turning it gently, finding severe red blistered areas and seared skin all the way up to the shoulder. Even the left side of Greg's face hadn't been spared, the skin red and angry-looking. Taking the kid's jaw in hand, Levi gently turned it into the light. The burns were ugly evidence that no simple accident had happened. These weren't just any kind of burns, the kind one got from scalding water, or even from fire. Something else had done this.

Levi sniffed at his fingers, catching a whiff of chemical-sharpness, like nail polish remover.

The kid didn't even try to answer and wouldn't look Levi in the eye. That told him more than a true answer.

"You've been monkeywrenching someplace local? Firebombing? After I told you not to? Knowing the damned Feds are on top of us? What the hell were you thinking?"

His inner parade of horribles took off at full speed. Who had defied him? What damage had been done? Was anyone besides this idiot burned? What consequences would there be?

Furious, he pried Greg's hand from his arm and shoved him into the side of the building. Greg bounced off the painted mural and slid down halfway before he regained his feet.

"Who else was there with you, huh?"

Some part of Levi's brain not burning with anger remembered belatedly they were out in public. He stole a look around to see if they were being observed by anyone, particularly law enforcement. He didn't spot anyone. "Who else, Greg?"

Greg coughed and swayed a little, a pitiful picture of failure. "Randy, Moff and Lee."

"Not Ron?"

Greg hesitated.

"Ron?" Levi repeated. He could guess, but damn it, he wanted to know. *And if I find out that Ron's mucked up any chance I had to explain things to Caryn Orlane, so help me, I'll...*

The kid shrugged. "He wasn't there." He scuffed one sneakered foot. "He gave us the stuff, though."

"Bullshit!" Levi slammed his hand on the nearest object, which happened to be the concrete wall. Two knuckles cracked, and pain shot up his arm. Blood dripped from his skinned knuckles. *Wonderful.* "How many hurt besides you?"

"I'm not sure, Levi, I swear. I started running when the worst of it broke. Ambulance showed up and some kind of law enforcement, I couldn't see who in all the smoke. I think it was volunteer fire maybe. But then they started yelling they needed oxygen, and one of the trucks nearly ran me down before it crashed. I saw blood on the windshield." His last words came out in a voice half-choked with tears.

"Blood?" Levi just stared a moment. "Is someone dead?"

Greg's voice was a haunted whisper. "I think so."

Levi scanned the street again. A couple of people had taken interest in their conversation. "Come on, get in my truck, now."

As he marched the kid over to his vehicle, Levi's temper threatened to burst. Alex had put him in charge of this damn group. If he and the others didn't intend to follow his orders, why would they have done that?

The obvious answer popped into his head. *Because of your connections...*

Did they think that he'd be able to bail them out? Surprise on them. Wasn't going to happen. He wouldn't tolerate this kind of stupid, reckless, negligent crap.

When they were safely in the truck cab and able to talk, he asked, "Who was in charge on scene?"

Greg shrugged. "Randy, I guess. He brought the

71

caltrops from his place, and scattered them all over."

Randy. That explained a lot. Ron Ranning's younger brother wanted nothing more than to outrank his big brother when they grew up. That petty jealousy had cost someone's life today. How many more lives would that envy ruin before they were done?

"Was Alex there?"

The kid just shrugged.

They sat in silence for a few long moments, then Levi started the truck. "Where should I drop you?" He gave Greg a sideways glance. "You need to get that looked at. It'll leave scars otherwise. You might even need a skin graft."

"Can't go to the hospital. Cops'll be looking for someone who's singed, you know that."

"Were you the only one?"

Greg shrugged, wincing when the frayed shirt edge caught his wound. "I don't think so. I heard a couple other guys yelling, but I couldn't hardly see nothin' in all the smoke. It was…it was chaos."

His eyes were wide, his expression a little stunned. He'd clearly been shaken by what had happened, not just to his own body.

The group was getting out of Levi's control.

He turned up toward the road that led to Big Mountain. "All right. I'll take you to my place. I've got some first aid there. Not much of a medic, but I can wrap it at least. You'll need to do the follow up care."

"Thanks, Levi." The kid's voice broke. Levi's heart filled with empathy, and his eyes burned with a flush of tears he quickly blinked away. Not that men weren't supposed to cry—he just hated seeing his guys hurt.

"You don't give me much choice," he growled. "Where did the rest of them go?"

"I don't know. Once the ambulance got there, most everyone had scattered into the woods. Randy said he was gonna give us all a rendezvous point, but that didn't happen. Not when I heard him, anyway. Maybe I missed it."

Feeling like he'd aged five years, Levi just nodded. "Don't worry about it. We'll have to have a meet to discuss this mess."

We sure will. And I intend to draw some harsh lines. Anyone doesn't want to follow them can pack up and move on.

What if they wouldn't? Yeah, that was going to be the big question.

The wolf pack was getting a little rough around the edges. The beta males whined at his leadership, but they wouldn't strike unless they saw he was weak. He couldn't let them see that, not if he wanted to maintain control.

On the other hand, if the more radical members of the group refused to stop, he'd have to find some way to disentangle himself. He'd always been in this for the non-violent, make-a-statement kind of alternatives. That was no secret.

Only lately had the more extremist ideas started floating around. Now the others were acting on those wild ideas. More people would die. And that, Levi wanted no part of.

As he turned onto the road that led to his driveway, a question entered his mind that first chilled his spine, then melted away in icy rivulets into his muscles, then his heart. What if they wouldn't let him go?

****

After an hour of soaking in cold water, some antibiotic creams, and layer upon layer of gauze bandages, Greg's arm was at least dealt with. Examination had showed burns on his side, too, but they weren't as bad. The face, Levi didn't feel competent to do much for. He was no plastic surgeon. He let Greg smear some cream on while Levi tended to his own wounded hand, and they left it at that.

Greg didn't share much else of any use, and frankly Levi didn't want to hear more lame excuses. He offered to drive the kid back into town, but Greg said he'd manage. At least he thanked Levi before he loped off down the driveway.

Once he was gone, Levi checked the online bulletin boards to see if anyone in the movement had stuck up an announcement of the event, wanting to glean what silver lining they could from the disaster. Nothing. A sigh of relief he hadn't even realized he'd been holding in escaped him. *At least the fools had the common sense to keep their mouths shut.*

The local news from KCFW led off with the bombing, though. Cameras filmed the fire in the background as one of the trucks burned. The coroner's car sat prominent on the scene, and a bloody man Levi didn't recognize sat on the back bumper of an ambulance, being treated.

Not one of mine.

More relief.

He'd score that a plus for not losing another of his own men, but minus several more points for hurting outsiders. If Ron wanted to blow up his own idiot self, that might be a public service, but when others not in the movement were hurt, it turned up the heat. The 'suspects' were listed as 'unknown ecoterrorists' but the public was assured that law enforcement had the situation in hand and expected to make arrests soon.

He was pretty sure that not only did law enforcement *not* have this in hand, but neither did he. Was it time to call Zane?

Letting the network's talking heads fade into a buzz of background noise, he imagined what a conversation with his brother would be like. Surely, it wouldn't go in Levi's favor.

Ever since they'd been kids, Zane had always taken the lead. Levi would assert his chance to control whatever game they were playing, insisting, "But you're my brother!"

Zane would give him the Look—that smarmy, superior stare—and say, "But I'm the mastermind. I'm the boss." And they'd play things his way.

Zane's law degree simply solidified that position. He used it like a sword or a shield, depending on the situation. The outcome was always the same. *I'm the boss.*

The only thing Zane hadn't won was this house and land. Their mother had given it all to Levi, when he'd stayed to care for her after Zane had left to find fame and fortune.

So, yeah, Zane might have some advice. But getting it would involve kowtowing and humility, and a lot of put-downs Levi didn't need right now. *No, thanks.*

Levi turned off the television. A heavy knock sounded at the door. His breath caught, his throat clogged with panic. Were they already here for him?

How did they know he was involved?

I definitely need that camera system installed. As soon as I get back.

He faltered, torn, in the center of the living room, unsure which direction to go. Take off out the back, running, or face up to what he had coming. Gun? No gun?

Either way, it's trouble.

He decided to handle it with courage, not cowardice.

Cherishing the long-shot hope that his visitor might be a Girl Scout or someone else with an innocuous purpose, he strode to the door and pulled it open. Another skipped beat when he found Caryn Orlane standing on his doorstep, dressed in uniform. Her face froze in an odd, polite expression when she saw him, and her gaze flicked to his bandaged hand. A sheriff's deputy came up behind her.

"Officers?" slipped out of his mouth before he could get his tongue under control.

Caryn cleared her throat and showed him her badge. "Mr. Bradshaw, I'm here on official business. Please accompany us to the office for a formal interview."

He noted her curious looks over his shoulder at the interior of his home and took that as a hopeful sign. At least she wasn't waving handcuffs at him. *Although he could think of situations where that might be a little more entertaining...* "Won't you come in, while I find my coat?"

She hesitated, then glanced at the deputy. He thought she might refuse.

"Both of you. Please."

He stepped backward, holding the door open, waiting for them to come in. The deputy said nothing. Caryn apparently decided he didn't constitute an immediate threat, and she walked in, eyes darting left and right, even up the stairs to the open second level.

"No one else is here," he said. He was actually a little surprised that the dogs hadn't come running. Usually they were on top of every threat or at least potential threat at the house. They must be hunting at the far limits of the property.

"Perhaps that's so."

He bristled at the smirk on the deputy's face. "It *is* so. I'm not a liar."

Caryn raised an eyebrow. "Right. Like when you said the monkeywrenching here in the valley was done and your team was moving on."

Well, she has me there. He did a quick scan of the kitchen to make sure he'd cleaned up after Greg's mess, and it looked as though he had. "They didn't do anything under my direction except leave town."

"Leave town." The deputy gave him an incredulous look. "So you're saying you don't know what happened this morning out by the dam?"

Now what's he up to? The incident was at Martin City. Did they expect to trip him up somehow?

He walked back toward the kitchen, pausing to glance out the sliding glass doors to the deck, taking a moment to think what to say. "I heard on the TV news that there was a fire up at Martin City."

"On the TV news, really. You expect us to believe that?"

Stung, he spun around to glare at them, locking gazes with Caryn, who seemed inconclusive. He wanted to appeal to her before this deputy got grabby.

"I was nowhere near there this morning, and I did not direct anyone to go there and do anything. The last I knew, the team was pulling together to head out to Billings. That's it."

The deputy persisted. "We'll check your alibi."

"I hope you do that," Levi snapped. "I'll give you a complete trip itinerary."

He stalked over to the chair where he'd tossed his black suede jacket and picked it up, angrily shoving his hands in the sleeves. He shot a glance over his shoulder at Caryn, to see her reaction.

Hell, I know I'm no angel, but I can't stand being accused of things I didn't do. Especially with her. I hate that look in her eyes, the one that says I just might be scum.

She observed his every movement, her hand near her gun. The grim look on her face said she was prepared to really shoot him this time, if it came to that. He had no intention of drawing on her; what had happened up in the woods was a gut reaction born of surprise, not the way he normally conducted business. Fortunately, because Rosie had been there, he'd been able to avoid the actual exchange of shots. *At that range, the result was pretty obvious.*

He kept his hands in clear sight, just putting his keys and his wallet in his pants pockets. "Is it all right if I call the dogs in?"

She hesitated, and his lips pursed tight.

Probably isn't a protocol for that, hmm? What does the BLM direct you do in the face of pet owners who want to be responsible?

She glanced around, her gaze fastening on the dog

door at the far end of the deck. "Why can't they use that?"

He saw where she was looking and nodded. "I guess they can. We'll just have to be careful going out. They get a little close in the driveway sometimes."

The deputy took a step toward the door. "Time's short. Let's go."

Again holding his hands clear, Levi walked back to the front door and opened it. Caryn took a final look around the big, mostly bare room, then went outside. Levi checked for the dogs but didn't see them. *Great guard job there, right?*

"So are you arresting me?"

She glanced over her shoulder at the deputy, then spoke quickly. "You're just a person of interest right now. We have questions. I expect you have answers."

I expect I do. I also expect they're not the answers you want to hear...

"Can I take my car?"

She frowned, but he went on, "So I can get home afterward and you don't have to drive me back." He shot a peek at the house, knowing how attractive it was. "Unless you want to come back on purpose. I hope you will, you know. I addressed an invitation to you today."

Her expression changed to one of confusion, and the deputy shot her a curious sidelong glance. *Maybe I shouldn't have mentioned that just then.* She looked at the ground, her expression unreadable. Finally, she said, "I don't care. Take your car. But if you're not visible in my rear-view mirror all the way down to Kalispell, you'd better bet it's the last chance I trust you."

The deputy growled, "I'll be on his ass all the way

there. Don't you worry."

Then the barking started, from behind the house, continuing all the way around the yard until all three dogs turned the corner of the house and launched themselves at the intruders.

Chapter Nine

The approach of three growling, barking, leaping dogs would have cowed a lot of people, but Caryn had grown up with big dogs, and she had some idea how to behave around them. Mike Thompson drew his gun, but she put up a hand to stop him.

"It's okay," she said.

She didn't run or retreat to her truck. Simply holding her ground, she turned her body slightly away, a less challenging stance, and crossed her arms, tucking her hands. She had a vest on, after all; unless they went for her head, she was in pretty good shape. She stonewalled, not meeting their burning eyes, until they were close enough to hear her, then she snapped, "Go home!"

She heard Levi yell "Down!" at the same time.

Already in mid-leap, one of two red-toned Rhodesian Ridgebacks punched her chest with its paws before it obeyed, knocking her several steps back. Its thick claws scraped her arm as it retreated. The others were called off, circling the humans, then finally ending up by Levi's feet.

"It's okay, boys," Levi said, hunkering down next to them.

Still amazed at the presence of two of these rare dogs in one place, she studied them with delight, finding them beautiful animals. The third dog, some kind of a pointer with a pretty mottling of color, seemed a little less friendly, shying away behind Levi, tail not wagging.

"Thanks for not shooting them," Levi said, a half-smile on his face. He watched the dogs carefully, whistling to keep them close and settled.

Mike reholstered his weapon, an unhappy V on his forehead. "Would have, if it wasn't for Officer Orlane."

"They're just doing their job," Caryn said. Now that the dogs were under control, she crouched and held out a hand, palm down, for them to sniff. The two Ridgebacks came up, curious, to meet her. When they were comfortable, she gave them a good rough scratch along the backbone.

"So this one is…Rosie?" she asked, as the taller one rumbled in appreciation.

"Yes. Rosie. Short for Rosenkrantz."

Now there was a high-faluting name for a dog, even one as regal as this one. Surprised, she glanced at the other one. "Don't tell me. Guildenstern?"

"Ah, you're well read, officer." He beamed. "And this pretty girl is Ophelia."

Caryn read the affection on the man's face as he turned to comfort the pointer. "She limps a little. Is she hurt?"

"She and a speeding car had a disagreement out here on the road about a year ago. We were lucky not to lose her."

We?

Caryn stood up and shot a look at the house. She hadn't seen anyone else inside, but that didn't mean there wasn't a Mrs. Bradshaw, or at least someone ready to be. The realization hit her empty stomach like a ball of ice. " 'We'?"

"The dogs and me." His tone was slightly amused. Did he think she'd sounded pathetic?

"I see." She cleared her throat, feeling a little stupid.

Mike coughed. "If we're finished visiting the zoo now, can we go? I've got a basket of paperwork waiting."

"Of course," Caryn said. She didn't like the look in Mike's eyes. He thought she was being unprofessional. *Probably because I am.*

"Caryn, I'll ride down with Mr. Bradshaw." Mike hitched up his pants and walked toward Levi, keeping a wary eye on the dogs. "Just to make sure."

Levi's face froze. "That's not necess—"

"It's no trouble," Mike said, with a cool smile. "You can drop me off when you come back out."

Caryn experienced a lightning flash of frustration, as she'd already determined that Levi's suggestion to drive himself down made sense. Something in his character justified trusting him, at least that far. Mike's persistence reminded her she needed more than trust with Levi. She had a duty.

Just because he's a fine dog man means nothing. People have died. Levi is likely involved. Get a grip.

Levi made a big show of saying goodbye to the dogs before he got in his truck. Mike climbed in the passenger side without incident. Caryn preceded them out the driveway, watching Levi's vehicle in her rear-view mirror, noting that the dogs followed for a few seconds, then sat down with sorrowful expressions. They probably matched her own.

****

Pondering the interrogation to come, she led the way into the BLM office. Sam came out of his cubicle to stand, hands clasped behind his back, watching as they paraded across the lobby, Caryn first, Levi second and Mike bringing up the rear. She didn't look at him. In fact, she wasn't feeling in any way proud about this situation. What she hoped, most of all, was that Levi would say something to clear himself of this crime. *That way I can continue to respect him. I want to be able to respect him.*

She took them to the generic conference room that doubled for interrogations, briefings and birthday parties.

"Can I get you gentlemen anything?" she asked. "Coffee, soda, water?"

"Coffee would be great," Levi said. "Cream, no sugar."

Just like I take it.

Mike took a seat between Levi and the door. "If you've got a bottled water, that'll do for me."

"You've got it." She stepped out, heading to the break room for two coffees and a water, and brought them back. Elbowing a curious secretary from the door, she nudged it closed with her foot, then set the drinks on the long oak table. "Here you go."

"Thanks." Levi's eyes had started to lose their twinkle under the deputy's focused stare, and his hand lay on the table, one finger tapping without rhythm. Maybe it was just the surroundings. Caryn felt any pleasure at being face to face with him slipping away as well. Better get this over with.

She dug a small recorder out of the drawer behind her, then took a seat across from him at the table. "Do you mind if I record this?"

Levi's finger stopped tapping, and his eyes went wide. "I thought you said this wasn't official."

"You're not under arrest," Mike said. "Doesn't mean this isn't important. In case you move on to do your monkeywrenching elsewhere, we'd like to have this information nailed down."

Caryn studied Levi, trying to guess what his sudden, trapped look meant. *I hope it's not what I think.* If he was involved with the Martin City deaths, she'd have no choice but to lock him up. No future for the two of them in that, now, was there?

The thought that she could lose any chance with him made her want him all the more. Her stomach tightened into a knot. She became even more determined to clear him.

"Come on, Levi. You keep telling me you're not involved in this. Show me."

He looked into her eyes, and something warmed in his face. He trusted her.

Let's hope I'm worthy of that trust.

"Fine," he said. "You can record it."

She nodded and flipped it on. "Investigation into incendiary incident, Martin City, June 21, 2019. Investigating officer is Caryn Orlane, Bureau of Land Management, assisted by Mike Thompson of the Flathead County Sheriff's office."

She gave Mike a nod, acknowledging the interdepartmental boundaries that sometimes became rivalries.

"With us for questioning is Levi Bradshaw, a resident of Big Mountain."

She paused to take a breath, and Levi lifted a finger

in her direction. "Isn't this where you should read me my rights?"

"Mr. Bradshaw, as Mike told you, you aren't under arrest. That means you're not in custody, and you're free to leave at any time. You could certainly consult with an attorney before speaking to me, and have that attorney present during questioning. I thought you came to help in this investigation." She eyed him. "You do want to help, don't you? Like any good...innocent... citizen?"

A flash of anger heated his eyes.

"Look, Ms. Orlane—Caryn. I can give you my whereabouts from the time of five a.m. today till the present moment. Here you are." He rattled off his morning routine, what time he went to town to begin his errands, when he picked up his suit at the dry cleaners, when he went to the post office, and when he remembered he'd left the dogs loose, so he decided not to stay in town for breakfast but went home instead.

"I hadn't been there but about an hour when you arrived. The rest of that, you can check with anyone in town. They'll verify where I was."

"I expect they'll verify anything you say," Mike said. "After all, you're pretty well known in Whitefish, right? Friends with everyone?"

Levi scowled. "So? I know what I did today. I've told you."

They glared at each other.

Caryn refocused the discussion. "Tell me what you know about the operation this morning."

A troubled expression crossed his face. She thought it actually made him look more appealing, a little Mr. Rochester from *Jane Eyre*. Those dark, brooding good looks had always excited her in the fictional version; here it was in the flesh.

"I told you. I saw it on the television news. Something about an explosion and some injuries."

She and Mike studied him, letting the silence drag on. It was a technique Caryn found useful. People were uncomfortable with silence. Often they'd talk just to fill that void, and when they'd used up their prepared story, sometimes they'd provide incriminating details, without intending to.

The door opened and Jessalyn walked in and handed Caryn a thick manila envelope.

"Pictures from the scene," Jessalyn said.

"Thanks."

Jessalyn took a long moment to eye Levi, then she left. Caryn opened the envelope and removed the photos to examine them. The color shots showed chaos. A number of people appeared in the photos, some injured, others in panicked flight. She leafed through them one by one, then shoved the stack across the table to Mike, who also reviewed them.

He took out a small pad of paper and a pen, then pulled out several pictures that prominently featured single individuals and laid them on the table before Levi. "Recognize any of these people?"

Caryn caught a glimpse of the picture and followed along. She didn't spot anyone she'd seen at the tree-spiking site, but then she hadn't had close contact with anyone but Levi that day. As Levi looked at the pictures, she watched his face. His eyebrows raised, created furrows of distress, and his gaze became troubled. He certainly knew the subjects. Now came the moment of truth.

"Well?" Mike prodded.

Levi glanced at Caryn, an apology in his eyes, before he turned to Mike. "Told you I wasn't there." He cleared his throat, adjusting his posture. "I want you to understand, I'm not in agreement with these sorts of terrorist acts. That's not what our group is about. Or it wasn't. We were just trying to bring attention to the pillaging of the old forests."

"You said you were moving on to other sites," Caryn said, her disappointment making her tone harsher than she'd intended. The sharp response caught Mike's attention. He eyed her curiously.

"Exactly. The discussion we had as a group was that we had finished our mission here. I thought they had gone on to the next location."

Mike's pen remained poised over the pad. "I don't suppose you want to share with us where that might be?"

"Not really." Levi glanced from Mike to Caryn, then his eyes returned to the photos. "Someone died, you said?"

"A volunteer firefighter. Good man, too. Left two kids and a wife." Mike tapped one of the photos. "He was overcome by smoke, and it set off an asthma attack. This ambulance—" He tapped another photo. "This one was trying to get him to the hospital, but your buddies littered the road with their damned spikes."

Levi leaned back in the chair, eyed closed. He took a deep, slow breath. "The group is splintering over the level of violence which they're willing to use. As I said, we began with the idea we could do some minor monkeywrenching and leave it at that. But there's an element of the group that wants to go farther." He gestured to the pictures. "I have consistently advised against such action and made it clear that if it were to occur, that I would disassociate myself from the group."

"How convenient." Mike's tone was dry and disbelieving.

Levi tensed so fast Caryn didn't even notice until his fist crashed onto the tabletop. "Convenient? It's not at all convenient. Look at this mess. A couple of troublemakers destroy the possibilities of saving the forests and kill innocents in the process! It's a travesty."

"What troublemakers?" Caryn asked. "Who are they? Help us get them off the land so these murders stop now."

"Murder?" Levi blinked at her.

"If someone dies during the commission of a felony—which these ecoterrorist acts are—then they can be charged with murder," Caryn explained. "Even if there was no intent to kill."

Mike sat up straight, then angled his tall body a little closer to Levi. "So are you willing to be an accessory to murder? Or are you going to come clean and let us know who's behind this?"

Mike was coming on a little heavy-handed, but Caryn was glad he had taken on the role of inquisitor. If she were to be true to her oath, she had to prosecute this case to the fullest extent. *No matter what I think about Levi Bradshaw as a man.*

Levi didn't answer right away. Caryn's heart sank. What was the problem? Why would he hesitate when given a chance to cooperate? Who was he protecting?

Levi looked at the pictures again, then stood up. "I'm not under arrest, right?" He watched Caryn for confirmation.

She nodded. "Right."

"Then I believe I've just remembered an important appointment I need to take care of."

Caryn stood up slowly, facing him. "You're giving up your opportunity to speak to us voluntarily?" With her eyes, she begged him to clear his conscience, to get himself off the hook. *Don't lose the chance that we can move past this...*

"I can't, not right now." He looked at her, his dark eyes speaking volumes. He didn't move until Mike fidgeted in his seat. Then Levi snapped into action and walked out. Caryn felt his departure like a huge vacuum sucking the air from the space where he'd been.

"He knows more than he's saying," Mike muttered.

Caryn swallowed down the snap response that came to her and shrugged, sinking into her frustration like a granite chip into the depths of Flathead Lake. "Guess that'll have to wait for another day," she said.

"Don't think your boyfriend's getting off the hook," Mike said.

Shocked, she stiffened. Had she telegraphed her feelings so hard that even a near-stranger could read them? "What?"

"Bradshaw," he said. "Boy, he's got a thing for you. Couldn't stop asking me questions about you all the way down the mountain. Guess he doesn't know you like I do. You'd never let personal feelings get in the way of your job." He grinned at her.

"No, of course not," she said, forcing a return smile. "Justice must prevail."

"It will, indeed." Mike gave her a respectful salute.

"Hey, Bob!" He waved to another deputy who was leaving the building. "Can you give me a ride?" He turned back to Caryn. "Pleasure working with you, but I have to get back to patrol."

"I'll let you know if we get IDs or more information."

Caryn walked Mike to the door and watched as he drove away, her thoughts in turmoil. When she turned around, Sam Evans was waiting for her.

"All right, Orlane. What's the scoop?"

Chapter Ten

Once he'd cleared the BLM compound, Levi wasted no time calling first Alex, then Ron, on his hands-free phone. Alex's phone rang through to voicemail, but Ron picked up on the second ring.

"Ranning."

"Ron, it's Levi." He checked traffic, then pulled onto Highway 93 behind a slow truck stacked with thick pine logs. "How's things in Billings?"

A hesitation before the answer. "Everything's on schedule, Leev. Something wrong?"

"I'd say." Levi glanced in the rear-view mirror, suddenly wondering if the BLM expected him to lead them right to those responsible for that morning's attack. No marked cars in sight, nor Caryn's silver truck. He worried he was being traced, but all the same, best to get right to the point. "Who told Randy to murder local ambulance volunteers?"

"Randy?" Ron sputtered. "Murder? What the hell are you talking about?"

"That little 'incident' up at Martin City. What a royal clusterfuck." He added the details he knew from Greg. "BLM's all over this. And the sheriff's department."

"Yeah?" Ron said something else, but his voice was muffled like he'd covered the phone.

"Yeah."

Another long pause before Ron spoke. Something was odd about this conversation. Was Randy there with him? *If he was smart, Randy would join Ron in Billings before the heat caught up to him.*

"Levi, when did you talk to them? The BLM?"

"Just now. They came with the sheriff and dragged me down to the office for an interrogation."

A choked sound on Ron's end. Apparently that hadn't been the right answer. Levi's collar was suddenly too tight. He opened the top two buttons and tried to catch his breath. Why wasn't Ron denying this? What was he hiding? *What have I gotten myself into?*

"Look, Leev, I'm having a meeting with some of the boys to discuss tactics. Why don't you join us? I'm sure they'd be glad for your input."

"Hell, Ron, I don't have time to drive all the way to Billings—"

Ron coughed, almost sounding like he was laughing. But that must be distortion through the cell phone. There was nothing funny about the current situation. Nothing at all.

"Actually, I came back to get a few things. We're out at the foot of the Blacktail, you know the side road that heads off to the west?"

Ron had lied about where he was. The fury that seeped through Levi's veins like hot mercury threatened to depose his intellect, the only thing that was keeping him from a total meltdown. Greg may well have lied about the source of their explosives.

And who do the authorities come after? Me.

He considered wryly that he'd wanted Caryn's attention. *Surely there was a better way to get it.*

The last thing he wanted was to be compelled to

turn in men whose work he'd respected. But somehow the focus had changed from saving the environment to giving the government a black eye—and that wasn't something Levi supported. A little civil disobedience to right a wrong was acceptable. A full-out militia attack on a government outpost was never part of the plans he and Alex had made. *And where the hell was Alex, anyway? Why wasn't he stopping this?*

Why hadn't he seen it earlier? These guys were so batshit cagey about their plans, he just hadn't put the clues together.

"Levi?" Ron prodded.

Levi sighed. He didn't have a choice. If Ron and his pals had committed to this course of action, even when it led to murder, then Levi had to stand against it. Not only because they were wrong, but because he needed to demonstrate the depth of his beliefs to Caryn.

"All right. I'll meet you there. When?"

"Now's good. See you soon." The connection clicked closed.

His hands clenched on the steering wheel. He should just turn the whole thing over to law enforcement and step back. Sure, he'd be caught in the fallout, but he was willing to accept responsibility for his part. He believed in the cause.

One last chance. Maybe I can talk them out of complete stupidity. If they won't listen this time…then I'm walking away.

****

He was halfway along the dirt road that led to the Blacktail when a huge 'boom' sounded off to the west ahead of him, rattling the windows of his truck. Black smoke floated into the air in the distance. *What in the hell was that? Sounded like a bomb. No...it couldn't be.*

Before he could assimilate the impact of that, a second boom went off. And a third. More black smoke, blowing toward the road. The closer he got, the air smelled hot, with a burnt, sulfurous blend that could have come straight from Dante's *Inferno*.

He knew that smell. What was it?

So much for his chance to talk them down. If those idiots were blowing things up so openly, it meant more trouble than he could control himself. Levi dialed 911.

"9-1-1," came the tired voice of the dispatcher. "What's your emergency?"

"Hello? I'm driving on Highway 93, and some explosions have just gone off. I'm not at the scene, so I can't tell you what damage there's been. But you'd best send some heavy guns out here, and I mean now."

Excited chatter at the dispatch center nearly drowned out her answer. He must not be the only one who called. "What's your location, sir?"

He glanced around for an identifying sign but didn't see one. Hell, he couldn't even remember seeing one. What was this? Bob's Road, named for someone who owned a spread along it?

"Can't tell you, ma'am. No signs. All I can say is I turned left off Route 93 just past the Conoco gas station."

"Can you remain on the line until we can pinpoint your location?"

Another explosion. "No, ma'am, I really can't." He hung up, pretty sure they could trace his GPS location anyway. If Ron and his buddies were right, maybe there was even a spy satellite watching him.

A hint of dust still hung in the air, so someone had

passed this way not too long ago. He wracked his brain to remember what was out here that might attract the environmentalists' ire. It wasn't far from the bison preserve. Maybe a logging interest was operating too close to a field of open pasture or something. *Not like the bison would appreciate living in a war zone, either...*

Intent on the road in front of him, Levi noticed belatedly that two red pickups had fallen in behind him, effectively blocking him in. He recognized one as belonging to Randy Ranning.

When he reached the end of the road, he found a small clearing surrounded by old Douglas firs. He pulled up near the other parked cars at the end, hoping at least to allow himself an easy exit. Randy smoothly drove in right next to him, boxing him in, jumping out of his truck when Levi did.

"Hey there, man," Randy said, a wide grin on his face. "Didn't know you were coming along this time." Carrying a cardboard box that claimed to hold bottles of an expensive whiskey under one arm, he came over to the back of Levi's truck. "Ready to play with the big boys?"

Levi suspected Randy really meant 'what did you hear about what we're up to?' No sense in giving too much away.

"All I've got is the usual. Won't that be enough?"

Randy looked over his shoulder at the buckets of railroad spikes in the back of Levi's truck. "Oh. No, I don't think so. We're not spiking today. Got something better going on. Something that'll really get people's attention."

Levi looked him in the eye. "Really? Maybe more

of those homemade bombs that killed those men at Martin City? Because murder is always a great way to get noticed."

Randy stiffened. "I don't think I like your tone."

"And I don't like the way you and your brother are perverting the focus of this group."

Levi studied Randy, wondering if he had a gun. Any sudden movement could be deadly. But the young man seemed focused on that box, which was clearly part of today's festivities. He suspected it was some sort of accelerant. Probably whatever had burnt Greg up when it lit up.

"Lighten up, Levi. Ron said you'd be cool about this once you found out. This isn't anything serious. He's just running an exercise, that's all. Letting the boys get a little creative." He moved a little more quickly so he ended up in front of Levi, those from the other truck falling in behind. Levi didn't recognize them. More of the militia, most likely.

Levi had a strong impulse to get back in his truck and go home. But his gut told him that wasn't the right choice. Someone needed to see this, to be able to report it if—no, *when*—something went wrong.

"Let's go," Randy said, with an intent look at the men behind Levi.

Levi wished he could get the gun he carried under his truck seat, but that move would be much too obvious at this juncture. *So I'll have to rely on my wits. Let's hope this isn't one of the days I'm only half armed.*

They walked up the path together, the others spread around him, effectively leaving him trapped in the middle of the group. His senses set on overdrive, he marched along, keeping their pace, studying the men and women with them, but none of them carried anything in their hands. Randy was the only one.

They came out of the other side of the woods at a construction site, several big pieces of heavy equipment parked for the weekend, standard setup, with a hydraulic crane holding a tank of diesel fuel high off the ground. The site appeared closed. Signs indicated the site of a future real estate and tourist cabin office. The business wouldn't seem to be particularly offensive, at least to a real environmental defense group.

But that isn't what this group is, not anymore.

Smoke and a hot blaze came from one of the larger bulldozers. Randy and the others ran ahead to join a dozen men including Ron, who watched with a jagged smile as the fire burned.

"Take cover!"

The group scattered. Levi ducked behind a large chunk of rock. Several of the younger guys, Randy and his cronies mostly, worked on some sort of mortar or potato launcher. A few seconds later, a bright fiery projectile sailed out of it and hit a dump truck. The impact nearly knocked Levi from his feet. Clinging to the rock where he hid, Levi peeked out briefly at the explosion, forced to turn his eyes away because the light was so searingly intense. He realized then what it was. White phosphorous.

He confirmed that a few seconds later when he could stand to look again. The fire dropped down in the machine, burning, as it always would, straight through the metal to the ground. Levi remembered from Army training that it would do the same to human flesh, too.

Nothing would put it out. It simply burned.

When the ground quit shaking, he looked around for Ron, a little disoriented by the ringing in his ears. Ron, along with Randy and his mysterious box, was over by the launcher, laughing and chatting it up with one of the other men, who had a spray paint can in his hand. Levi took advantage of the post-explosion lull to join them. Ron's delighted expression looked like he was watching something on the delectable level of a stripper show. Levi wouldn't have been surprised if the man was sporting wood.

He asked, "So tell me, Ron, what's the purpose of this destruction? What have these people done to the environment that makes them targets?"

Ron's anticipatory look of excitement faded for just a moment. "Everyone's a target, Leev. I wish you'd come to see how true that is. Just because you've got the hots for some BLM chippie, that doesn't change the facts. Our own government has betrayed us. After that last election, there's no question that the wrong people are running the country. How long do you think it'll be before they come crashing down on us with all the damned weapons at their disposal, hmm?" His eyes were wild, and spittle actually formed at the corners of his mouth.

It was all Levi could do to avoid taking a step back. He was afraid to do it in the face of this insane rant, not sure whether Ron might take the gesture as provocation, proof that the world was truly spinning on this paranoid axis.

"Seriously? This is a militia thing? You're just blowing up the world before it blows you up?" *Do you know how crazy that sounds?*

Levi hoped like hell he hadn't said that last part aloud, but he was having a hard time focusing. The acrid smoke burned his nose and choked him. None of these guys should be out here without proper equipment—gas masks, a fire extinguisher in case things got out of hand.

"Hell, no, Leev. We haven't got serious about it yet. This is just some mischief the boys wanted to try out. That last bit, out at Martin City? That was just a little test run to make sure our troops can defend themselves if they have to."

How could Ron sound so cold about this? "Someone died!"

Ron shrugged, a detached look in his eyes that gave Levi chills. "Not any of our guys. That's what it's all about. Us versus them."

Levi looked in the box that sat between their feet, seeing each of the divided sections that formerly held a liquor bottle now held a metal bit of ordnance. Twelve of them. Enough to destroy this building and most of this pasture, leaving it in ashes.

Randy tossed the spray can to one of his buddies who loped over to spray paint the initials of the environmental group on what remained of the burning bulldozer.

"Besides," Ron said, "now that little tree-hugging group you used to run will look like it grew some balls. People'll take you seriously, right?"

Grinning like he'd just given Levi a Christmas gift he'd coveted since he was a kid, Ron dropped one of the projectiles into the launcher tube.

Bastard has no idea how lunatic he sounds. I've got to get out of here.

"That's it," Levi said. "We're done. You play your little revolutionary games all you want, but I'm not part of it anymore."

He turned to walk away, but Ron leaned over to snatch his arm. "Not so fast, you son of a—"

Ron yawed off-balance when he yanked Levi closer, then his outstretched leg caught Randy, who lurched sideways. Randy grabbed the launcher for stability and then it went off, shooting almost straight up. The projectile slammed out of the top and flew through the air, landing right in the middle of the nearby diesel tank, just as if there'd been a target painted on it. Several people yelled warnings before the tank went up in a huge bright-white fireball, sending small pieces of metal flying. The shock knocked all of them and the launcher to the ground.

Caught in the open, Levi felt the heat of that burn sear his face and the bare skin of his arms. The ground shook like an earthquake, and Ron released him, stumbling away, toward the gigantic fire, bellowing something Levi couldn't understand through ears that had suddenly plugged up. Levi's eyes burned, too, and the light faded until all he saw was darkness.

"Someone help!" he called out, racked with nausea. But no one did.

Time passed in a nightmarish fog, pierced by the sharp shriek of sirens. Sounds of a war zone echoed around him. Running feet passed him by where he lay on the ground. Other voices called out for help. Some just screamed in agony.

"Please help," he said. He pushed himself upright, but couldn't keep his feet. He fell to his knees, still praying that someone would come to rescue them as the fires burned, swallowing up all the air. He choked on the smoke, gasping for breath.

"Here's one!" he heard someone call. His arm was grabbed and he was yanked up, sending waves of pain through him. Before he could beg them to stop, he slipped over the edge into unconsciousness.

****

He woke up to total blindness and the sound of beeping, weight heavy on his face and arms.

Where am I? What is this place? Am I...dead?

The memory of his last waking moments fading in slowly, he tried to clear his face, but found his arms secured so that he couldn't. "Hello?"

His voice was muffled, something covering his nose and mouth. "Hello?" he called, louder.

No answer.

The skin of his face hurt, stung like he'd fallen asleep at the beach without sunscreen for a week. His arms, too, heavy and wet. Even the inside of his nose felt seared. His throat hurt. Everything sounded so loud!

What most disturbed him was that he couldn't see. He remembered the 'blinding' light, but hadn't anticipated that it was literal. What immediately came to his mind was the utter dismay that he wouldn't be able to set eyes on Caryn Orlane's face again. That would be devastating.

He listened hard for a clue to where he was, the gradual sounds of the hospital ward coming into focus and recognition, the intercom calling for a doctor, the beeping increasing as he became more frantic, obviously a monitor of some sort.

If this is a hospital bed, then there must be a call button.

Anxious fingers felt around for a buzzer, and he finally latched onto one just in reach of his right hand. He pushed the button multiple times.

"Yes?" came a harried female voice.

"I need help," he said. "I can't get this off my face. What's happening?"

"Mr....Bradshaw? Someone will be with you in just a moment."

"All right." He didn't let go of the call device just in case they forgot.

After what seemed like hours, footsteps came close, several sets. A female voice. "Glad to see you're awake, Mr. Bradshaw. How are we feeling?"

Small soft noises all around him, several hands touched him, adjusted his IV, apparently, checked...whatever nurses checked. The weight on his face moved. He realized it was an oxygen mask. How sick was he?

"You tell me. I'm thinking I don't want to be here. That's what I'm thinking."

"What? And miss out on the opportunity for us to care for you?" The woman laughed softly. Her voice was a little gravelly and sounded older. "Your bandages are just fine, keeping your burns damp so your skin can recover."

She changed the mask for a nasal cannula, her fingers gentle as they tucked the plastic tubing behind his ears and tightened the cinch under his neck. The nasal parts rubbed against sensitive tissue, but it was infinitely better than the smothering mask.

Better get the bad news out of the way first. "Am I blind?"

A moment of hushed silence. *That wasn't good.*

"You'll have to wait for the doctor to answer that question," the nurse said.

His heart sank. "That means yes, doesn't it?"

Another voice, farther away, more familiar. "That means that the doctor gets paid to do the diagnosing, not the nurses."

What was *she* doing here? Was she worried about him? His heart lightened, despite his debilitated state. "Caryn?"

His nurse's voice took a distinctly scolding tone. "I'm sorry, Mr. Bradshaw isn't allowed to have visitors at this time. You'll have to leave."

"Oh, I think he's allowed to see me." A pause, followed by murmurs. *She must have flashed her badge.*

"Fine, but don't stay too long." Waves of disapproval came off the nurse's tone.

"Is it necessary for him to be restrained now that he's conscious?"

A quick confab among the nurses. "That's up to doctor to release him." Said with a note of self-satisfaction, just before a herd of footsteps left the room.

He listened a moment but heard nothing. "Caryn?"

Her footsteps approached the bed, heavy boots, not soft-soled nurses' shoes. "I'm here."

He paused a moment. "So...official business?"

A smile in her voice. "Mostly."

"Mostly? Does that mean that you wanted to visit, because it was me?"

"Partly."

"Good. I mean...I'm glad."

Her question about the restraints tipped him off

that he wasn't handcuffed—as in he wasn't being viewed as a criminal. Not out-and-out so, anyway. Even though she'd come officially, she'd admitted that part of her motive was personal. At least a little. That lifted his spirits even higher. He tried to ignore the 'official business' part as long as possible.

"I'd get up, but…"

"Not a problem."

A chair scraped across the floor, then her voice came from lower down, not standing above him anymore. "Let's get the hard part over with, all right? I have some questions for you—"

A sudden suspicion that she'd brought Mike Thompson along with her chilled him. Certainly that made it more official—but his concern leaned to his sense of some competition for Caryn's interest in the sheriff's deputy. "Are you alone?"

"Are you kidding? That inferno Saturday called out every law enforcement officer in a twenty-mile radius, even the tribal guys. We're spread thinner than diet butter on dry toast."

Her words laid a strip of fear right down his midsection. "Saturday? What day is it now?"

"It's Monday afternoon."

Two days? He hadn't been home in two days? What about the dogs? What about…his companions?

"Are the rest of them all right? Anyone else get hurt?"

"I think ambulances brought in four here to the Regional. One got life flighted down to to the burn center in North Colorado. Several more showed up at local urgent care offices. As if no one would put together a dozen flash burns and two explosions and total up a set of guilty faces."

So many… A bitter taste filled his mouth, threatening to choke him. *Damn Ron Rannell. Look what he'd done now.* At least maybe he'd slow down now that he'd hurt some of his own with these crazy ideas. "How many injured altogether?"

A pause. "Fourteen. One dead."

"Dead?" He gasped. "Who?"

"Your buddy Ron. Burned to death on the scene. That phosphorus is nasty stuff."

A wave of nausea seeped through him. *Guess old Ron will definitely slow down under the circumstances. What an inglorious ending to a life.*

He took a shuddering breath. "Damn it. So unnecessary."

The pack had turned…the pack had turned.

Silence fell between them. In that space of time that stretched out like an abyss, his helplessness gnawed at him. Buckled to a bed, unable to see—what the hell use would he be to anyone from here?

There was only one thing he could think of. He had to reveal the identities of those in the group, and their culpability for these events. *Crimes*, he reminded himself. These are crimes. People are dead. No more wiggle room, excusing their actions as 'environmentally necessary.' He wanted Caryn's respect.

And most of all, I need my own.

"Levi?" she asked softly.

"Still here."

Well, duh. Not like I'm going anywhere soon.

"I heard the nurses talking at their station before I came in. Apparently most of those who came here had a similar sunburned appearance and optic paralysis. They were saying the patients have gradually recovered. I expect they'll tell you the same."

Relief at her reassurance slipped away, elusive in the wake of the news about Ron's horrible death. "Yeah, okay."

"Okay?" She sounded surprised. "That's it? Okay?"

He sighed. His skin itched a little and he wished he could scratch. Probably why they'd put on the restraints, to keep him from pulling off his bandages.

The door opened and someone's firm footsteps echoed on the linoleum, walking around to the other side of the bed from Caryn. "So, Ms. Orlane, you're satisfied we're taking good care of your friend?"

Caryn cleared her throat. "Seems so. The nurses—"

"Told him he'd have to wait for me. Exactly right." The doctor's big male voice boomed around the room, hurting Levi's traumatized ears. "Mr. Bradshaw, I'm Dr. Mountjoy. I don't believe we've met medically, although I remember your mother. A lovely woman."

Now that was a marvelous name. Mountain of joy. Who wouldn't want that?

Focus, damn it.

The doctor cleared his throat. "Mr. Bradshaw, what you've experienced is a flash burn due to phosphorus exposure, similar to what welders get if they're not using proper protective gear. You slept through the worst of it, so we were able to treat the damaged corneas. We haven't been able to determine the extent of the damage to the interior of your eyes, but we're hoping to be able to do this as the blistering and swelling goes down."

Levi didn't want to hear any of this. His breath came in gulps and he felt dizzy. He couldn't be blind. He just couldn't.

"Mostly first-degree burns, but a few are a little deeper into the skin layers. At this point, we believe the wounds will heal on their own, without need for skin grafts."

"W-When can I go h-home?" Levi asked.

"Well, aren't you ambitious?" The doctor's voice resounded with cheer, almost too much. "We need you to stay a few more days. Phosphorus burns are nasty things, and we don't always see the worst of the systemic symptoms for at least four days and as much as eight."

Eight days? I can't stay here eight days!

But the doctor kept right on talking. "You took it worse than most of them. We nearly sent you to Colorado."

"I c-can't—"

"You will," the doctor replied firmly. "This toxin is nothing to mess with. You could die from poisoning and internal symptoms that haven't even evidenced themselves yet." A long pause. "Mr. Bradshaw, you're obviously free to leave, against medical advice. But if you go, you are taking your life in your hands. Your injuries need time to heal undisturbed. The restraints will help protect against inadvertent touching."

"But—" Levi's frustration boiled over. "There are killers out there! Don't you understand? Dangerous people!"

The doctor coughed discreetly. "I'm sure that has something to do with Ms. Orlane's presence. You're here to interrogate him?"

The last was clearly directed toward Caryn. Levi held his breath for the answer.

"The sooner we get answers, doctor, the fewer patients you'll be sending to the morgue."

"Hard to argue with that. But the man needs his rest. The nurses will be monitoring. If they tell you to stop, you're done."

"Understood."

"I'll be back to check on you later, Mr. Bradshaw. If you need anything, just let us know."

"I need to go home," Levi growled. "I've got responsibilities. Dogs…sorting things out…"

"Soon."

The doctor's footsteps headed for the door, and Levi caught the bit of a whistle as he turned the corner. That left him vulnerable, with a law enforcement officer—even one as sympathetic as Caryn—ready to hear what he had to say about everything that had happened. Could he count on her to understand his side? Or was he about to dig his own grave?

Chapter Eleven

Caryn's gut had twisted in physical pain when she'd walked into Levi's hospital room. The sight of the man who intrigued her, all bandaged and burned, horrified her. He could have been killed.

While others in her unit might consider Levi had simply gotten what he deserved, something deep inside her couldn't accept it. The link formed between Caryn and Levi at that first encounter told her to believe him when he said he wasn't at Martin City, even though she felt he'd held something back. He seemed the kind to protect innocents. Maybe someone had gotten caught up in this mess who shouldn't have.

Besides, emergency records confirmed that his cell had called in a report on the explosions. So he was on the right side, wasn't he?

Why had he been there at all? He'd apparently left her office and headed straight out there. Why?

Interrogation under these circumstances was out of the ordinary. Levi was likely under the influence of drugs and couldn't give informed consent. But Sam Evans had made it clear he wanted these guys nailed before they had time to scatter. Several less-injured participants in custody had given wildly divergent stories. A walk-through at the scene revealed the grass trampled in every direction, pieces of hardware and debris dispersed over the whole pasture and swerving deep tire tracks indicative of hasty escape. Perhaps chaos had ruled, but truth was truth.

The officers had rallied at the BLM office for a briefing, during which deputy Mike Thompson made reference to Levi's comments regarding Caryn. Sam rolled his eyes, but in the end, assigned her to get what she could from him. "If he likes you, Orlane, he may tell you more than one of the guys. I can't afford to be choosy. We can't lose this bust."

Over the snickers of Robert and the others, she'd left the office and headed straight for Kalispell Regional. She'd waited patiently while all the medical personnel had come and gone. Now that she and Levi were finally alone, all she could think was how pitiful he looked, swathed in white gauze, sucking oxygen from a face mask.

He coughed dryly. "Water?" he asked.

Frustration, with him, herself, and the situation, left her throat in an irritated growl. She poured ice water from a plastic pitcher on the bedside table into a disposable cup, filling it halfway, then handed it to him with a bent straw aimed at his lips.

"Thank you." He emptied the cup. "Another, please?"

Wondering if he was medically allowed to have water, she hoped the fact it was sitting here on his bedside table was a sign. She refilled the cup and gave it back. He slowed down as he came to the end of that one, then relaxed on his pillow with a little sigh of relief.

So strange to see him this debilitated when he'd always seemed a little larger than life.

"So you want answers," he said in a raspy voice

barely louder than a whisper.

"Sure do." Caryn retook her seat, then shoved her hand in her pocket for her recorder. In light of Mike's prodding, she wanted everyone to know this session had been one hundred percent on the up and up.

"Got your recorder?" he asked. That demonstration of his presence of mind startled her, but reassured her that he might be okay to talk, despite his medication.

"Yes." She set it on the edge of his bed, in a place on the white sheet not covered with betadine or bandages. "I have your permission to record?"

"Sure. What does it matter now?"

His defeated tone tugged at her heartstrings. At the same time, her law enforcement side lit up with the fire of new discovery. This was the sound of a man on the ropes. She'd have what she needed. She could almost smell it.

"Let's start at the beginning. Could you state your name, and your permission to record this session?"

He did so, adding, "I waive any need for counsel. I'm doing this of my own free will."

"Thank you. Please tell me what was going on at that construction site on Saturday. And what were you doing there?"

He shifted uncomfortably on the hospital bed. "Remember I told you that my environmental group had...well, two factions? One that was truly dedicated to civil disobedience in protection of the trees, and another looking for more violent action?"

"I remember." Caryn sat poised to take notes, but instead found herself doodling geometric shapes, mostly triangles, as she listened.

"After I spoke to you the other day, I called Ron

Rannell to see what was going on. He and…" A long pause, then a deep breath before he continued. "He and his brother Randy have been all fired up about adding the bulk of their militia group to the eco group, thinking they can use it as a cover to strike out at the government that's coming to take their guns. You know, 'repressing their civil rights.' Apparently they believed that my connections, which had bent the rules for us a few times as a protest movement, would cover them for these more deadly acts."

"Did you promise them you could?"

"Hell, no." He coughed again. "Water, please?"

She gave him another half-glass, which he slurped down.

"I'm sorry," he said. "I haven't experienced anything like this before." He breathed quietly, resting, then began again. "Ron seemed very upset that I'd talked with you. I'm sure he thought I'd shared things about him, about the others."

Levi told her about his trip to the explosion site, his voice in a monotone. Watching him, unable to see his eyes, or the changes of expression of his face, or even emphasis with a gesture, made the tale almost surreal.

"Once I realized what he had there on Saturday, I tried to get him to see reason, but he was fired up on adrenaline. They wouldn't stop. They launched the device and…"

"And here we are," she completed for him. "What about Martin City? Were these same men involved there?"

Levi's fingers twitched, and he moved restlessly under the sheet. "My skin feels like a thousand ants are crawling over it."

Caryn considered what she knew about burns. "That's good, then. It means you haven't destroyed the nerve layers in your skin."

"Fantastic." He tried to scoot farther up his pillow, without much luck. "Can you raise the head of the bed?"

She glanced out through the window to see if any of the nurses were handy. Would the restraints allow him to sit up? She couldn't see why not. "Maybe a little." She dug for the button that would elevate the bed, then raised it a few inches. He continued to fidget, and she wondered whether he was just stalling her. She took her seat again.

"Were you aware that the militia group had gained a leadership foothold in—"

"Look, what do you want me to say?" Levi's voice ached with anguish. "You want me to say I'm sorry for what happened at Martin City? I'm sorry as hell, but it wasn't my fault. God knows that was the last thing that I wanted! My boys, my own recruits, we've been working at defending the environment, just quietly making our point known, all above board and according to the monkeywrencher handbook, which I'm sure you have a copy of back at your office."

He turned his face away. "It's weary work and we're always looking for extra hands. When Ron and his guys came along a year ago, I was delighted to have help. But when more of them joined up, Ron stepped in and bent and twisted my direction. He subverted a bunch of the guys to go off on these sexy missions with bombs and splash. And look what it's come to!"

She'd never seen a clearer example of surrender. It almost made her feel guilty to pursue her inquiry, but then that's what she was supposed to do, wasn't it? She was supposed to rout out injustice and protect the property of the United States.

But all I want to do right now is protect this man from any more harm. He's been punished enough.

"So, Ron…?" she prompted.

A harsh breath shuddered through him. "I told him after what happened at Martin City, that we were done, that the groups couldn't work together anymore, but he just laughed at me."

"And then he tried to kill you."

The words slipped out before she could control them. She'd drunk up all the frustration he was spilling and claimed it for her own. She could relate to co-workers or other cops taking over what she felt was her territory. It happened a lot up here, where some things were under the jurisdiction of the tribal authority, some was state, some was local, and she was a Fed. But no one had dared to toss her far enough under the bus to get blown up. The gall made her angry.

"What?" Levi said.

The astonishment in his tone stopped her interior rant. "Isn't that what happened? They called you up there, then set off these killer homemade bombs?"

"I…"

Levi's hands clenched into fists for a second, then, with a quick gasp, he released them. He must have pulled on his damaged skin. Her heart went out to him. He wasn't a bad guy. *He wasn't a bad guy. He wasn't. Here was her chance to clear him.*

"So you're confirming that your group—Ron's group—was responsible for the incident at Martin City."

115

He chewed his lip, then nodded. "Yes."

She tapped on her cell to open the file of suspects already collected by the BLM, and read off the names, one at a time, getting his confirmation of each one. "Who have we left out?"

His jaw tightened and fingers twitched, the bright line on his monitor peaking in a faster rhythm. He opened his mouth to speak, but nothing escaped his chapped lips. One long, labored breath, then another. She didn't know what was happening, but it didn't feel right. *Too much water?*

Her gut was validated in the next seconds as two nurses came swooping in the door, one to each side of the bed, adjusting and tsking at each other.

"You'll have to leave now," the gray-haired one said.

"But—"

"Now." The nurse eyed her, her gaze like rock.

Caryn nodded and gathered her things, slipping everything into her bag before she took one last look at Levi. The nurses checked his bandages, yielding a moan of pain from him. He seemed oblivious to her presence and impending departure.

"Levi, I'll check on the dogs," she said, pitching her voice to be heard over the monitor.

"Alex," he murmured. "Find Alex."

"Alex who?" she asked.

"Enough!" one nurse said. "You have to go. Visiting hours begin at two."

Frustrated at the change in circumstances, Caryn couldn't get out of her mind the thought that someone had tried to kill Levi. "I'll make sure security checks on you, all right?" She eyed the nurse. "No one suspicious gets in here, you understand me?"

The other nurse shooed her out then, practically a physical shove into the hall. Each step Caryn took after summoned further determination to punish these people, not only for the deaths they'd caused, but for the agony they'd caused Levi.

Continuing through the lobby to the security desk, she stopped to show her badge and ask the favor of having someone keep an eye on Levi's room. The stocky uniformed guard assured her he'd be able to do that, with a little smile that had an invitation for coffee in it. Before he could ask her, she thanked him and left the building. *Got enough complications in my life right now, thanks.*

In the parking lot, she got in her truck, locked the door, then dialed the office on her cell. Caryn watched the parking lot as she talked, studying each person she saw. How would a nurse know who was "suspicious"? Most of the hospital visitors looked the same. It was that kind of town.

The secretary routed her through to Jessalyn Brown.

"Didja get anything?" Jessalyn asked with a smile in her voice.

"I did. Mr. Bradshaw was very forthcoming. They're holding him here at Kalispell Regional for a few days. I'll email you the file when I'm done here. Anyone else come up with something?"

"Nothing earthshaking. Not about this, anyway. But, there is something else."

"What now?"

"The tribal police unit's asked for you, in person. That pagan group camped out on tribal lands this week

117

without a permit."

Caryn closed her eyes and groaned. *Didn't Cynthia listen to anything?* Now she'd have to drive an hour out of her way south to Pablo to the tribal headquarters. And another hour back. *And I promised to stop in and check on Levi's dogs, which is half an hour north.* And Niabi would probably want food too.

How can I be in three places at once?

Better for her to deal with the pagans, though, especially if her sister was involved. The promise she'd made her father to look out for her younger sibling was made years before her promise to Levi. She sighed.

"All right. I'll swing by there. Stand by for this email."

"Will do."

Caryn hung up, then accessed her email to send the information. She also found an emotional email from her sister Trescha celebrating news in her perpetual on again-off again relationship with her boyfriend Gunnar. Apparently he'd asked her to move in.

Terrific. Maybe that means she wasn't on site for the pagan group's illegal incursions today. Hey, I'm due a break. I'll take it.

She sent a brief congratulatory note to Trescha, as little tongue-in-cheek as she could make it. After all, it wasn't the first time her sister had madly lost her heart. Not even the first time it had happened with Gunnar. Who could guess how long this infatuation would last?

Finally ready, she pulled out of the parking lot and headed south on Highway 93.

****

When Caryn walked into the tribal law enforcement office, her ears were assaulted by raised female voices screeching in protest.

"How dare you keep us from the pure land? You, of all people, should know what it feels like to be separated from nature!"

"We have rights, too!"

"We destroyed nothing, we left nothing. How are you harmed by our presence?"

The older, heavy-set woman at the front desk wore a handmade tribal-patterned vest over her uniform shirt. She sized up Caryn and jerked her head toward the sounds of discord. Caryn gave her an awkward nod and moved along.

She found the officer on duty, Addison Montoya, cornered behind his desk while four women stood in front of it, gesturing wildly in emphasis. When he spotted her coming in the door, he stood up, his dark eyes flashing both relief and further annoyance. That caught his lecturers off guard, and they went silent, following his gaze to find Caryn.

She, in turn, was just thrilled to see her sister wasn't there.

"We got a call...?" she offered tentatively.

"Yes." Montoya moved his muscled form from behind the furniture to stand next to her. Tension came off his body in waves. Caryn wondered how long ago this confrontation had started.

The tribal officer read from a yellow pad in his hand. "The Earthenkrafte group made plans to invade the tribe's sacred space at Kootenai Falls, and—"

"We're not invading!" complained a short woman wrapped in blue scarves, who stood just in front of Cynthia Fallingstar. Caryn didn't know her, but her clothing seemed to be made from natural fibers, knitted, woven or otherwise, and her wide-set blue eyes overflowed with innocence and honesty. "We want to share in some of the spiritual energy of the forest there. Surely it can't be meant only for the native Americans."

"You are…?" Caryn asked.

"Patricia Park," the woman replied, straightening her shoulders, trying to look taller than her five-foot-two height. "I've come all the way from Oregon to participate in this sacred ritual. We intend to proceed with the utmost respect. Just to be able to stand where the first people once stood and share in that energy. Don't you see how important this is?"

Caryn shrugged. She'd be the first to proclaim the beauty and inspiration of the deep forests of northwestern Montana. Her commune with nature was one of the best parts of her job. But why did it have to be at that exact spot?

She turned to Montoya. "So they haven't gone yet?"

His jaw set in a firm line as he eyed the women. "They've been asking landowners all the way out to Libby for a rental spot. The thing is, they haven't gotten permission from the tribes. Without that, they will be in violation of the law and subject to arrest." He pointed at Cynthia. "You know this, because the same thing happened last time. The tribes won't give you permission. So you'd better make other arrangements."

Cynthia glared at Caryn. "Are you going to stand for this?"

"Me?" The sharp query caught her off guard, and Montoya, too, because he gave her a pointed look. "This isn't my call."

"You won't even stand behind and honor your

sister's beliefs? Hasn't she taught you anything about our bodies' need for peace and meditation?"

Caryn burst out laughing before she could stop herself. "Peace and meditation? Trescha?" Realizing too late she had let the woman engage her, she controlled herself and stood shoulder-to-shoulder with Montoya. "What my sister does is her business. What happens at Kootenai Falls is tribal business. If they say no, then this conversation is done."

"But—" Patricia ventured.

"Done," Caryn said firmly. "Now, why don't you move along and let Officer Montoya get back to his duties, hmm? We have thousands of miles of forested land in the state that you can use to conjure the wood spirits and natural energies. What about the vortex lands up in Columbia Falls? That's got the reputation for all sorts of magical powers."

Patricia turned away, her cheeks gently sagging with disappointment. Cynthia frowned. "That place is a tourist trap and you know it. Obviously you don't understand the importance of a true connection with the earth."

Montoya snapped, "I think you're the one who doesn't understand, ma'am. You can't just usurp someone else's sacred space. Your soul is not connected to the waterfall land, and it never will be."

This was going nowhere. Caryn looked at her watch. Two more stops to make an hour or more north. She wouldn't reach home before dark. Before Cynthia could shoot back and start the battle again, Caryn raised a hand.

"Look, I don't care if you go out in the field across the road and lie down in the grass to connect to the earth. You can't do it in here. You can't do it at the Falls. Neither Officer Montoya nor I can change that. Go through the right channels. I've got bigger things to investigate—people's deaths. We don't have time for this."

She sidled over in front of the desk, then started walking toward the Earthenkrafte delegation. They backed away as she came closer. Montoya recognized her intent and joined her. They backed the women out of his office and down the hall toward the door, step by step. Caryn continued to meet their eyes, letting them know she was serious.

The Oregon woman's big blue eyes cradled hurt like a sick child, very near to tearing up. The leader's determination never faltered, even as she was being evicted. The other two women had said nothing, but Caryn recognized the one as Judy, the waitress from Montana Coffee Traders, the one who had commented on Levi's good looks. Those turquoise contacts were unmistakable. Judy remained in the background, silent support, but before they left, she gave Caryn a wink.

Caryn and Montoya stood at the door, once they'd gotten the ladies out, making sure the entrance was blocked against a return. The women apparently acknowledged defeat, at least for now, because they went to their cars and departed.

"Your sister's one of those wackos?" Montoya asked.

Caryn shrugged, then crossed her arms. "My sister doesn't know what she wants to be when she grows up. I doubt it'll happen any time soon."

He took a deep breath, then let it out, still watching the parking lot. "The council said this is the absolute last time. They've been warned. When they next come on tribal land, we're arresting them. Even a big sister in the BLM isn't going to save them."

She frowned and turned to him. "I would certainly not expect you to do anything differently because of me. Who asked you to do that?"

He cleared his throat. "Came down through command. Chief to chief, I guess."

So Sam did look out for her once in a while. A small smile came to her lips. Nice to know he had her back, at least on this. But she couldn't justify protecting Earthenkrafte over this. Someone was going to get hurt, and then a line would be crossed.

"Thanks for giving me a call. Next time…well, you all do what you have to do. These people are grownups. Actions have consequences."

He nodded and opened the door for her. "Have a wonderful afternoon, Officer Orlane."

"You too, Officer Montoya."

She felt his gaze on her back as she headed to the parking lot, eagle-claw sharp. No wonder he was sore about special treatment for the protesters. She'd never asked anyone to give them a break, though, and she wouldn't. Next time Trescha made a wild and romantic gesture, Earthenkrafte's flavor of the week, she'd be up her own creek.

Maybe that would be good for her. Dealing with the grown-up consequences of her choices, instead of having me rescue her all the time. Dad would forgive me, if Tresch learned a lesson, right? All baby birds need to fly from the nest. Learn by doing.

Settled in her own mind that's what would be best, she gunned the engine and pulled out to retrace her steps to Kalispell and on to Big Mountain to see about Levi's dogs.

Chapter Twelve

A cloud cut across the July sun as Caryn turned off the main street in Whitefish to head north over the bridge to Levi's house. The graying skies matched the fading of her mood. She contemplated her situation—even what she was doing right now, well-motivated or not, felt wrong. She was about to go into the home of one of their suspects with no warrant and no overt permission. What if she found the single key—the one e-mail, the cans of accelerant, the 'smoking gun'—to bust the whole circle and lock away the bad ones?

Her job dictated she should nail Levi Bradshaw with anything she found.

But it wasn't the "right" thing for a friend to do.

Turning her attention to the busy sidewalks, she chuckled at the rosy, flushed faces of the summer tourists who'd likely spent the day on the shores of Glacier Lake without enough sunscreen. Just because the temperatures were below seventy didn't mean they couldn't burn as in the hot desert hundreds of miles south.

She'd made the same mistake when she'd first come to Montana from California. It didn't take long for the lesson to sink in, though. Fortunately, working in the forest depths helped protect her from too much sun. She enjoyed nothing more than standing on the forest floor, looking up through the delicate lacework of the leaves overhead, a constantly changing kaleidoscope of light. Often, by remaining still she could hear the call of hawks and other birds overhead and sense the cool breeze on her face. It was how she imagined heaven must be.

Which brought her back again to her drive to Levi's house.

Misguided as their tactics might be, Levi and his original group believed the beautiful woodlands of the Bitterroot had to be protected. She'd invested in a career to accomplish this task, and he'd committed to even break the law if necessary, to do the same.

That much would have endeared him to her all by itself. The fact that his brooding good looks had seized her heart as well doomed her to…what? How would she deal with the fact that they stood at polar opposites in the corners of the legal system, while standing as close as could be in everything else?

She pulled up to the front gate of Levi's Candy Cane house, her heart sinking as she realized the ornate wrought iron portal was closed. She'd forgotten that. How would she get inside?

The Ridgebacks were already barking and jumping up on the gate, aggravated by the intruder on their master's driveway. Caryn couldn't see the pointer—what was her name again? Ophelia. Odd that Levi would pick the name of Hamlet's doomed admirer for the shy rescue dog. *Or maybe he was subconsciously "rescuing" the play's heroine by building the dog back to health and keeping her safe…*

Cutting off her silly romantic imaginings, Caryn put the truck in park and climbed out. Her boots crunched on the stone of the driveway as she walked over to see if she could find a method to jimmy her way inside. When she approached the black metal gate, the dogs sniffed the air and stopped barking, tails now wagging in greeting.

"Good boys. Now how can we get in and feed you, hmm?" she said in a soothing tone. "I bet you're hungry."

Tails continued to wag. Ophelia appeared up the driveway, much closer to the house.

Caryn put her hand on the gate and pushed toward the house. Nothing. She pushed harder, stymied, and finally kicked it in frustration. Her vehemence startled the dogs, and they barked again.

Their reaction brought a swell of embarrassment that only increased as someone in a red pickup drove past, eyeing her suspiciously. At least she wasn't in uniform. She could pass as an unidentified friend, right?

She gave the passerby a little wave, then turned back to the dogs. The Ridgebacks watched her, tails now still, and Ophelia had ventured closer, but her tail hung down, pathetic.

"Sorry, guys. I should be able to do better than this, with all that fabulous police training."

She tried to recall whether she'd seen Levi using any sort of remote-control device, but she didn't remember it.

"Open sesame?"

Nothing.

Well, it was worth a shot.

She grabbed hold of the metal again and pushed as hard as she could, but she only got the narrowest of movement. "Oh, come on. This can't be so hard!" She yanked the gate toward her. It magically swung open.

Shocked beyond movement for a moment, Caryn was frozen when the dogs came joyfully leaping at her, tails once again in action. Laughing as they tried to lick her face, she patted their wiggling bodies as she could and reassured them she would fix their missing meal issue momentarily.

She hurried to the truck, drove it inside, then got out and closed the gate behind her before the enthusiastic canines could get out on the road. They followed her to the house, dancing around her as she climbed up the steps to the porch.

"I don't suppose Levi leaves the house door unlocked, does he?"

A rhetorical question that, sadly, had the answer she expected. He didn't.

"All right then, we have to be a little more clever."

Practically tripping over the frantic dogs, she continued around the porch to the place where she remembered there being a doggie door. Luckily, Levi had installed one large enough for the Ridgebacks, so size wasn't an issue. Caryn did have quite a battle competing to get inside. Waiting on hands and knees for the dogs to precede her, she'd begin her way inside to get nearly bowled over as one or the other would shove his way back out to see if she was coming. If she tried again, they tried to beat her inside. Finally, she pulled out her "now-shut-up-and-listen" police voice.

"Sit!" she bellowed.

Both dogs, inside this time, twitched and immediately sat up tall.

"About time," she muttered, crawling in quickly before the spell broke. She sprang to her feet just in time before the two broke into a chorus of vigorous yelps and a tango around the empty food dishes.

"Now, where do we suppose we'd find dog food?"

The dogs were no help, so she hunted through the cupboard under the sink and then the closet next to the stove. Ophelia nudged Caryn's leg with her nose.

Caryn reached down to pet her and found that nose dry. "Water. That might be a good idea. I can find that."

Taking a crystal pitcher from the counter, she filled it from the faucet water, then divided it evenly among the three bowls. The dogs lapped it up within seconds. Mindful of their owner's reaction to too much water, she added a little to each bowl again, not even half full. While they were distracted with quenching their thirst, she poked through a couple more cabinets and found a warehouse-sized bag of a pricey dog kibble and several cases of canned dog food. She grabbed some of each. The dogs now bumping her in their eagerness, she set bowls on the counter to fill them. When she'd assembled them all, she set them on the floor, taking a moment to pet each dog as she gave it food.

Her mission accomplished, she left the animals unceremoniously crunching and licking, and walked out of the kitchen, taking a moment to admire the home where Levi lived.

The large open rooms had polished hardwood floors that shone like mirrors, Persian-style rugs in burgundy, gold and blue adding a homey touch. While there wasn't a lot of furniture, what she saw was well-placed and suitable for one occupant. In the study, the fireplace was fronted by a well-worn rag rug, looking comfortable as if it was a frequent sleeping spot for the dogs. So many books! Shelves lined the walls. No wonder he'd pulled classical literature names for his pets.

Knowing it was none of her business, but tempted beyond her ability for self-control, she went up the hardwood steps and their padded green carpet runner that went all the way to the top. Something drove her to learn personal details about this mysterious man who'd entered her life at the muzzle of a gun.

Once upstairs, she noted more raw wood, many of the rooms, particularly on the left side of the hall, sat unfinished and empty, except for the detritus of construction. Surprised at the contrast between the beautiful rooms downstairs and these, Caryn walked along the hall, peering into each room. Judging the stacks of materials, she guessed some of these rooms had been empty a long time, years perhaps. That alone made her curious. What did one man need all this house for? Did he intend to have a wife and a busload of children? What dreams had Levi owned that he'd set aside?

The three rooms on the right side of the hall, however, were a different story. She stepped into the first room on the right and found herself mesmerized by the panorama out the broad window and sliding glass door that led onto an upper deck overlooking the lawn. Beyond the hill below was the real stunner—the blue-gray waters of Whitefish Lake. The view was breathtaking.

She stepped outside, and for just a moment, she imagined herself sitting here on one of the stripe-cushioned lounge chairs as evening set in, listening to the birds and crickets, looking out onto the lake painted with sunset colors. As night curtained the area, the boat lights on the water below would sparkle like stars.

Stars...

She glanced up, imagining what Montana's big sky would look like, this far from town. She'd bet she could see the Milky Way and hundreds of constellations, all laid out for her study and enjoyment.

A quiet yip behind her tore her away from the postcard-like panorama. One of the dogs, she thought it was Rosie, studied her from the doorway, head cocked curiously. It seemed fairly plain the dog was wondering either what she was doing here alone, or where Levi was.

"He'll be home soon, boy. The doctors are taking good care of him now."

Rosie's amber gaze, deep-set and intelligent, didn't leave her face.

"Really. I promise."

She left the deck and knelt beside the dog, first scratching him behind the ears and finally giving it a hug, moving slowly despite its apparent acceptance of her. The last thing she needed was her own visit to the hospital for a dog bite, and Levi's dog locked up pending a rabies analysis. But Rosie tolerated her and even gave her face a lick.

"Come on, boy. I really shouldn't be here anyway."

She headed back for the stairs, only to be stopped by a passing glimpse in a mirror in the room at the head of the steps. What had to be Levi's bed was tumbled as if he'd just climbed out of it, his sheets a medium tan, with a coverlet bearing some kind of alpine print in earth tones. The air bore a faint scent of aftershave or cologne, something extremely appealing, with a little spice to it. Curious, she checked the several bottles on his mirrored dresser, sniffing each one until she found the culprit. She inhaled it deeply, feeling it speak to her whole body.

There it was. Her new favorite.

Her gaze slipped up and caught her guilty expression in the mirror. She looked away and continued her exploration, trying to rationalize it away as "part of her job."

Ridiculous. You've already decided that you can't use anything you find for your work purposes. This has nothing to do with work.

Fine.

Just…fine.

She rummaged through a couple of drawers, determining that Levi wasn't a big T-shirt wearer although he had plenty of tank-style undershirts. Definitely a denim jeans guy. Nothing else of interest in the drawers. Across the room, she found a huge walk-in closet, thinking it was perhaps half the size of her camper. Only the rack on one side held any clothes, and that wasn't even a full rack. The rest of the space was taken up by boxes labeled "Dad's" and "Mom's" and "Zane's."

Zane…that was a name she hadn't heard from him. It was clear no one else had a room here, so who was the mysterious Zane? Where was he? Was he part of this ecotage business, too?

Was that who Levi had wanted her to call? He'd asked her to call someone, there where he was losing it at the end. Zane didn't sound right, though. Who had that been?

Her mind wandered but was brought sharply back into focus when her cell rang. She saw it was the office calling. Did she really want to get pinned down about where she was? Guilty, she let it go to voicemail.

"All right," she said to herself. "You've done what you came for. Time to go."

She started to leave the bedroom, then paused. She crossed the room to the dresser and took a tissue from the box there, spraying it with the cologne that loved her senses. Before she put it in her pocket, she took a long sniff. *Yes.*

A sound from behind startled her, and she stiffened. Movement in the broad mirror caught the corner of her eye, but she saw no one. She instinctively took a step back, regretting that she'd left her gun in the truck. "Who's there?" she demanded.

Ophelia inched into the doorway. Caryn's face flushed. *What an idiot. Of course it's the dogs.* Something in the way the dog's head hung down tickled Caryn's empathy. She hunkered down and held out a hand. "Come here, girl."

It took several patience-straining minutes, but the pointer inched closer until she was within reach. She sniffed Caryn's hand, and then her pocket, and her tail wagged once.

"You like that, too, my friend?" Caryn said with a smile. She grabbed a worn flannel shirt laying nearby and gave it a short spritz of the cologne. The dog took a whiff and then laid down. When Caryn put the shirt on the floor, the dog rolled on it, then curled up as though she were ready for sleep.

That made Caryn laugh, and she stood slowly, so as not to spook the anxious dog. "Hopefully, that will hold you until he gets back in person, okay?"

The dog's tail thumped against the floor multiple times.

"Good enough."

Caryn glanced at her cell, the message notification bugging her. "I'm going, I'm going..." She hurried down the steps. Levi's study sat there, ready for her to plunder, the top of it covered with papers. Her conscience prickled, and she chewed her lip, torn, then turned away to check in the kitchen. The dogs had eaten all the food she put out. She refilled the bowls, hoping they wouldn't just gorge themselves, then get sick, but she didn't see any kind of special feeder-container to release over time. She'd have to trust them. Same with the water.

I imagine if they get hungry or thirsty enough, they'll find game and a stream in the woods. Not much else I can do.

"You guys be good, now," she scolded. The two males studied her, as if analyzing the tone, then went to occupy the rug in the office. She went halfway after them, then stopped.

No.

She wasn't here because of business. She was here to do a morally correct favor for someone. A friend. Someone she hoped was a friend. Someone she yearned to be friends with—and more.

If she went in, she'd want to scour through whatever she found there. Was it better not to know? Because if she did root through Levi's personal information and found evidence of his crimes, they would lose any chance to become the friends she so dearly desired to be.

Setting her jaw, she picked up her keys and left the house, locking the door behind her.

Chapter Thirteen

Levi was vaguely aware of what went on around his hospital bed over the next two days, grateful to be able to just shut it out when he became too frustrated to cope. With his eyes bandaged, there wasn't much to see anyway. He remembered Caryn's promise to set a guard on his door, though, and knew it wasn't to lock him in. He was in danger.

Why hadn't Alex come to see him?

In light of the two incidents and deaths involved, Levi needed to talk to Alex even more desperately about salvaging what they could of their original monkeywrench team. They must cut ties completely with Rannell's men and women. Amputation was the only way to resuscitate their credibility.

Meanwhile, nurses and therapists came and went. The doctor stopped in periodically. A woman from social services even dropped by to see if he wanted any family notified. The only family he had left was Zane, and he was pretty sure Zane wanted no part of this. He told her no.

He'd expected that Greg or one of the other moderates in the group would come by to check on him, or perhaps to warn him what to say—or what not to. But none of them did. Not even Alex.

Something felt wrong with that. He'd known Alex since they were kids on the mountain together. Alex wouldn't abandon him just for this choice. Hell, Alex had brought the Rannells in! Why wasn't he here apologizing?

The morning of the third day, Levi pulled himself out of his lethargic haze and asked one of the nurses for his cell phone.

"I'll ask Doctor if you're allowed to have it. We don't want you getting yourself worked up," she said, a cheery grin in her voice as she changed the dressings on his arms. The bandages were much lighter now, just a gauze covering instead of the heavy packs they'd used earlier. "All right, I'm going to give you something to keep you comfortable."

He snapped, "No! No more drugs."

Her footsteps drew back as though he'd slapped her. "Excuse me?"

"No more drugs. I have things to do."

"Doctor won't—"

"Get the doctor in here. Now."

She hesitated, then backed away. "I'll see if he's available." Her footsteps led away from the bed, then the whoosh of the door sliding let him know she'd gone out.

That felt good.

The first smile he could remember in days came to his lips.

A rush of adrenaline hit his system, preparing him for the verbal battle with the doctor. Levi had been in this bed long enough. Time to get out and deal with the world.

Dr. Mountjoy came bustling in, setting the ubiquitous laptop that held all the patient charts next to Levi on the bed. "Now what's this I hear? You're giving the nurses trouble?"

"No trouble," Levi said. "I just want to make some calls to make sure my animals are being cared for and to take care of business."

"Let me check a few things first, shall we? I'd like to try to remove the bandages on your eyes, if that's all right."

"Hell, yes, it's all right. Do it."

"Please keep your eyes closed, Mr. Bradshaw. It'll be pretty bright since you're not used to natural light. Nurse, will you dim the lights, please?"

"Of course, Doctor."

The doctor's fingers, cool and smooth, touched Levi's arm, then his face, then unwrapped a gauze bandage from around his head. With each circuit, Levi could swear he saw a little more light. "Now I'm going to remove these eye pads. You'll be more comfortable if you keep your eyes closed until I tell you to open them."

The pads were removed, and chilled air rushed across his face, making him shiver. He faithfully obeyed the doctor's command, trying to be patient. A light shone on his face and flicked away a couple of times.

"How are you doing, Mr. Bradshaw?"

I'm a nervous wreck, a penned-in wolf. How do you think I am?

"Fine," he said aloud.

"As I told you, you received a flash burn, similar to what welders get if they're not using proper protective gear. The eyes are a delicate part of the body and more easily damaged. We'll find out now if any permanent injury has taken place. I'm going to put some anesthetic drops in your eyes, one at a time, all right?"

He nodded, almost afraid to speak. In so many fields he was a strong, vibrant man; here, at the mercy of modern medicine, he felt abandoned in the wild.

His right eyelids were carefully separated by the doctor's fingers, sending a shock of light right into his brain that actually hurt, then the same on the left side.

"Now blink your eyes a couple of times to spread those drops around."

He blinked his eyes, the action burning at first, but then the pain faded. He looked around the room, finding things a bit blurry, but he wasn't blind. *And I can still look at Caryn's beautiful face. Thank God.*

"How is it?" the doctor asked.

"I think it's all right," he said. "Still a little stiff-feeling."

The doctor nodded. "That's to be expected. We'll leave the lights half-dimmed for now, until you adjust."

"Thank you." He glanced down at his arms, wrists still fastened loosely to the bed. Peeling red skin peeked out from around the gauze. *Jeez, I really did it up right.* He wanted to curse Ron Rannell for his idiocy, but then Ron had gotten the ultimate punishment. Nothing Levi wished could make it worse.

"Now that you're visual again, I don't think we'll need these," the doctor said, and he released Levi from the restraints. "Just be careful not to rub your affected skin. The blisters are still healing. Overall, you're recovering quite well. Faster than expected."

"Good. Thank you." Feeling more like himself at last, he focused back on his purpose. "Could I have my phone?"

One eyebrow raised, the doctor studied him like he

was a small boy standing in front of his mother's favorite vase, broken in pieces on the floor.

"For Pete's sake, I'm a grown man!" Levi burst out, much louder than he'd intended. The lab tech passing outside his room stopped to stare. "I should be allowed to call people on my own damned phone!"

The doctor's frown morphed gently into a smile. "Well, I see you're feeling better, indeed. I'll leave orders that your phone can be returned from your personal effects immediately." The doctor left.

Levi wiggled himself into an upright position on the bed, negotiating the IV and oxygen tubes, which both threatened to lasso him. *So there. I won.* Allowing the glory of the self-righteous victory to sink in, he realized as the minutes passed that it hadn't been much of a fight at all. Just a test.

"At least I passed," he muttered.

The nurse came in with his phone, handing it to him like it was a king's scepter. "Here you go, Mr. Bradshaw."

"Thanks."

She hesitated, as though he might fall out of bed from the weight of the phone, or some other tragedy would unfold.

"I'm good," he assured her. When she didn't budge, he made shooing motions with his empty hand.

"Nothing I can do for you?" she asked.

Frustrated, he growled, "Fine, fine. Could you raise the head of the bed?"

She hurried to do his bidding, adjusting it so he could sit comfortably. "Now, don't you wear yourself out calling all your girlfriends!" she scolded.

He stared at her, a little confused, as she went back

to the nurse's station across the hall. 'All' his girlfriends? Just who'd come by while he was sleeping? Caryn had come once a day, but she'd left a written note if he wasn't awake. He was deeply grateful she'd volunteered to care for the dogs. Their well-being weighed heavy on his heart. His instinct about her had been true. She was definitely the woman for him, if they could only resolve this 'tiny' issue that stood between them.

Not wanting to waste more time, he tore himself away from the memory of Caryn's green eyes and dialed Alex. No answer. No voicemail. Nothing.

He vaguely remembered asking Caryn to check on Alex. Maybe she knew more. He dialed her cell.

"Orlane," came the clipped response, when she answered on the first ring.

"Caryn, it's Levi."

A surprised pause. "Levi? Where are you?"

He almost laughed. "What? Did you think I was out spiking trees or something? I'm at the hospital. Did you contact Alex Sullivan?"

"That's who it was." She took a deep frustrated breath. "I didn't have a last name, so I couldn't."

Disappointed, Levi took stock of himself and made a snap decision. "Where are you?"

"Just stopped for some coffee at Colter."

Perfect. She wasn't even two miles away. "Come get me," he said.

"What? Are they discharging you?"

"Yeah. They don't know it yet. Just come. Quickly. I'll…I'll work it out."

He clicked off before she could argue with him.

"Better make sure I'm not going to collapse right

out the door," he said, keeping one eye on the nurse's station. Carefully he slipped the oxygen tubing off, over his head, taking deep breaths, then more shallow ones. He didn't feel light-headed or dizzy.

So far, so good.

He'd been brought in unconscious, so he didn't know where any of his belongings had ended up. He scanned the room for closets. *There.*

But if he was going to escape, he'd also have to disentangle himself from the network of sensors, needles and tubes that still confined him. In the movies, all the heroes just ripped that stuff out and went on their manly way. He wasn't sure he was quite that reckless. Or knowledgeable. With his luck, he'd rip open a vein and bleed to death before he could leave the building. Then who would take care of his pets, hmm?

"Levi, nice to see you up and around, man."

The voice from the door startled him, and he twisted around to see who had called his name. The young man wearing hospital scrubs sat in a wheelchair just inside the door. He was one of Ron's guys who'd been there the day of the explosion. Levi couldn't pull the guy's name out of the fog in the back of his mind, though.

"Hey. How are you doing?" he asked politely.

"They let me out, just long enough to take a cruise down the hall." He wheeled closer, his blond hair hanging in lank locks to his shoulders and a several-day scruff of a beard. Holding up his hands, he grinned. "No handcuffs."

"Did they say you were under arrest?"

The young man shook his head. "Nah. They're looking for bigger fish, I guess. You?"

"Me?"

What did he mean? Was he under arrest, or was he a bigger fish? Neither applied. "No, I'm not under arrest. Yet. Guess it depends on whose fault they ultimately determine this to be."

The young man snorted. "Guess we know it's the gov'ment's fault for being so communist we have to take up arms, right?"

Levi kept a look of utter disdain and disbelief from his face. "Right. Whatever you say."

Movement outside the glass caught Levi's eye. Caryn had arrived, two Styrofoam cups in hand, and a curious expression in her eyes. The young man glanced over his shoulder and scowled.

"Hey, it's the BLM cop. What's she doing here, Levi, huh?"

Levi stared straight at the window. "How should I know? Probably has more damned questions about your boss."

"Yeah? Bringing you coffee like your best pal?" His eyes got a little wild, and he backed up his wheelchair so he blocked the door. "C'mon, Levi, what are you doing? You're not going to rat us all out, are you?" The young man's voice rose, taking on a ragged edge. "You turning on us, man?"

Levi eyed him. "I'm going home, pal. That's all. Just going home. Hope you're all better soon, and you can go on home to your family, too."

The man kept his wheelchair squarely in the door. "You'd better not say anything to her! You'd better stick with the program, man, or you know someone'll be after you like an old hound. Ron's dead, but there's more of us—"

Caryn stepped up behind him, finally in earshot. "Is there a problem here? I can come back later."

"No, come in," Levi said. He'd heard enough. Taking a wild guess as to which of the wires attached to him was a crucial monitor, he ripped it off, wincing as it took hair with it. He watched the nurse's station across the hall. Sure enough, several of the women glanced up, and then came at a run.

"Here, now! What's going on?" scolded the head nurse, the one who was always chewing him out. "You're supposed to be lying down." She turned to study the man in the wheelchair. "And you've had just about enough exercise. Get back to bed."

Her attitude would have cowed Patton. The man opened his mouth, then closed it, turning to wheel his way out, glaring at Caryn as he passed. He shot one more hate-filled look at Levi through the glass before he left.

Caryn slipped inside, taking a position out of the way, and set the cups down on a countertop. "What was that all about?" she asked.

The nurse and her aide bustled around the bed, trying to get Levi to lie back down, but he was about finished. "I'm leaving," he said.

"I don't think so." The nurse straightened the sheets and wrestled with the tangled oxygen line. "You're not healed yet. Doctor will want to check you. He'll do rounds again this afternoon."

Levi took a deep breath, his heart racing. The implications of what the man had said were setting in. He glanced at Caryn, saw lines of concern digging into her forehead. "I can't wait until this afternoon. I'm going now."

"Nonsense." The nurse continued to putter with the bedsheets.

"I'll do it myself," he threatened, reaching for the IV line.

"Don't you touch that!"

Caryn twitched when the nurse barked, as did the aide. Levi's hand jerked away from the offending IV.

"I'm not going to let you just rip that out. Blood everywhere and who knows what internal damage," the nurse grumbled. "If you want to leave against medical advice, you have to sign a form releasing the hospital from liability when you get infected and die. I'll have the doctor bring it to you." Stern and unsympathetic, she wagged a finger in his face. "Don't. Move."

"Yes, ma'am." He sat straight and still, very aware of all the tubes. The nurse stormed out, the aide in her wake.

Caryn leaned against the counter, sipping her coffee. Watching her, he realized that he'd really let down all his walls when they'd last talked. She'd found him at one of the lowest points of his life. The insight brought him a wave of embarrassment. Here he wanted to impress her, wanted her to like him, and he'd degenerated into a defeated warrior.

I've got to turn that around somehow.

She cleared her throat in the awkward silence. "So...wasn't that Terry Gable in the wheelchair? One of the militia boys?"

That was it. Levi nodded. "Guess your timing wasn't the best."

She shrugged. "You said come. I came."

The matter-of-fact tone with which she admitted this gave hope that despite his infirmity, perhaps she could still invest in some relationship between them. But doubts made him deflect the thought, with faint humor. "With coffee?" he asked hopefully. "Real coffee? Not hospital stuff?"

"Oh, right. I'd forgotten in all the excitement." She handed him a cup. "Do I need to look into Mr. Gable further? That sounded like a warning."

He tried to minimize it. "They just talk that way. Makes them sound tough, you know."

"I see." The dissecting look she gave him let Levi know she saw very well. She didn't take it lightly, despite his disparagement. "So, if that didn't spur this big jailbreak, what did?"

His gaze slid to her, then the door. "Jailbreak? Are there guards outside?" His voice caught.

"Not while I'm here."

"What, then?" His troubled gut clenched tight. "Are you here to arrest me?"

"No. Don't be in such a hurry to go to jail. Every time you see me, you assume I'm going to lock you up." She bit her lip, chewing it a minute. "Actually, the consensus of the evidence shows you didn't arrive on the scene until after the launcher was set. The other witnesses admitted you didn't even know about it." More softly, she added, "I think this puts you in the clear."

Her slight smile was a lifeline. He let it wrap around his heart. "And you're still here."

She nodded slowly. "I'm still here." She adjusted her stance, rocking her weight onto her heels. "You realize you're probably an idiot, signing yourself out against medical advice?"

"Yeah, maybe. I've got animals to feed—"

"I told you I'd taken care of that. I went up to the house and fed them every day. They're fine. They just miss you."

"You didn't have to. That's really something. Really something." Relief showered over him. "I owe you. But that's not the only issue on the table. I'm still going." His jaw set and he rubbed his eyes, then sucked in a sharp breath of air. "Damn it, that hurts."

"Exactly my point," she said. Her self-satisfied air was annoying and endearing at the same time.

He paused, opened his mouth as if he was going on, but at that moment, the doctor stepped in, clipboard in hand. His broad face set into a jolly flavor of disbelief. "I hear you want to leave us already. What's the rush, my friend? Are the nurses mistreating you? I hardly think so."

"I have business that I need to attend to. You've all been great. Just give me the form. Whatever you want me to sign. I've just got to get out of here. Now."

The doctor shared a puzzled look with Caryn. "Something you said?"

She raised her hands and stepped back. "I just arrived. Not my fault."

Levi didn't want this to break down into a conversation between the other two. *Damn it, I should be able to control my own future!* He pitched his voice into a more insistent mode. "The *form*."

The doctor set his clipboard on the edge of the bed.

"Mr. Bradshaw, please. You've been through a horrendous experience. You could well have died. Still might, if you're not cared for properly. I want to make sure you understand the seriousness of your condition before you make a rash choice."

He pulled a small flashlight from his pocket and shined it in Levi's face.

Levi hissed when the brightness hit his sensitive eyes. "That doesn't prove anything."

The doctor kept on checking, moving on to the gauze on Levi's arms. "You've got to choose some better playmates, sir. Playing with fire is not for grown men."

Annoyed with the lecture, Levi snatched the clipboard, took the pen and signed his name.

The doctor eyed him with skepticism. "You didn't even read that. It could have been my lunch order for today."

Levi hardly took a beat. "Was it?"

"No." The doctor read the paper, then lifted his hands in surrender. "You're free to go."

Relieved, Levi worked to give the doctor a smile that was more than half-hearted. All this drama was starting to sap his energy. "Thank you. I'll invite you to my next Friends of the Pines fundraiser. We have great wine."

The doctor deadpanned, "I'll look forward to that, as long as we skip the pyrotechnics. I'll send the nurse in with home care orders." He left the room with a cryptic look at Caryn.

A nurse appeared to remove the IV and other attachments, and methodically added fresh bandages on his arms. She added, "Here are your discharge instructions. Sign at the X."

With increasing impatience, Levi scribbled where indicated. "Where are my clothes?"

The nurse hesitated. "I'd thought someone hung them in the closet." She went over to check that out.

"Here they are."

"Great. Thanks." His tone was dismissive enough to chase her out, and she went away. He eased gingerly out of the bed, the pull on his healing skin making itself felt in multiple locations.

"What can I do to help?" Caryn asked.

"First, you could not laugh at the hospital gown." Inching closer to the closet, he held the flimsy cloth sides closed to cover as much of his dignity as he could.

She chuckled. "Wouldn't dream of it. Want me to wait outside?"

"Yes. No. Let me see if I need help," he said. A sharp smell of smoke came from the open closet door. "Ugh." His pants hung on the hanger, and boots sat in the bottom. "Doesn't look like there's a shirt here."

She glanced at his burns. "Probably burnt when you were."

"Right." He grabbed the pants, then limped into the bathroom.

The attempt to get dressed was a slow business as he adjusted to the aches and pains the accident had inflicted. At one point he caught a glimpse of himself in the mirror, one eyebrow half seared off, his hair rumpled and wild, the scars on his cheek like that of a demented pirate. How could anyone even look at him?

You said come. I came.

Caryn's words buoyed him up. She'd accepted him for who he was. He'd get through this. *They* would get through this.

But once he tried to pull up the burnt and shredded pants, it was apparent he couldn't leave in these. One strong breath and they'd disintegrate. He stuck his head out the door. "I need clothes," he said. "These aren't going anywhere."

Caryn frowned. "Do I look like a magician?"

Embarrassed enough, and annoyed that his brave attempt to get out of here was falling apart on the details, he snapped, "Haven't you ever seen a movie? There's always a closet of scrubs handy."

"You want me to steal hospital scrubs?" Her eyes widened and her jaw dropped. She nearly spilled her coffee.

"Like you said, I'm sure they'll include them in the bill. I'm not leaving this building naked."

He closed the bathroom door, waiting. How about it? Was Caryn too much a cop to break the rules for him? As the seconds ticked by, he thought perhaps she was. More waiting. Damn. He'd misjudged her.

The door opened suddenly, and a set of turquoise scrubs came flying in at him. The door closed. No comment.

A smile creeping onto his face, he shucked the hospital gown, leaving it on the floor. He chuckled and pulled on the loose-fitting scrubs, which were much more comfortable and certainly more substantial. On to other problems, now that he at least had pants.

"Where's my truck?" he said, coming out into the room.

"How should I know? Do I have to keep inventory of all your belongings? I'm guessing not here at the hospital."

"Can you find out? Otherwise, how am I going to get home?"

"It probably got towed." She pulled out her cell and texted a message.

The nurse's aide popped in with a bag of personal

belongings and a handful of pharmacy slips. "Nurse Hammond said you need to get these filled." She handed them to Caryn. "Make sure your husband takes these on time, so he doesn't relapse."

Caryn took the papers, amusement tickling the corners of her mouth. "I'll do that."

The aide smiled, pleased, and scooted back out.

Levi growled as he tried to shove his feet into his boots, a task that proved too difficult. "Did she just put you in charge of me? What the hell. Today just gets better and better."

"I guess." Still smirking, she handed him the bag.

"You don't happen to carry spare sandals, do you?" He caught another glimpse of himself in a mirror and frowned. "Not so pretty anymore, huh?"

"Why don't you just go barefoot for now?" she said before draining her coffee cup. "You'll be home in no time."

"All right. I don't have that far to go."

"You mean, 'we,' don't you? I guess I'm driving, since you're without wheels."

He looked around the room gathering up anything that was his. "You'd do that? I can't ask after all you've already done."

"What's another trip to Big Mountain, right?"

"Oh. We're not going there."

"We're not?" She paused en route to the door.

"We're going to Alex Sullivan's house."

A wrinkle of concern squeezed up between her brows. "Why there? Is he militia?"

"No. He's a childhood friend of mine that was part of my crew. I haven't been able to raise him on the phone since before the accident."

Caryn tossed her empty cup in the wastebasket. "Maybe he's just laying low."

That brought Levi up short. He hadn't considered that possibility. Perhaps everything was just fine. But something nibbled at his gut that disagreed. "I need to check it out anyway."

"All right," she said with an exasperated sigh. "Let's go."

As they walked down the hall, people stared at Levi's bandaged, blistered arms. Some whispered. He ignored them all, head held high. *Hey, my stupidity earned every one of these scars. Get over it.*

His determination carried him to the first floor, then out to the parking lot, where he avoided the bright sun and the stares of passersby to climb into the passenger seat of her truck, ignoring his pain as best he could. Only then did he lay his head back against the headrest, eyes closed. He reached over to take her hand and squeeze it, hoping it reassured her he wasn't about to drop dead.

"I'm good. Let's check out Alex's," he said.

Chapter Fourteen

Levi walked beside Caryn on the way to her truck, keeping up until the sun came out from behind a cloud. The bright light hit him full in the face and he stumbled over the concrete.

Caryn grabbed his elbow. *Bad enough I'm traveling around with a confessed monkeywrencher—I definitely don't want to have him break his neck on my watch.* "Whoa now, you'd better stay upright or I'm going to turn you around and walk you back inside," she said.

He let her steer him into the passenger seat. "Guess maybe I wasn't quite one hundred percent. Hate hospitals, though. Especially the Nazi nurse tactics."

She rolled her eyes. "They were caring and invested in your well-being. Unless you're going to claim they beat you when all your visitors left."

He muttered something she didn't catch, but nothing in his tone sounded like a legitimate complaint.

"That's what I thought." She studied him a minute as he pulled the visor down and then hunched down, eyes still shaded with his hand. "I've got a baseball cap behind the seat, I think. Maybe a pair of flip flops too."

He dug around gingerly and pulled out a cap with the San Francisco Giants logo. Putting it on his head, he pulled the brim down over his eyes. She closed the passenger door and walked around to the driver's side, then got in.

"Are you all right?" she asked.

He murmured, "Be fine. Don' worry."

She started the truck, noting she'd have to get more gas before they went too far. Driving back and forth to care for Levi's pets had seriously strained her budget. *And I'm not sure I can bill that to the department as a legitimate expense, even if it's related to our case.*

"So where's Alex's place?"

"Off 40, over by Trumble Creek Road."

He directed her to the other side of Whitefish, at the foot of the mountain, where they pulled at last into the short gravel driveway of an unassuming white single-story house. A dog barked from the back yard, but Caryn couldn't see it from where they parked.

"How vicious is the watchdog?" she asked.

"Pete?" Levi snorted. "Lick you to death before anything else." He opened the door and slid off the seat.

Caryn stared at the house, seeing no signs of life. "Is that his pickup?" she asked, noting the large blue Dodge truck in the back.

"Yeah." Levi had his cell in hand, dialing. He listened for a minute, then put it back in his pocket. "Still no answer."

"Doesn't look like anyone's home."

Levi continued walking toward the back of the house, ignoring her. Caryn followed reluctantly, glad she had her weapon loose in its holster at her side. Something felt *off*.

They rounded the back corner of the house and found a black Labrador tangled in the light twenty-foot chain that secured it to the doghouse. The food and water dishes were both empty.

Levi scowled. "Alex would never leave Pete that way." He glanced at the house.

"Anyone else live here?"

"No, Alex lives alone. His girlfriend stays sometimes. But not often. I don't see her car." He let himself into the pen that surrounded the dog run. The Lab seemed frantic to welcome him with licks and a tail wagging like a metronome. "Hey, boy," he said over and over, soothing the dog while he worked out the kinks in the chain.

While he was occupied, Caryn walked closer to the house, peering in the uncurtained windows, beginning with the kitchen. Electric worry sizzled along her spine. Any officer knew better than to get into a dicey situation with no chance of backup. She could be about to engage in a shooting match with someone who might or might not be a militia sympathizer. She and Levi had an understanding. This guy? Not so much.

She took her gun in hand, and eyed Levi. He'd finally gotten the dog untangled. He dumped some water from a nearby jug into its dish. "Come on. If we're going in, let's do it."

She located the back entry, a heavy metal door without windows. No kicking this sucker in. "Do you have a key?"

"I do." He straightened slowly, with a sheepish grin. "It's at home in my desk."

The day just got better, right?

"Brilliant."

You know the day is better, because that man is up and around and looks like he's going to make a full recovery. You should be giving thanks, not complaining.

Caryn mentally kicked her inner nag in the pants and returned to her survey of the inside. "Well, what do you propose, then? Breaking and entering isn't exactly on my list of things to accomplish today."

Levi walked over and turned the handle. It opened easily, swinging wide to invite them inside. "How about we just go in?"

The fact the door wasn't locked failed to comfort her. And she was the one with a gun.

"Wait," she said, reluctant to proceed, but even more reluctant to let him go first if danger awaited them. "Let me secure the place. And don't touch anything!"

He held up his hands in mock surrender. "Yes, ma'am, Officer Ramjet. By all means."

She glared as she passed him, and his smile faded. Pausing to listen at the threshold, she heard only the low hum of appliances. The kitchen was immediately inside the back door. A quick glance showed her nothing of concern. She stepped inside, arm extended in front of her with her gun at the end of it.

"Alex Sullivan? Bureau of Land Management," she called.

No response.

Levi pushed past her, careful to keep his wounded arms clear. "Alex, come on, man, this isn't funny."

Still nothing.

The hallway, living room, and the bathroom were all the same: nothing. Caryn thought belatedly about the militia group's explosives and the possibility they'd wired this place to blow. "Levi, maybe we'd better—"

"God damn it!" came Levi's yell from a back room.

"What?"

She hurried to catch up with him, fully expecting to discover a body. She was happy to be disappointed. Levi stood in the middle of a room that appeared to have once contained a dust devil. Clothing lay scattered and twisted all over the floor, and several boxes of papers sat next to a shredder, halfway through the process of being destroyed. The only surface not covered with clutter was the empty desktop. It showed the dusty outline about the size of a computer case.

Levi turned to her, his jaw slack, eyes wide. "He's gone."

Despite her relief that he hadn't gone boom, or found his friend dead, she realized the crisis hadn't passed. "You think he's packed and left? Or did someone do it for him?"

Levi murmured, "He wouldn't leave the dog unless…" Oblivious of her orders not to touch anything, he yanked open the desk drawers, one at a time, scrounging through them, his voice growing tight and distressed. "You never leave your pack. You never leave your pack. You…*never*…leave…your…"

Hunched over the last drawer, he dropped it, empty, on the floor.

Silence stretched out, second after second.

"Levi?" she whispered.

"He's gone." This time, the two words were infused with dark clouds of despair.

Caryn moved closer, then lightly put her hand on his shoulder.

He suddenly turned to her, putting his arms around her, clutching her for comfort like a worn teddy bear. Startled, she set her weapon on the desk and embraced him. The dog barked faintly outside, then subsided. Stillness billowed around them until Caryn felt herself swallowed up, consumed by it. When she couldn't stand it any longer, she gently untangled herself, then looked into his face.

"So he left on his own?" she asked quietly.

Tears in his eyes, Levi nodded. "I trusted him. I thought we were standing together against the militia. But…"

She studied the pile that had come from the drawers, unable to make out anything that looked particularly valuable. "What were you expecting to find here?"

"Airplane and race car models we built, back when we were kids." He gestured at an empty shelf. "Files, personal papers. Alex kept everything he cared about in this desk." He glanced out the window. "I can't believe he left Pete."

She shrugged, thinking the same thing. No one should treat a dog like that.

"Maybe where he was going, he couldn't take a pet. Or he left in a hurry."

Though she hadn't phrased her thought in a question, multiple answers popped into her head as to why a monkeywrencher who knew militia folk might bug out in a hurry. Was he worried that BLM was after him? Or that the militia was?

Levi swayed and grabbed the back of the chair in front of him. It rolled forward and hit the desk with a crash. He fell to his knees.

"Levi!" she gasped. She reached for his arm, then pulled back, afraid she'd hurt him. "Come on, let's get you home."

He murmured muffled protests, but let her slip an arm around him, carrying some of his weight as they made their way through the cluttered mess. She got him into the front seat of the truck, but he insisted she bring the dog.

For a split second, she wondered if she really wanted that poor neglected animal in the front seat with them, but it surely looked like no one was coming back for it any time soon.

"Fine."

She stalked across the yard, the dog watching her as it barked and ran along the fence. She wondered how she'd convince him to come with her, a stranger. "You'd better call him," she yelled.

When she stepped inside the fence, the dog sat, as though it awaited her touch. She let it sniff her hand and then awkwardly released the chain from the thick collar. Levi didn't even have to do anything. The dog sprinted for the truck and jumped in, curling up in the center of the seat, his head on Levi's lap.

By the time she got in, Levi had taken off the hat and tucked it between his bare arm and the dog, minimizing touch. "You all right?" she asked him.

"Mm-hmm." He laid his head back, eyes closed. Then his head slumped a little to the side. By the time she made it back to the road, he was snoring.

Poor thing.

She headed for Big Mountain, stopping in town to fill the prescriptions she'd shoved into her pocket when they'd left the hospital. With no idea what pharmacy he'd prefer, she just picked the closest chain drug store drive-through, while Levi slept on. The tech told her she could just wait there, and they'd get started right away.

After she'd passed the paperwork on to the pharmacist, the clerk studied the three of them with open curiosity. "Is Levi all right? Heard through the grapevine he and his boys got into some real trouble."

"He'll be fine."

Caryn drummed a finger on the outer edge of her steering wheel, wishing time could move faster. One thing she preferred in a city like San Francisco, where her dad had lived till his death, was the anonymity of a large population. With Levi half-dressed and asleep in her car, she was sure word would get around in no time through her connections, or his, or both.

Although that shady Brad Pitt lookalike at the hospital seemed plenty ready to run and tell someone about me being there to see him. Not altogether pleasant.

Small red flags popped up all around the edges of her consciousness. She wasn't worried about her job at this point; she could certainly spin keeping an eye on Levi to her advantage under the guise of getting more information for the investigation. And what the locals thought about her work didn't really matter to her a whole lot. She was more worried about the militia—if they'd do this to one of their own…

She glanced at her companion. His jaw slack, one hand on the neck of the sleeping dog, he seemed so vulnerable, not at all the suspected monster who'd held a gun on her at their first meeting. Her hand reached out to caress some part of his skin that wasn't red and blistered.

"Well, here you go!"

Caryn jerked back at the cheerful squawk of the

girl at the window, handing out the thick bag of medication. She stared down the girl till her smarmy smirk faded.

"Is that it?"

"Ten-dollar co-pay." The girl leaned forward to catch a look at Levi, surely making note of his condition. "Don't look like he's got much in his pockets, though."

Irritated, Caryn dug in her purse and paid the girl. "You have a great day," she snapped before she pulled away from the window.

Continuing to the Candy Cane house, she made a mental list of things she needed to do once she got Levi settled. She'd call in to the office, check on the status of the rest of the investigation, then see to any new assignment Sam had for her. No one had called to update her, so the investigation must be stalled. Maybe she'd gather something further from Levi at home. The fact that Alex had split might be fodder enough to feed the analysis team for the afternoon. *What could that be about?*

Levi stirred when she pulled up to the gate. She jumped out and opened the old gate, then got back in and drove up to the house. When she turned off the engine, she took a fleeting look to see if he was feeling better. As if he could sense her attention, he opened his eyes. He fumbled for the cap, pulling it on, low over his face again, then shared a sheepish smile.

"Sorry. I didn't mean to fall asleep."

"You're exhausted. Should have stayed at the—"

"No, we're not having that conversation again." He studied the big white pharmacy bag on the dashboard. "What's that?"

"I don't know. Whatever the doctor ordered for you."

He grimaced. "I don't need it."

"Take it or don't." she said, opening the door. "You owe me ten bucks either way."

The dogs came running to meet them. Pete scrambled over Levi to get out his open door, barking happily, the answer a Hallelujah Chorus of canine greeting. When the dogs realized Levi was with her, it crescendoed, and they greeted him, too, with great enthusiasm.

He slipped out of the truck, landing hard on his feet. His second step, he stumbled and grabbed the open door for support before the ecstatic dogs could knock him down.

"Oh, hell," Caryn said. "Just stay there."

She scrambled out the door and proceeded to the other side of the truck, gently edging her way past the dogs to slip her arm under Levi's. She held the animals back so they didn't aggravate his injuries and supported half his weight at the same time.

"Stubborn man," she grumbled. "Let's get you inside." He balked, but she hauled him upright and kept walking, the dogs close around them as she made a beeline for the door. "Give me your keys."

"Well, that's a little forward, don't you think?" He wavered on his feet, and his hand came up as he tried to make a point. Then he tripped over her feet and nearly knocked them both to the ground.

I should have insisted he stay in the hospital. How's he going to be able to take care of himself here?

"What can I say? I just don't like to waste time." She held out her hand. "The keys?"

He fumbled in the hospital's personal effects bag, cursing under his breath till he found them. He pointed them at the lock and pushed his hand in that direction, but his fingers trembled. She laid her fingers over his and guided the key, then helped turn the lock to click it open.

The two Ridgebacks, impatient now, disappeared around the side of the house, Pete on their heels. Ophelia sniffed Levi, as if she couldn't figure out what was wrong with him.

Once inside, the dim light allowed him to pull himself together. "Kitchen," he said. "Have to feed the dogs."

"All right."

They proceeded slowly to the kitchen, where the dogs waited, watching their every move as they came in the room. Their water and food dishes were all empty. Levi started for the sink, and Caryn could only see a hundred ways he could get hurt even more.

"Look, I've been feeding them all week. Why don't you sit down, and I'll do this, all right? You're making me nervous."

She expected an argument, but he capitulated, dragging one of the kitchen chairs aside to lean on instead of her. He sat down heavily.

"They each get one scoop kibble, half a can of wet food, and a hard-boiled egg."

"The full gourmet treatment, hmm?"

She smiled and filled the dishes, setting another one out for Alex's dog. Pete went at it as though he hadn't been fed for weeks, even growling at the other dogs when they showed interest in his food. She moved his bowl to the side, where he could have a little space.

"Now, settle down, boys. Plenty to go around!"

Finding hard boiled eggs in the fridge, she gave them each one, then studied the group until she felt they'd finish without incident. "I didn't know about the eggs. Some routine. They're lucky dogs. Very beautiful."

"My pride and joy." His faint smile seemed a little stronger than it had been earlier. "You really came up here every day?"

"I did. I told you, in the hospital, but I didn't think you'd heard me."

"Your notes reassured me," he said, "knowing they were being taken care of."

His gratitude made her heart do something warm and twisty.

"You probably should have stayed longer. The dogs would have been fine."

He took off her cap and laid it on the table, then went right on as if she hadn't spoken. "You seem to be a dog person. Do you have a puppy at home?"

Caryn shook her head. "I don't really have the space. But I'd like to." She tried to erase that wistful note from her voice. "My dad had dogs. I miss them."

A pause. "'Had'? So he's passed, then?"

"He died a couple of years ago. He was a cop, too."

Feeling overexposed, she focused on putting the containers of dog food away, then leaned against the polished gray granite of the kitchen counter. The gray expanse wrapped itself along two walls, looking brand new and expensive. "I'm sure you wouldn't have liked him, considering the crowd you hang with."

"I told you, I'm done with that particular crowd."

He fell silent, and the only sound was the gobbling

of the animals as they filled their stomachs. Pete looked ready for more, continuing to lick his bowl long after every chunk of food was gone. The dogs eventually finished and headed for the den. The growls and yips of gentle dog play came from the other room, but finally settled down. Levi continued to sit on the stool, alternately watching her and looking out the window.

Caryn wondered what she should do. She'd brought Levi home—even gone above and beyond with the run to find out about his friend. Her duty was finished.

But she didn't feel comfortable leaving him to fend for himself. What if he had a relapse? Or a playful dog tore open his healing skin? She'd feel terrible if something happened to him. Besides, she found it hard to keep her eyes off his muscled body, even with the partly-healed scars.

She distracted herself with something practical.

"How about some clean clothes?"

He looked down at his thin scrubs as if he'd forgotten. "Sure. Bedroom's upstairs, first door on the right. There's got to be a button-up shirt in the closet. Something light."

His bedroom? Her heart skipped a little beat as she remembered she knew exactly where his bedroom was—but certainly didn't intend to tell him she'd already been in his closet and smelled that devilish aftershave.

"All right, I'll be back in a flash," she said. She started for the stairs, but he caught her hand and pulled her to a stop. He looked into her eyes with true tenderness.

"Thank you. You don't know what it means for

you to look out for me like this. Surely, you've got no good reason to."

So close she could still smell the analgesic cream on his skin, she thought about kissing him. "I'm glad to help," she said. "I have plenty of good reason."

Before he could say anything else—or she could do something stupid—she forced herself instead to pull away. She hurried upstairs, finding an appropriate short-sleeved shirt. She had to stop one more time to take a look over that panoramic deck. Definitely breathtaking.

Apparently she took too long. He called up, "Can you find it?"

"I'm good," she said, tearing herself away. She hurried down and gave him the shirt, avoiding his inquisitive look. "That's some view."

He smiled. "It is, isn't it? That's why I moved my stuff in there. Growing up, my brother and I had the room across the hall."

"Is that Zane?"

A sharp look in her direction. "How do you know about Zane? Were you investigating him?"

"No, not at all," she said, defensive. "He—the boxes in the closet... I wasn't spying. Just... I'm observant."

"Oh. I suppose so." He tentatively slipped his arms into the shirt, wincing as they rubbed across his burnt skin. "Couple days, the doc said, right? Then I'll be back to normal."

"That's what he said." She stood to the side, unsure what to do, her arms crossed.

"You want...coffee or something?" he asked. "I can do that much at least."

She jumped at the chance to be useful. "Stay there. Tell me where everything is."

He directed her around the kitchen, giving her the opportunity to scope out his neatly- arranged cupboards and stacks of dishes that hardly looked like they'd been used at all. The coffee came in bean form, roasted at the ubiquitous Montana Coffee Roasters. By the time the coffee was ready, she had a pretty good idea of where to find most anything.

She set out two cups, then poured them both some of the steaming brew, adding some cream to each cup.

"Let's sit in the den," he said. He took one of the cups, leaving her to bring her own, and moved slowly into the other room. Wood was already stacked in the fireplace, and he put down the coffee long enough to light it. When he took a well-worn chair by the fire, Ophelia came to curl up at his feet. Caryn took the chair next to him, the whole scene feeling very domestic. He watched her with an odd half smile.

"Is there a joke I'm missing?" she asked.

"Not a...joke," he said. "Just something nice. I remember my mother puttering in the kitchen. The way you moved brings back memories of her."

Now I remind him of his mother? I'm not even thirty! How did I do that?

Dismayed, she struggled to keep her expression complacent. "Well."

He laughed softly. "Sorry. I didn't mean that the way it sounded."

More silence, growing more awkward as the seconds passed. She ought to do something to settle him in, make her feel comfortable leaving him. After all, she had her own pet to feed and her own obligations to fulfill. She checked her watch. Nearly six p.m. The office was long closed. No one had called, so apparently they'd functioned fine without her.

"You don't have to stay," he said, with a pointed look at her wrist.

"I feel like you shouldn't be here alone," she confessed. The time stretched out into what she'd always heard called a "pregnant pause."

Find some reason to justify why you're still here.

She could have gone into business mode and asked him more questions about the case.

That doesn't feel right. Not when he appears so weak and wretched.

"Do you want me to take a walk around the perimeter to doublecheck that you're safe? None of the militia coming in here now that they know you're home?"

He shook his head. "They won't get past Rosie and Guildy."

Nothing else to do. Go home.

She spied the pharmacy bag. "Here. Take your medicine." She handed it to him.

A frown replaced his smile. "I don't even know what they put in there." He ripped the paper open and set the three containers on the table, making a huge business of reading every page of the warnings and contraindications.

She took a deep breath, wishing for patience, and sipped the coffee. It at least, was the one thing that had gone like she'd expected that day—it was delicious.

By the shape of the bottles, she could tell one was eye drops, which she would have expected. She couldn't read the labels on the others, but he finally popped them open and took several. "Might as well drink the Kool-Aid," he muttered.

They sat in companionable silence for several more minutes, then he took a remote control and pointed it at a flat-screen television on the wall. "What music do you like?"

"Music? Anything but opera and whiny country crap."

He snickered, flicking through digital music till he found a soft rock channel. The sound of piano started playing, and Levi tucked the remote away. "No broken hearts and honkytonks for you?"

The sparks she'd noticed between them remained, no matter how she tried to deny them. *How can I even think this could end well?* "No broken hearts at all," she said, a layer of steel coming into her words she really hadn't intended. To cover her flustered reaction, she took a big sip of coffee, then choked on it.

"You okay?" He started to get up, but she waved him back into the seat.

He sat down, then studied her over the rim of his mug. "You know, all this time, I've been hoping to get you alone in my house," he said. "And now that you're here, I'm too exhausted to do anything about it."

She chuckled, secretly delighted to hear him reveal his feelings. But that probably really meant it was time to go. The length of the day on her emotions was taking its toll, and her own fatigue was setting in. "Fully understandable. Look, everything's handled, why don't you go to bed? The dogs will alert you if there's a problem, and—"

He set the coffee down and stared at the fire. "Would you think I'm too pathetic if I asked you to come up and wait until I fell asleep before you left?"

"To—to your bedroom?"

"Please do." He held out his hand. "No funny business, I promise."

She hesitated, but finally, compelled by her determined belief in his trustworthiness, she took it. His skin was warm, his hands slightly callused—a man who spent a good amount of time chopping wood and doing hard work. His fingers slid over hers, massaging them.

"Good, strong hands," he said.

Nonplussed, she struggled for some response, but couldn't find one easily. His touch gave her feelings she hadn't had for a long while. She hadn't had time to indulge in emotion while she focused on her work, her career, her independence. Her body responded with a shudder that seemed to pierce all the way to her soul.

His eyes registered the movement, and his lips twitched. They stood up at the same time. Trying to re-establish an appropriate distance between them, even while holding hands, she asked, "Do you need me to carry you upstairs?"

He snorted. "Thank you, no. Being back in familiar surroundings and knowing my fur babies are fine makes me feel better all in itself. I'll be good in no time."

They traversed the stairs slowly, Caryn noting the white grip of Levi's other hand on the stair rail as he made his way up. But, true to his word, he made it under his own power. He disappeared into the master bath and closed the door.

Feeling at loose ends, she straightened up a little, tossing what she guessed were dirty clothes into a wicker basket by the closet. The water ran briefly behind the closed door, then turned off. She didn't hear any worrying sounds, like a collapse, so she continued her fussing, finally making the bed and turning down the blanket and sheet on one side so he could get in.

When Levi emerged, he'd changed into baggy pajamas with faded blue stripes. He surveyed the room and his eyebrow went up. "I don't recall hiring a maid."

She mock glared at him. "You couldn't afford my rates, believe me. Come on. Get in." She gestured to the bed.

Ophelia popped her head around the corner, Pete following close behind.

"She doesn't let you out of her sight for long, does she?" marveled Caryn.

"She really doesn't." Levi sat on the edge of the bed and snapped his fingers, calling the dogs to him. He gently rubbed behind each of their ears. "Go lay down," he said.

They obeyed, retreating to a worn braided rug at the far side of the room. He lay down, pulling the covers over his legs. He patted the broad empty side of the bedspread next to him. "I saved you a spot."

Her head argued that she would be crossing a line if she did what he asked. Her heart leaped at the chance to simply let go of the rules and the inhibitions she'd held for so long and allow herself to be human and give and take comfort from the ability to touch and reassure.

The intimacy they'd built over the day and their discoveries finally made the decision for her. She climbed onto the bed and scooted close to him.

"You're sure this is comfortable?" she asked, concerned for his nearly-healed wounds.

"You have no idea," he murmured, eyes closed. "Thank you."

She lay back on the soft pillows and smiled, even though he couldn't see her. *No, thank you.* With her other hand, she reached for the lamp's small knob, and turned it off. Twilight dimmed the room, but it was still light enough to see. She checked on the dogs, finding them sleeping companionably. She raised up on her elbow, watching Levi drift off to sleep. In the half-light, the scars from his accident were concealed in shadow, and she could almost pretend he was whole again. She smoothed the hair back from his forehead, thinking they should have brought his medicine upstairs in case he needed it later.

The thick down bedspread felt so good beneath her. She wiggled lightly, making herself a little space next to him, intending to get up in five or ten minutes when Levi was solidly asleep. The cicadas began to sing outside the open window. Despite her silent, half-hearted protests, their song lulled her to sleep.

Chapter Fifteen

A rhythmic thumping woke Caryn as the early sun streaks of dawn painted the wall across the room in soft shades of orange and ochre. A heavy weight lay across her midsection. She was under the covers...and where were her pants?

She jerked upright to a sitting position as the mysteries unraveled. Pete was scratching on the floor near the bed, thumping his rear leg. Her jeans lay on the floor next to Pete. And the weight that held her was a sleeping Levi's arm.

What did I do?

Levi stirred and turned to face her, leaving his arm right where it was.

"It's drafty up here," he said. "Easy to get hot, then cold, then hot and cold." When she stared at him blankly, he grinned. "You shucked your pants about halfway through the night. But then you were shivering, and I tucked you in with me. I told you. No funny business."

"I—I see."

A chill ran through her. It must be one of those drafts. Or maybe the warmth that awaited her under the covers. "How are you feeling?" she asked, trying to distract herself.

"Almost human." He studied her intently. The scrutiny made her wonder if she had a muskrat on her head or something equally egregious. She ran fingers through her hair, trying to tame it.

"I'll make some coffee," she said, starting to get out of bed.

"Not so fast." His arm tightened around her and he pulled her down next to him. He looked into her eyes and inched closer, his lips seeking hers. Then he kissed her.

She wanted him to stop. She wanted him to continue. She…wanted him.

"Oh, Caryn," he whispered, with such longing in his voice that it nearly broke her heart. She turned her face up to accommodate him, the soft brush of his mouth stimulating her. His lips fastened onto hers again, his embrace pressing her close against him.

Long-hidden feelings rushed through her body, the sparks of attraction turning into flames of desire. His hands moved up and down her back, always holding her firmly, not letting her escape the heat that built between them. Conscious thoughts of warning, reminders that they should keep a professional relationship, worries about his medical condition, danger signals, all went off in her mind, in the very back, where the rush of adrenaline and passion squelched them down into a little box and then slammed the lid on it.

Half afraid to touch him, she whispered, "I don't want to hurt you."

"I'm a big boy," he breathed into her ear. "I'm not worried about broken hearts."

"No, idiot, I mean your skin. Remember, the hospital?" She did pull back just far enough to look into his eyes.

"Oh, that. Don't worry about that."

She could swear he giggled. "I *am* worried about that. You could get an infection, you could—"

"Yeah, but I have drugs. Beautiful, beautiful drugs." He kissed her deeply, then confessed, "I can hardly feel that burn any more."

"Really."

"I have a different burn now, honey, and it's telling me to take you before you can get away."He pulled her close again, his hips against hers. She felt the very physical manifestation of the burning in his loins right up against her leg.

She knew she should say no, but her body was screaming yes. When he started to kiss her again, any will power she had left faded away. She was lost.

She caressed his cheek, looking into those eyes that called to her. Inches apart, they studied each other, his hand coming up to smooth her hair, to slip down her arm, and finally to cup her chin, lifting her mouth to his for another long, sweet, hungry kiss.

Anticipation welled up inside her, and she moaned, his touch tingling every part of her. He was a wonderful kisser, sometimes light and feathery, other times demanding and hard, taking her breath away and leaving her dizzy.

She lost track of time then, as he slowly unbuttoned her shirt and removed it, leaving hot kisses on her skin, nipping at her neck, making her feel like a container of white phosphorus, about ready to explode and burn. Frantic to be with him, she turned slightly to let him unhook her bra, and he tossed it aside, holding her to his hips and rolling to his back so she sat astride him.

"There," he said. "You're not touching anything

that was burned."

Feeling free and wild, she arched her back while he caressed her full breasts, pinching her nipples between his thumb and finger, rolling them until they ached with pleasure. She leaned forward, teasing him, dangling her breasts close to him till he seized them in his hands, pulling them down to his mouth, where he sucked on them like he was a hungry baby. Another moan escaped her, and her hips moved of their own accord, sliding into a rhythm. They fit perfectly together.

Time disappeared as she rode him, and she closed her eyes, savoring the sensations that filled her and made her blood run hot. Pleasure coursed through her, but she didn't want to find release, not just yet. He seemed to sense her sweet delay and let her go.

She laid down and curled close to him again, both on their sides, facing each other. He slid one leg over hers possessively, and kissed her again, his mouth hot and wet and everything she wanted. When he went for her neck again, she shuddered, then lifted her head to delicately drag her tongue around the edge of his ear, her fingernails digging into the skin of his back. That triggered something in him, because he held back no further. He flipped her onto her back and drove into her, mad with passion, his eyes closed, and his lips whispering her name.

That first orgasm was a sudden thing, crashing over her all at once when he pressed inside of her, exploding into the silent fireworks she'd been building to since he first touched her. As he continued to plunge and buck, she found herself coming again and again in what seemed to be an unending ride. Finally he gasped and pushed deep, his own release filling her.

Time seemed to stand still for several moments, the two of them frozen in place, the only sound their synched breathing, coming hard and fast after such an athletic performance. Then he groaned and disentangled himself, lying down next to her, welcoming her into the curve of his arm to cuddle.

When she caught her breath, she asked, "Are you all right? I didn't hurt you, did I?"

He chuckled. "Oh, no, officer. No police brutality here. I should ask the same. I hadn't expected to be quite so…energetic. It's been longer than I would have liked since the last time I…you know."

Oh, how I know.

"No, I'm good. Better than good." A smile had fastened itself to her face and she couldn't seem to remove it.

But this whole thing isn't good and you know it.

She shut off her inner critic and concentrated on the warm, protected feeling she got from being in his arms. A light breeze came through the window, brushing across her nakedness, making the hairs on her skin stand on end. She shivered.

"I lost the sheets," he said. "Want me to get them?"

"No. I don't want to move…or for you to move either."

He sighed with relief. "Deal."

Gradually the other noises of the natural world floated in with the fresh air. It was the sound of the world outside moving on, blissfully unaware that for she and Levi, the world had changed, forever.

****

Levi lay on his back, grateful for the pain medication numbing his body, allowing him to spend time appreciating the beautiful woman who now lay in bed next to him.

Who would have guessed this would be where his wild adventure would end up? If nothing else proved that his life was on an insane track, this would definitely be the topper.

Or maybe it was a dream, induced by the drugs. Maybe it wasn't real at all.

His hand went to touch her, lightly stroking her arm, verifying that in fact she was very much real.

Good.

As much as he wanted to extend these magical moments with Caryn, it was so hard to keep his eyes open. Between the usual post-coital sleepiness, the post-accident exhaustion and the post-hospital drugs, he really didn't stand a chance.

Caryn, too, seemed to be fine just relaxing in silence, letting things simply be. It was so soothing…

When he woke up, she was gone.

The pain medication had worn off, too. His quick twist upright rubbed his arms against the sheets, stinging him badly, and he let out a string of curses.

Stumbling into a pair of sweatpants, he stubbed his toe on the bedpost, then ran his knee into the open dresser drawer. Continuing the spray of obscenities, he yanked the pants up to his waist and limped out to the stairs, hobbling down them as fast as he could. Halfway down, he heard sounds in the kitchen, and hesitated a moment, wondering if he should retreat and get some protection. *I didn't seal up that dog door before we went upstairs…*

But it wasn't a threat he heard at all. Instead, gentle female laughter filled the kitchen, along with the sounds of pots and pans in use. And something smelled suspiciously like garlic cooking.

He peeked around the corner into the kitchen and found Caryn hunkered down on the floor, playing with the dogs. She wore yesterday's jeans and one of his long-sleeved shirts, the cuffs rolled up to fit. Her hair was loosely tied back, framing her face in softness. Several pans steamed on the stove. He got a little heated just looking at her, remembering their earlier encounter, but she was fully engaged in her current activities. *Too bad. I could have done with a repeat. Once my arms quit burning.*

"You can come in now instead of spying on me," she said, without looking up. "You walk as lightly as a grizzly bear."

Embarrassed, he stumped in. His eyes felt like they had sand in them. He frowned at the eye drops, but knew they'd help. He took another round of pain medication, too.

"Thought you'd left."

"I hope you don't mind that I made myself at home. I wanted to make sure you had breakfast, at least."

"I don't mind at all. Wish you'd stay longer."

Her wistful smile tugged at his heart strings. "Wish I could. But I've got pet responsibilities of my own."

"Oh? I thought you said…" Confused and still a little woozy, he replayed what she'd said about her dogs. No, they had been her father's dogs. "Not dogs, then."

"No. Not dogs." She grinned and scratched behind Rosie's ears. "I don't live in a…house, exactly."

"Your apartment doesn't allow animals?"

"It's not exactly an apartment, either."

He hesitated, cocking his head curiously. *What wasn't a house or an apartment?*

"I live out at the Hungry Horse campground in a motor home."

Well, that was a new one. "Really? Year round?"

"Suits my lifestyle." She shrugged and looked away.

"So what kind of pet do you have then? A cat? A hamster?"

"An iguana. She's about four months old." She left the dogs and rinsed her hands, then tended to whatever was cooking.

Iguana? Northern Montana was hardly tropical— weren't lizards tropical?

Levi shuffled to the coffeepot and poured himself a cup. She already had one near the stove, so he didn't offer. "You know, lady, nothing about you ever turns out like I'd expect."

"Is that good or bad?"

She smiled as she scooped soft scrambled eggs and slices of ham onto plates.

The breakfast aroma filled the kitchen. He identified the bacon and coffee easily, but was that dill? Some sharp cheese, maybe Parmesan or Asiago, lay like snow dusted across the top of the eggs.

All that, and she can cook, too. She's a keeper.

"It's good," he said. "Usually I like when people are mysterious. I have to puzzle out the truth about them. Challenges are fun."

"At least for women," she said, sliding one plate across the top of the granite island to him. "Your working companions must be harder to decipher."

Bam.

And there it was. Back to the tough law enforcement attitude.

From the way she casually slid onto a stool and started eating, Levi could tell that she hadn't intended to be cruel with her comment, though it stung him to the heart. For her it was matter of fact, part of her work, part of *her*. Would she ever be able to separate herself from her work so that she and Levi could enjoy a relationship out in the open?

That's a problem I can't solve right now.

"Right. Better keep up my strength."

He took another stool at the counter and dug in. He'd been right about the dill, and the garlic, too. After days of bland hospital food, this was a real feast.

Though he was curious about her day, the fear that it centered on investigating him discouraged him from asking. He hadn't participated in the fatal tragedy at Martin Lake, but he'd lied to her about Greg. Once she knew he hadn't been truthful, it would be much harder to convince her that everything else, including his feelings for her, wasn't a lie too.

She didn't say anything either, and that worried him more. What had happened between them was spur of the moment and driven by need. Hers had proved to be every bit as strong as his. He wanted to affirm that glowing connection between them. Did her silence mean she regretted it?

He opened his mouth to address his concern, but he was interrupted when the sounds of "I'm Walking on Sunshine" came from her pocket.

She grabbed the phone and excused herself, hurrying out to the porch to take the call, leaving him puzzled and curious as to whose call was that important. *And with that ringtone, too.*

I bet it's not that stick-up-his-ass boss.

Finding some small amusement in the thought, he finished his breakfast and cleared the table, resolved to be dressed and ready for whatever else Caryn might need. If she needed him at all. And he sincerely hoped she did.

Chapter Sixteen

The distinctive ring tone identified Caryn's caller as her sister Trescha. Caryn checked her watch. It was a quarter to ten in the morning. Trescha never got up before noon.

What the hell has gone wrong now? Why does it have to come up while I'm here?

Come to think of it, why am I still here?

Memories of their early morning lovemaking reminded her exactly why she was here. The spontaneous interlude reassured her that her feelings for Levi were genuine—and mutual.

Once she'd cleared the door, she answered. "What is it?"

"Real nice, sis. Way to make me feel welcome."

Caryn heard it all in her voice, which held a snap, but was torn by tears. "You don't call me anymore unless something's wrong. What's happened?"

"It's G-Gunnar. He threw me out."

I knew I never liked that long haired hippie freak.

Funny her granddad's term came to mind when describing the guy. Trescha had fallen for him from the very moment she'd seen his dark puppy-dog eyes at one of the pagan gatherings. He'd scorned her at first, preferring the pretty blonde wood nymphs who circled Cynthia Fallingstar like a pack of faery dogs, but when they all turned him down, he "settled" for poor Tresch.

Caryn had tried to warn her. Did Tresch listen? Did she ever?

"Did you kick him in the nuts? Afterward, I mean?"

"Care, d-don't be that way! I love him!" Her sobbing continued. "Wh-what am I going to do now?"

Caryn rolled her eyes skyward, thinking she'd like to pay a visit to Gunnar herself and teach him how to treat another human being. *No matter how much you hugged a tree, it still couldn't keep you warm...*

"Tresch, you're going to be fine. The guy is pond scum—"

Trescha cut her off with more tears. "I shouldn't have been so demanding. Maybe he'll take me back."

"Trescha, don't you dare!" Caryn growled. "Where are you now?"

Her sister sniffed. "I'm on the street in Kalispell by the North Bay Grille."

Caryn pictured her slender sister, standing outside the restaurant, her long bangs hanging in her eyes, her cheeks streaked with tears, clutching her handmade cloth purse as she waited next to her flimsy cardboard suitcase box.

"Don't go crawling back to him. Make him think about what he's done for a few days. Maybe...maybe he'll come around." *Or maybe I'll have more time to make you see the light.*

"But where can I go? Can I stay with you?"

With a pang of guilt, Caryn realized this solution would be self-serving as well. "Actually, I'm not home. But that works out. I needed someone to feed Niabi anyway. Why don't you take a lift out to my place? You have a spare key. I don't know exactly when I'll be back."

Caryn mulled over her options. With someone to watch over her pet, she could stay longer with Levi. Maybe once he was rested, they could improve on their impromptu morning skirmish.

"Where are you?" Trescha asked.

"Ah...working."

"All day and night?" The tears had stopped now that Trescha had a new indiscretion to focus on.

Caryn made a face, grateful her sister couldn't see it. "Look, just go, hang out, rest, relax. Have some wine. Make the bastard wait. He'll appreciate that you're worth fighting for."

She sniffed again. "Y-You think that'll work?"

"You bet. I sure think you are. You're my pretty, wonderful little sister. And everyone ought to love you as much as I do."

"Aww, Care, you're the best."

Caryn was almost glad for the distance the phone put between them. If they'd been in the same room, Trescha would have gone into her over the top squeezy, huggy, touchy feely mode, which always went on too long and gave Caryn the willies. "Yeah, whatever."

After an awkward pause, Trescha suddenly asked, "Wait. What should I say if someone calls? I mean since you're not home. Should I tell them where you are?"

"It's...ah. It's work-related. Anyone who needs me has my cell number." Caryn rolled her eyes. She had no landline. No one would call. No one would even know. *And that was just fine with her.*

"When are you coming back?"

"I don't know, Tresch. Don't worry about it. Just

sleep in my bed. If I come back and you're already sleeping, I'll crash on the couch. There's some food in the refrigerator. I *think*." She paused to mentally inventory her larder. Enough greens for Niabi, maybe some bruised fruit."You know, maybe there isn't. Better take something with you."

A deep sigh so dramatic it pierced the phone air waves signified Trescha's agreement. "Thanks, sis. You're the best."

"Yeah I know. Don't break anything."

"Hey! What do you—"

Not wanting to begin another round of complaints, Caryn hung up and cut her sister off. She took a deep breath of the pine-scented air, then walked out to get the newspaper that someone had tossed over the gate.

Levi's attention zeroed in as she walked back inside. "Trouble?" he asked.

Caryn shrugged and slid her cell into her pocket. "Family." When he kept staring, she added, "My sister's having boy trouble again. No big deal."

"Do you need to go?"

There it was, her perfect exit excuse. Whether she went to see Trescha or not—and she wouldn't—she could gather her things and leave, the rest of the day an empty slate before her.

Some echo of Trescha's trouble stirred within her, and she made up her mind. Her own regret at being alone ratcheted into overdrive. Surely both sisters weren't doomed to live without a man. After the tumultuous beginning she'd had with Levi, Caryn wanted the chance to turn it into something real.

"No. I'm fine. Let me notify the office I'll be out."

She sent a quick text to the BLM secretary that she

was under the weather and wouldn't be in until later. If her luck held, no one in the gossipy, everyone-knows-everyone-else little area she patrolled would have seen her come home with Levi, and she'd be in the clear.

If her luck ran as usual? That was something she'd have to deal with when the time came.

Levi had put on some violin-laced classical music. "You got the paper. Good. Do you want more coffee?"

Twenty minutes later, as they sat in heavy leather chairs on opposite sides of the low table in the den, sipping from steaming cups and reading sections of the paper, Caryn considered once again the easy domesticity they had fallen into. Could fall into permanently, if they chose to. But if they were to make this succeed, they'd have to put this investigation behind them. She glanced over to gauge his mood, to see if he was up to a serious discussion.

Levi leaned back against the wing of his chair, editorial page of the *Daily Inter Lake* propped up in front of him, his eyelids drooping along with his head. Even as she watched, his head lolled back onto the cushion and the paper slowly descended into his lap.

Not yet, apparently.

She grinned, touched by the innocence of his sleeping face, and went back to reading the local news.

The fire crackled down into embers, the dogs spread out in front of the fading warmth. Outdoors it would soon be 70 degrees, but in the shadowed hollows of the drafty old house, the fireplace took the remaining chill from last night's air. The pendulum of a large wood-framed clock ticked loudly, setting a rhythm. She found her breath aligning with it. The atmosphere was so quiet and comfortable. Nothing to do. How long had it been since she could say that?

Her gaze swiveled over to the desk and its papers. While Levi slept, she could discover anything she cared to about him, his business, his correspondence. Perhaps she could even discover exactly who in his group was the mastermind of the violence and criminal activity. She could solve this case and put it behind her. Behind them. They'd be free to move forward.

She bit her lip. What kind of relationship could they have if he couldn't trust her with his most private papers and thoughts? None.

But...

Resisting the gnawing temptation, she got up quietly and set the newspaper on the table. A tinkle of dog tags greeted her as they all noted her movement. Only Ophelia followed her outside onto the upstairs deck. She surveyed the view for several minutes, identifying businesses in the valley below and all of the mountain peaks she recognized. A shame Levi's mother hadn't launched the bed and breakfast she'd intended—this view alone with a tray of good mountain food would make the reservations worthwhile.

She settled into one of the Adirondack chaises, adjusting the cushions until she was comfortable. The bright sun tired her eyes, and she closed them, the afterimage of the mountains and sky remaining on the inside of her eyelids for several seconds. Ophelia stood beside the chaise and licked her hand. Caryn chuckled and moved her legs to allow the pointer space to curl up with her. Then she let the buzz of the noon insects and the soft breeze send her to rest.

****

Someone shook her shoulder.

"Hey. Caryn, you'll be burnt in…oh. Looks like you already are."

"Hmm?" She came awake quickly, sitting up, brushing the dog off the chaise with her sudden movement. "What?"

Caryn took in the scene, dazed with sleep. Levi stood, blocking the sun overhead with his body. "You were sleeping," she said.

"Seems like it was nap time all around." He smiled and held out his hand. "I'm serious about the sun. You're burnt."

Instead of taking his hand, she felt her face, finding he was correct. Her cheeks were hot and slightly painful to touch. "Damn." She stood, rueful smile tugging at her lips. "Guess I'd better find a cold cloth."

"Sure. C'mon in."

He led her to the small bath downstairs and showed her where everything was, even though she already knew.

"I'll get some ice water for you," he said, leaving her to tend to her situation. "Lemon?"

"Ah, sure. Thanks."

Eyeing herself in the mirror, she wondered just how she'd convince Sam she'd been sick when it looked like she'd spent the day out boating on Flathead. With a groan, she ran a thick terry cloth under cold water and applied it to her face, praying it would take the burn down. Sneaking a glance at her phone, she found one missed call, and saw it was nearly four p.m. The worst hours of the day for sun, and she'd done herself the favor of lying out, exposed. She deserved the stupidity award for the week.

Taking the cloth with her, she walked to the

kitchen, where Levi had a tall glass of water waiting.

"The sun will suck life out of you. You need to rehydrate," he said.

"You're the damaged one." She studied his arms and face. He'd changed since she'd left him, now wearing a plain white T-shirt and jeans. The healing scars remained, but they didn't look worse. He'd be all right.

She guzzled half the glass of water, its crisp clear taste reinforced by the slice of citrus. "Mm, thanks," she said.

"Comes out of the well. Good mountain stock," he said with a wink.

Feeling more alert, she checked her missed call. Trescha. "Now what?" she muttered. She hit the auto-call, waited for her sister's response. She'd probably locked herself out of the RV. Or maybe let Niabi out. Whatever it was, it was bound to be annoying.

After ten rings, the call went to voicemail. Unlike her sister not to answer. Usually she was desperate for contact.

"Hmm."

"Work?" he asked from the other side of the kitchen island.

"No, sister. Again."

"Is she in town?"

"No. I sent her out to my place until she and Gunnar straighten things out. They probably will, even though I think she's better off without him. She's never strong about these things."

He came around the edge of the granite piece, stopping behind her to tenderly rub her shoulders. She started to jerk away, afraid it would hurt, but apparently whatever burn she had hadn't gone through her shirt.

"Relax," he said, stepping close enough she could feel his breath on her neck. "You're safe here."

The rhythm of his fingers moving along her shoulder felt wonderful, and she surrendered.

"And you?" he asked. "You're overly strong about these things, to compensate? Duty before self?"

Her breath caught at the irony of the comment, considering her earlier thoughts. She let him think it was his massage that caused it.

"Duty's important, yes. It gives me a focus, a direction. I can't spend my time lollygagging around like Tresch, a butterfly flitting from cause to cause, one man to another. She believes there's something out there for her, an answer to her dreams. Prince Charming and a beautiful world."

Levi's tongue clicked. "Shame, shame. We have a beautiful world right outside, in these woods. Don't disillusion me."

"But no Prince Charming," she declared.

Was there a hesitation before he replied? "No one's perfect, I'm sure."

"No." She diverted herself from the discussion with another drink and application of the cold cloth to her face. "I'll have to get some cold cream or aloe."

"Let me see what I've got," he said. He released her and left the room.

She tried Trescha's number again. Still voicemail. Maybe she'd solved whatever problem she had.

Well, not by herself. The girl was a helpless jumble.

Gunnar better not be at the RV. I'll arrest him for trespassing.

She shoved her phone in her pocket. Levi returned with several tubes of cream, and she sorted through to find one she hoped would work. She retreated to the bathroom to use the mirror, making sure she didn't miss one reddening inch.

"Do you want me to make dinner?" Levi said when she came back. "I feel much better."

She called Trescha again. Still no answer.

"I don't know. This feels odd. I may have to go out there."

"Here's an idea. I need to pick up my truck at the impound lot anyway. Why don't we take a ride into town, then we can go out to Hungry Horse and check on things?"

"You should rest—"

"We'll be driving. How taxing can it be?" His lips curved in a mischievous smile. "What would happen if I had a relapse, hmm? I'd need a vehicle, right?"

Already twitchy about her sister, Caryn refused to be responsible for something happening to Levi as well. "Fine, I'll drop you off. Let's go." She grabbed her bag, making sure she was armed. "Feel free to stop me from shooting Gunnar if he's there."

He raised an eyebrow. "Noted." He headed out to the truck. She was pleased to find him much steadier than he had been the day before. At least his healing remained on track.

Possible scenarios unreeled in her mind as she drove to the city lot. Levi's thoughts seemed to run in the same direction.

"Maybe she's gone out for a walk," Levi said. "You know how it is. Nice day like this, you start walking, you get snarled up in the beauty around you.

191

All of a sudden it's hours later."

"She'd still answer her cell."

Levi shrugged. "Not if she hiked out of range."

That thought had occurred to Caryn. Hungry Horse was a serious hit-and-miss area for cell reception. But she also knew her sister.

"Right, but even though Tresch wants to love the Earth and all its plants and creatures, when she actually has to get out there and meet them, she doesn't do so well. Things like mud. Snow. Cold water. Animals with teeth." She hit redial. "She wouldn't go that far."

No answer.

"If she's so freaked by creepy-crawlies, how is she staying there with your baby dinosaur?"

She scowled. "Funny. It was a spur of the moment thing, all right? Solved two problems. Tresch being suddenly homeless and Niabi needing a babysitter while I'm up at your place."

"Maybe she and her pagan friends went off for a sun ceremony since she was there."

Now that was a possibility Caryn hadn't considered. Usually when her sister was emotionally wounded, she retreated and hid in comfort. But she could see how Trescha would be persuaded to let the group camp with her, so she didn't have to be alone.

"Yeah. Maybe." She just wished the sick feeling in her stomach would pass.

At the lot, Levi paid the penalty fees on his truck, muttering about the police tape on it. "Makes me feel guilty as hell." He ripped it off and tossed it in a rusty barrel nearby. "Get in," he said.

"I've got my truck. You can go home." She'd worked herself into a full-blown worried state now. If they hadn't been clamped firmly on the steering wheel, her hands would have trembled.

"Right."

The look he gave her seared through any bravado she had left. The better part of an hour with no response was not like social Trescha. Something wasn't right. She parked her truck in the city lot, putting her BLM placard in an obvious place on the dash and locked it up.

Then she climbed in the passenger side of Levi's truck, her toes beating an anxious staccato on the floorboard, reaching for an accelerator that wasn't there.

She castigated herself silently. She should have gone straight out; she would have saved twenty minutes. She'd know what Tresch had done, and they'd have solved the problem already.

It would be dark before long. They had to drive faster. She glanced at the speedometer, saw that Levi was already driving five miles over the legal limit. A sigh escaped her.

They zoomed up to the edge of town, and Caryn put her hand on Levi's arm. "Slow down. There's only one cop here and he loves to give tickets."

He obediently took his foot off the accelerator and cruised leisurely through town, picking up speed as soon as he crossed out of Whitefish. Hungry Horse was a few rough roads beyond, and shortly after, he slowed just long enough to pull the Chevy into the campground driveway. He accelerated down the stone path, wheels spinning hard enough to send rocks flying.

Caryn's nerves, already frayed, stopped her breath in her throat as they crossed the last fifty feet. The bright beams of a burnt orange sunset illuminated the RV's front window, revealing half a dozen bullet holes and splintered glass. The side window, too, was reduced to shattered fragments.

"What the hell…?"

Levi's truck slid to a stop on the far side of the camper, and she bailed out before he cut the engine.

Caryn's voice choked on her sister's name. *Why were there bullet holes in her camper? Had Gunnar attacked Trescha? He could have found Caryn's personal weapon in the back. How would Caryn get her sister out of this one?*

"Damn it," Levi muttered, pistol in hand. He shoved his way past her, heading for the door.

Wondering where Levi's gun had come from, emotion poured over her like cold honey, drenching her in slow-motion sense of time. She should have been first. She had training. But her feet felt mired in quicksand. Finally forcing herself onward, she grabbed the Glock, following Levi around the front fender of her motor home.

Niabi's well-being came to mind, but only because she didn't dare let other thoughts squeeze through. With the window shattered, the iguana could easily have escaped. She studied the ground in passing for any sign of the lizard's long claw scratches in the dirt but saw nothing.

"Be careful when you open that. Niabi might be loose."

"Yeah," he said. He turned the handle with his left hand, gun ready in his right, and pulled the door open, then looked inside. He stiffened, then glanced at her over his shoulder. The look in his eyes told her only things she didn't want to know.

"What? Let me in."

She reached for the door, but he blocked her with his body. "Honey, you don't want to go in there."

Alarm pulsed through her at his tone. "What's happened? Trescha?"

"Caryn, I'm so sorry." Levi reached for her, but she shoved him aside.

Her first glimpse was of her sister's hand on the floor, stretched toward the door as if reaching for help, cell phone nearby. She climbed the two steps into the RV. Trescha lay on her side between the table and the stove, face turned away, several bloody wounds on her back that had pooled blood on the stained linoleum. Tears blurred Caryn's vision as she knelt down to check for a pulse, despite the evidence before her.

No answer.

No pulse.

Caryn sank down onto the steps, tears running down her cheeks. She should do something. She knew she should, but she couldn't. Whoever had done this had sucked the life from her as surely as they'd done it to her sister.

She gritted her teeth, trying desperately to avoid the hot wave of guilt and loss that threatened to wash her away. Police mode. It's how one handled bad situations. Put emotions aside, and just the facts, ma'am...hang on to professional decorum.

My sister's dead.

Caryn's gaze slid across the side of the RV to the bullet holes. Whoever had done this was too much of a coward for a face-to-face shot. They hadn't come near the door. A high-powered rifle? She looked back over her shoulder. Where had the shooter stood?

Who was she kidding? You could practically go through the walls of an RV with a baseball bat. It could have been any kind of gun.

"I'll call the police," Levi said.

"I *am* the police," she whispered, bitter negation choking her. It couldn't be real.

It was real.

When she found the bastard who'd done this...

Wait, wait. She couldn't handle this herself. Police. Yes. Falling back on protocol, she nodded numbly. "Call," she said.

Some part of her consciousness noted that Levi walked away and had a conversation on his cell. She could only stare at that limp hand.

Trescha had never hurt a damned flea...how could this happen? It wasn't fair!

Denial settled over her like a stinking, drenched blanket. It couldn't be true. Was Gunnar really that cold, that he'd kill Trescha for leaving him? In a whirl, her mind sorted memories for hints of potential violence, but she couldn't recall any, not now.

Even so, she should have been there for her sister. Trescha had come asking for help, and Caryn had failed her, miserably.

Levi returned to her side, his hand warm when he placed it on her shoulder. "What can I do for you?"

Caryn shook her head. "There's nothing to do until the sheriff gets here."

Movement through the open door of the cupboard over the cab grabbed Caryn's attention, bringing her to her feet, gun in hand.

Levi's movements paralleled her own. A split

second later, she focused on the shadows inside and knocked his gun down, putting her own away. "It's fine." She closed the door between them and crossed to the cupboard, broken glass crunching under her boots. When she held out her arm, Niabi scrambled up, all the way to her shoulder, taking refuge under the front fringe of her hair. Her pet's familiar sassiness was gone, replaced instead by a desperate cling. Caryn slid a hand down her green body, assessing her condition with a light touch, though the iguana pulled away and snapped at her.

"It's okay," she whispered, knowing that in fact, nothing was okay.

At least Levi was here. The warmth of his presence spread around her like a shield. But she couldn't hide within it, not now. She had business to attend to.

My sister's dead.

Her heart ached. The instinct to start cleaning up pulled at her sleeve, but she ignored it. *Not until the investigative team does its work.*

Trescha's body kept drawing her gaze like a magnet. She shook herself and petted the lizard. "We've got to get out of here."

Caryn gently disentangled the iguana from her hair. "I'm sorry, baby, I know you don't want to be in here, either, but I've got to wait for backup. You'll be fine." She placed Niabi in the cage, fastening the door closed, then wrestled it to the door of the RV, kicking it open with her foot. Levi tried to take it from her, but she wouldn't let go. They ended up setting the cage on the hood of his truck. Caryn leaned against the fender, breathing hard.

"The sheriff's on his way," Levi said. He held his

arms open. "Come here."

Until then, she'd been able to keep her emotions frozen in the shock of what they'd found. Once his arms closed around her, her defenses broke and the tears came freely. He didn't say anything, just held her close. It was exactly what she needed.

They were still locked together when the sheriff's office team showed up ten minutes later, sirens blaring. There weren't but six cars in the western end of the county, and five of them had come here to investigate. Gratitude choked her up, and it took a few moments before she could speak to the elderly but robust sheriff, John Folden, whose wide-set blue eyes were full of sympathy.

My sister's dead.

"John, I—" She couldn't say the words aloud.

He fiddled with his thick white mustache. "I understand. Whatever we can do to help, Caryn." He glanced toward the motor home. "She's in there?"

Caryn nodded.

"All right then." He gestured to his second in command, a recent hire Caryn didn't know, to come speak with her, then he went to the open door, leaning inside to peek at the body.

Caryn sensed that Levi pulled back, trying to appear invisible, and she reached for his hand. His presence made her feel secure in the face of this insanity. She needed that strength, especially when the sheriff's deputy started firing questions at her.

"Have you disturbed the scene at all? Did you move her?"

She gave him the stink-eye. "Really? What kind of a cop do you think I am?"

He shrugged. "Honestly, I don't know, ma'am." He turned his attention to Levi. "What's Bradshaw doing here? Heard he got blown up or something."

"Could we focus on the crime?" It was all she could do not to take a swing. *Good thing Levi's got my hand, or I'd plant it in this idiot's face.* "He drove me out here."

The sheriff's deputy peeked at his notepad. "So that's a no? You didn't move her."

Caryn growled. "No. I didn't move her."

"Does she have any enemies?"

"Trescha? None I can think of."

"Does she live in…there…with you?" He eyed the motor home like it was a roach motel. To Caryn, it felt like he'd kicked her in the stomach.

"No. Well…yes. Not really."

The deputy raised a suspicious eyebrow.

"She'd been living with her trashy boyfriend in Kalispell. He kicked her out and she had nowhere to go. So she was staying here for a few days."

"You weren't here?"

"No."

"Where were you?"

Caryn's eyes narrowed. "You think I'd do this?"

He didn't miss a beat. "I didn't say that. I'm just building a record, Miss Orlane."

Maybe that's what annoyed her so much. That as far as he was concerned, she was just 'Miss Orlane.' A civilian. *Nobody.*

A nobody who'd done nothing to keep her sister safe…

"What about this boyfriend? You know his name?"

"Gunnar something. He hangs out with the

199

Earthenkrafte Circle pagan group."

The deputy's eyes rolled. "Terrific. Was she with them, too?"

"Yes."

"They've been having some scuff-ups, too, haven't they? With the Kootenai?"

Caryn frowned. She couldn't imagine the tribe finding the pagan intrusions worth retribution of this magnitude. "Yes. But I don't think this... Don't be ridiculous."

About that time, the techs pulled up, and the sheriff pointed them to the RV. They snapped pictures outside the camper, then inside. Once he had them working, the sheriff came over to them, his eye on Levi.

"We'll finish up here as soon as we can, Caryn." His voice rasped like sandpaper on granite, very different from his usual commanding tone.

"Thank you," Caryn managed, scrabbling inside for that professional face. If she could just hold onto it for a while longer, she could get through this.

"Can we talk?" He moved as if to guide her away from Levi, but she felt anchored to him. Her hand clenched tighter to Levi's, a link to the world away from that horrible sight inside.

"I—I'm fine here."

In a half-scolding voice that echoed of her father's, the sheriff continued, "Caryn, I hope you know what you're doing with this man." He glared at Levi.

Levi cleared his throat. "Innocent until proven guilty, isn't that how it goes, Sheriff?"

"Don't bandy words with me, son. Doesn't matter that I've known you since you were a kid, not with the company you've been keeping. Your group's on a rampage, and I don't intend to stand by much longer. If I had my way, you'd all be locked up!" His eyes blazed, and he tucked his thumbs in his belt and looked out at the horizon long enough to count to ten.

"It's all right," Caryn whispered. "Can we just go on? You're not thinking this has anything to do with them anyway, right? Trescha didn't even know them."

The sheriff's eyes peered right into hers like lasers. "You want straight talk? Okay. Is it possible that the shooter made a mistake? That they thought they were taking you out?"

A wave of cold splashed over her, and she shivered. Her fingers tightened on Levi's.

She let her professional mind run with the thought. If she'd been on the job, it might have been her first question to the witnesses on the scene. Of course it was possible. Someone gunning for her could have seen a woman inside the camper, particularly if it wasn't well lit, and could have assumed it was her. Absolutely.

My sister could have died by accident. Because of someone's stupid mistake.

Because someone wanted me dead.

"I suppose it is."

Her field of attention expanded to the whole area. Could someone be watching now? Scanning the faces of the campground neighbors who'd gathered just outside the lengths of yellow police tape that measured off the area around her motor home, she read curiosity, thirst for drama, some sympathy reflected in the flashing red and blue lights. Most people in the campground knew her by name. She'd lived there for several months, and it just wasn't that big a town. Once they spotted Caryn, several waved, looking relieved, but that didn't answer unspoken questions about the victim's identity. Could any of them have seen anything?

Her line of inquiry was followed up quickly by the deputies, who divided the inquisitive crowd to ask questions. Caryn's gut instinct had been to volunteer to help, but the sheriff and Levi gently discouraged her. Without anything specific to do, her mind sought escape in flights of thoughts, paranoid trails of dark smoke and deep pits of despair. The touch of Levi's hand brought her back to earth every so often, but for the most part, she just felt lost.

My sister's dead.

****

The techs seemed to take forever, now working under bright flood lights they'd set up outside the RV. She must have zoned out a couple of times, because the sun disappeared below the horizon and the stars came out without her noticing. Even the most curious neighbors had wandered back to their homes for supper by the time a large red SUV spun to a halt at the edge of the perimeter, grabbing the attention of everyone on the scene.

Her BLM boss, Sam Evans, bailed out of the vehicle, breathing hard, his gaze shooting from person to person until he finally focused on her. "Orlane!" he bellowed.

Shocked at his arrival, Caryn remembered only belatedly that she was holding hands with one of their most wanted. Exchanging glances with Levi, Caryn let her hand slip out of his. *What this must look like... Screw him. I don't care what it looks like.*

But somewhere deep inside, she really did.

To her surprise, Sam ran over to hug her, picking her right up off the ground. "Couldn't believe when I heard it on the scanner," he mumbled in her ear. "Knew it couldn't be right."

Stunned at his unexpected affection, she patted his shoulder to comfort him.

He finally set her on her feet and looked her up and down. "You're all right?"

She nodded slowly. "I'm not hurt."

Sam marched over to the sheriff, his unbuttoned jacket flapping open. "What's the story, John?"

The sheriff glanced at Caryn, an inquisitive eyebrow asking her permission before he answered. She debated withholding the information, since it was her personal life, and none of BLM's business. *It's not like it won't be public record before long.* She shrugged, then nodded.

The story didn't seem any less dramatic told by an impassive third-party. The ending remained the same: the last relative she had in the world was dead.

Sam listened, his expression fading into a grim scowl. When John finished, Sam started for the camper, but the coroner's office was already there, carrying the ends of a blanket-draped stretcher to the back of their black car.

"You have somewhere else you can stay, Orlane?"

Caryn chewed her lip. The last thing she wanted was to confess to Sam where she'd spent the night before. Better to lie, for everyone's protection.

"Yeah, I'll grab a hotel room."

Sam's gaze snapped to her right, where Levi stood. She guessed that Levi's face had revealed something hers did not. *Wonderful.* Sam studied her for a few endless moments but didn't say anything. He reached out to squeeze her shoulder.

"If you need anything, let us know."

"Of course, Boss. I'll do that," she said, with no intention of doing so. But then she remembered she'd left her truck at the impound lot before they'd come out here. She took the keys from her pocket. "Can you have someone get my truck from the Kalispell city lot? Just drop it at the station?"

"Sure, honey. I'll get it tonight."

He looked from her to Levi, and back to her, then visibly cut off something he wanted to say. Instead he growled some instructions at the sheriff and exited the scene. His absence left a vacuum, a space where she felt cherished and cared about. Was that why he was constantly gruff with her? Covering some sort of fondness? She couldn't imagine that if Robert's apartment had been shot up he'd have barreled in to embrace Robert.

I should be grateful he feels that way. Looks like I need all the friends I can get.

What was she expected to do next? Sorting through possibilities, but still too disturbed to focus on any one of them in particular, she suddenly understood on a much deeper level the people she'd dealt with on a tragic scene. Often, she'd become impatient talking to them, wanting to get past the upheaval and disorder to the solving of the crime. Life was very different on this end of the conversation.

John came over before he cleared the scene. "We got her phone. You want to look and see if any of the other electronics in there are hers?"

"Sure, I can do that."

"Is there anything else you need? Anyone we can call? We can notify next of kin, if you'd like. Whatever makes your road easier."

"Her only next of kin has been notified," she said, the words tasting like dirty plastic.

A moment dragged by as he processed that, then he nodded. "We'll let you know if we find anything. In the meantime, you be careful." He studied the motor home. "Need some help getting enough things for a few days?"

She considered the mess inside. "I should clean that up—"

He shook his head. "Don't worry about it tonight. It's late. Just get a few things. Plenty of time to deal with it by morning light." He eyed the cage. "You're taking that?"

"Yeah." Caryn mulled over Niabi's reaction to being carted twenty miles to share a house with Levi's dogs. *Well, honey, if I'm put out, you are too. And none of it brings Trescha back...*

For some reason that final reminder really punched her in the gut, and her whole body reverberated with the pain of loss, like plucking a single harp string. Her tears began and she couldn't seem to stop them. Racked with sobs, she would have fallen, if Levi hadn't caught her in his arms, lending her his strength, her usual resilience abandoning her in the face of this crisis.

I'll get through...I'll get through. I just need to get a handle on this.

She fought to catch her breath. Eventually the determined effort and the warmth of someone who truly cared about her restored her equilibrium.

"Ready?" Levi asked.

"I'll just get a few…" Caryn shuddered. Marching to the RV before she could lose her nerve, she took a deep breath and went in, carefully stepping over the plastic sheet covering the spot where the body had been, trying to ignore the broken glass. If she was going to get through this, it had to be done like a surgical strike. In. Out.

She shoved a week's worth of clothing into a duffel bag, then a few of her books, her shampoo and other personal care products. Socks would do instead of slippers; she was wearing her hiking boots. Maybe some sneakers for just around the house.

A quick look around the bedroom revealed no other clues. Nothing had been rummaged through or sat out of place, other than Trescha's own belongings, most of them scattered on the floor where she liked to keep them. *It was really just those few shots, and her life was over. No other intentions or motive. Just perhaps the wrong woman, wrong place, wrong time…*

Her emotions threatening to swallow her again, Caryn shut that door in her mind and turned to stuffing a cloth grocery bag with treats and food for Niabi. She'd seen what Levi kept in the refrigerator. The vegetarian iguana could starve to death there.

She snatched up her valuables, her camera, computer and the like. Trescha didn't have any here, as far as Caryn could tell. Just her phone. She wondered what the investigators would find on it to be of use, whether about Gunnar, or just enough to shed light on the ongoing feud between the pagan group and the native Americans.

Not my concern at the moment. I need to focus on being safe. So I can come back and kick these sons of

bitches right in the teeth.
    And I will.

Chapter Seventeen

Levi kept his eye on Caryn while driving back to his place, more than a little alarmed at the cold complacency that had settled over her. Sure, she'd had that one collapse, but this had to be heartbreaking. Instead, she was shutting down. And he didn't like it.

In the rear-view mirror, he caught a glimpse of the iguana malevolently staring back at him through the cage bars. It hadn't stopped flipping its tail and smashing against its food dish since they'd started driving.

Apparently it didn't like this either. Or his truck. Or being torn out of its home and moved. He shut his window halfway to keep the lizard from being chilled in the breeze.

Though he was no stranger to violence or death, the sight of Trescha's body lying in her own blood had shaken him deeply. Caryn's vision of her sister as flighty, random, maybe even misguided might be true. None of those things should be a death sentence.

Who are you kidding? You know who they were aiming for.

His fingers gripped the steering wheel as if it were the guilty man's neck. As much as he'd wanted Caryn to be in his home, a part of his life, this was obviously not the way he would have chosen it to happen. But she'd be safe there even if he had to lay down his own life to ensure it. Time to ignore his own wounds and tend to hers.

"Hey," he said softly, reaching to touch her arm. "Penny for your thoughts. Or maybe a whole dollar."

She continued to stare out the windshield. "I'm not having much in the way of coherent thought, Levi. Sorry you're in the middle of this." She took a deep breath and let it out. "Guess I've just pissed off someone to an extreme."

"Theories on who?" he asked. He knew what she'd say. But maybe she needed to say it, get it out in the open.

Her laugh was harsh, with an edge that scraped his skin. "Does it really matter? Something I did cost Trescha's life and—"

"No, it's not your fault! That was the act of a third person, independent of you. You're not to blame for that."

"Like hell." She hunched down into the seat.

"We can't be sure that the shooter meant to hurt you. Trescha's group has plenty of detractors, too. Her ex is still floating around out there. Or it could have been completely random—some kids out target shooting that went out of control."

A long silence. "You don't believe that."

She was right. But he didn't want to consider the possibility that she'd come that close to death. Neither of them pointed out the obvious corollary: once the shooter discovered that he'd killed the wrong woman, he'd come looking for Caryn.

"Okay. You're right. I don't believe that."

She nodded slowly. He took it as an indication she was ready to move on. "Good. Then we're on the same page."

He turned off onto Route 2. "So the question becomes, who do we suspect?"

She closed her eyes, grounding her back into the gray upholstery of the seat. "I can't believe it would be anyone from the tribes, even if they are out for revenge on Earthenkrafte."

He tended to agree. "Why would they have blamed you for your sister's acts?"

She stared down at her hands in her lap. "Oh, I don't know. I suppose they could call it selective enforcement when I didn't arrest the pagans after they defiled the Native site."

It seemed to stretch logic to make that explanation fit. Levi knew his share of the local Kootenai leaders; this wasn't their style. "That doesn't make sense."

"I don't think so, either. I've stood by them one hundred percent on this philosophically." She picked at non-existent nails. "Besides, why would they go after either Tresch or me? The movement has much more obvious leaders."

He nodded, taking the turn to Columbia Falls. The streetlights revealed the small city to be a sparkling delight by night, people still walking the streets from evening visits to the community restaurants and bars. People who had no cares, hadn't just lost their last relative—

Niabi shifted in her cage, knocking the water dish loose, and a small spray came over Levi's shoulder into his ear. He swerved but recovered quickly.

"Geezus, what was…" *Was that water? I so hope that was water.* "Sorry. That was unexpected."

Caryn took a short stack of tissues from the console

between the front seats and patted him dry. "You've been baptized into Niabi's family," she said with the soft ghost of a smile.

She turned in her seat, extending a couple of fingers toward the cage. The iguana pulled away, tail whipping back and forth, and snapped at her. Caryn withdrew her hand and sighed.

"Can she actually hurt you? If she bites, I mean?"

"Oh, yes. They have teeth. When they get upset, it's not just the teeth. They clamp down and don't let go. It's pretty traumatic." She kept her eyes on the cage. "Poor thing. Iguanas can be fairly anxious. I don't know how long Tresch might have been there. The smell of blood in the air alone would disturb Niabi to no end. Having to leave in a strange vehicle adds to her distress."

She clicked her tongue at the lizard but didn't try to pet it again.

He could almost hear her thoughts return to self-blaming mode. "Hey," he said. "So I'm baptized. I'm proud to be part of that tribe. And anything that includes you."

She looked up at him, her face pale in the reflected light from the street. Suddenly she scooched over onto the console, slumping to put her head on his shoulder. Instinct drove him to slide his arm around her, despite the strain on his healing skin. She didn't move as they drove through Whitefish, silently depending on him. Their breaths slowly came into synch, and he wished they could remain like that forever, joined and sheltered, away from anyone who could hurt them.

When he turned onto the road up Big Mountain, the heavy traffic—for this time of year, anyway—

surprised him. In winter, vehicles with chains, loaded up with ski and snowboarding gear, out of town visitors as well as locals, were drawn to the lodges and ski slopes on the top of the mountain. But this was July. What could be so fascinating?

Three separate vehicles slowed as they approached his driveway, and then sped on past. *What the hell?* He didn't like the looks of that. Not at all.

He stopped to open the gate, glad he'd locked it before they left. Caryn slid over and drove on through so he could close it behind them. The dogs met him almost at once, their tails straight, ears perked, tension clear in every muscle of their body. Something had spooked them as well.

Had the shooter been there already? Did they already know Caryn was staying with him? How long would it be before the murderer realized he'd shot Caryn's sister instead?

He secured the gate and added the chain and combination lock.

When he got back in the truck, Caryn had moved back to the passenger seat, shoulders tight against the door. Her face set like stone, she glanced from left to right. "What is it?"

"I'm not sure. The dogs are bothered about something."

"You think someone's been here?" She was already digging in her bag, likely for her sidearm.

"Sit still," he said.

He pulled the truck to a stop near the garage, close to the edge of the stone-filled drive. This vantage point let him see over the edge into the yard and its gradual descent to the lake. The full moon was up now. Once he got out and walked to the brink, he had a good view. No intruders were openly visible. The dogs stayed close to the truck, too, which told him that no one was likely down that way.

"What is it, boy?" he asked Rosie, giving a comforting pat on the head. "Has someone been here?"

Even Pete stuck close to Levi as he walked around to meet Caryn, since she hadn't waited for him to open the door. She surveyed the house, bag on her shoulder and gun in hand.

"You should go in," she said. "I'll do a perimeter check."

He patted his pocket, where he'd put his own pistol. *Good thing her BLM boss didn't pat me down. Not that I'm a convicted felon. But...*

He smiled. "I'll help you. My invalid days are fading into the past. No time to be weak."

She hesitated, as though to argue, then waved a hand. "Fine. Not like you'll listen to me anyway."

That made him laugh. "You're getting to know me, aren't you?"

He whistled and snapped his fingers, and the dogs followed, still agitated, but that energy wasn't directed at anything in particular. So whether they'd been here and gone, or whether the odd traffic had them rattled, he assumed that for right now, he and Caryn weren't in immediate danger.

All the same, it didn't hurt to check...

"You take the front," he directed, with a nod of his head in the direction he meant. She quickly moved across the driveway, Ophelia following on her heels. Levi took the back of the house. He scanned the open yard all the way to the tree line by the lake, then up the hill on the east side of the house. Rosie, Guildy and Pete heeled him all the way, their tails finally wagging in a more friendly manner as he finished. He and Caryn met on the far side of the house; neither had anything to report.

"Didn't spot anyone," Caryn said, "but that doesn't mean they didn't leave any presents behind. Be careful when you check the doors."

"Good idea," he agreed. They each re-patrolled the area they'd scanned the first time, this pass checking each window and entry for signs of tampering.

All Levi found was a lot of dust and some spider webs in the corners of the entryways. No obvious fingerprints or other signs of meddling. When he met Caryn back at the truck, she had two sets of pliers in hand, one small, one larger.

"Are these yours?"

Levi squinted at them. "Yeah. Were they over by the bay window?"

"Yes."

"Guess I left those there last time I had to fix the hinge."

She studied them a moment, then handed them to him. "No sense in giving anyone the wherewithal to break in, I suppose." She tucked her gun away and looked in the truck. "We'd better get Niabi inside. The cage needs to be someplace warm. If you've got a heat lamp, that will help protect against drafts."

"I think we have one in a closet upstairs. My mother used to use it for her knee. We could put it in the study and keep a fire going."

She nodded. "That's a good idea. Even the residual heat will help during the day."

She opened the truck door and bent down to look inside. "Wow, you've really got that wedged in here." She reached for the cage and drew back quickly when the iguana snapped. "We'll need gloves. Heavy gloves."

"Sure." He ducked into the garage and found a heavy leather pair his father used to use for planting trees. "Why don't you let me get it? These are probably too big for you."

Levi spent several minutes working the cage loose, trying not to spill the seeds and other food all over the floor of his vehicle, but he was only marginally successful. Knowing the loss Caryn had already suffered that day, he was determined to make sure she kept this bit of family. When he finally had the cage out of his car, he adjusted his handhold, mindful of Niabi's nips at his fingers.

He carried the cage to the house as if it were a trophy, letting Caryn open the doors before him like a royal footman. The dogs followed them, sniffing curiously. Caryn found a folding table in a closet and she set that in an area where the warmth of the fire wouldn't be too much, but would remain to keep Niabi's area warm even when the fireplace wasn't lit. Rosie, in particular, seemed affronted by this scaled intruder in her house, half-growling as she paced around the table.

"Come here, boy," Levi scolded. "We'll be fine now. One big family."

Even as he spoke, he half kicked himself for bringing up the subject of family. Caryn's eyes welled up, and she turned away from him, surreptitiously wiping away tears.

He watched her for several long moments, wanting to comfort her, but sensing anything overt would just hit the brick wall of her whatever remote place she'd retreated to. One step at a time.

"Hey, I've got a great idea. Let's break out another bottle of that merlot from last night."

"I should get my things from the truck," she said.

"I'll get them. You relax."

He was already on the move to the kitchen, where he uncorked a bottle, letting it aerate while he went out to bring Caryn's few possessions. He loaded them up on a serving cart his mother had left in the pantry, then drove them inside and down the hall to the guest room. He imagined she'd like her own space to work in, whether or not she chose to use it after dark.

I'd feel she was safer wrapped tight in my arms, that's for sure.

When he returned to the living room, he carried a wine glass in each hand, their crimson contents sloshing promisingly. Caryn had started the fire, creating a certain homey atmosphere. Her boots sat by the end of the hearth. She stood before the fireplace, arms crossed, hugging herself a little, rocking back and forth in her stocking feet. She seemed transported to another place.

Not wanting to disturb the quiet, settled air around her, he approached her slowly, nearly silent in stocking feet. "Cara?"

Startled, she whirled to face him, coiled like a taut spring, one hand raised to defend herself. Aided by his instantaneous retreat, she barely stopped in time. They stood there a moment, breathing hard, both jazzed by a rush of adrenaline, an echo of the day they'd first met.

The tension got the dogs started barking and

circling around them, and he had to get control of himself in order to reassure them. "Sorry!" he gasped. "I didn't mean to startle you. I should have known better. Hush, Rosie! Ophelia, down."

Having miraculously not either dropped the glasses or snapped their delicate stems when she scared him, he held one out to her. "I brought you some wine. I think you could use it. And maybe several more."

Her hand trembled as she reached for the glass. "You shouldn't sneak up on me. Especially like that. I'm serious."

He waited until she had a firm grip, then took a step back. "I'm sorry," he said again.

"I know." She swirled the ruby liquid in the glass, watching it a moment before she took a sip. "I can't help it."

He stepped closer and slipped an arm around her. "You're fine. Don't worry about anything else tonight. I've brought everything in, put your things in the guest room, and locked the truck and every door into the house. We'll be fine. Both of us."

She clung to him in a needy way he'd never seen in her before. "We won't be fine. Not until we figure out who did this and take them down."

He didn't reply, he just held her. Now that the adrenaline rush had started to fade, real exhaustion set in. His knees wobbled; she must have noticed.

"Come on, let's sit," she said, walking him to the love seat near the fire. He sat and drew her down next to him.

"Sorry. Your hero ought to be a man of steel." He put the smile on his face, but it was weak and they both knew it.

"My hero," she repeated softly. She looked into his eyes. The licking flames reflected off of her face, deepening the shadows under her eyes until they appeared almost hollow-cheeked. His hand came up, almost without his bidding, to cup her cheek, wanting only to unburden her, let her know she was loved.

She drank the wine in a few quick gulps and set the delicate glass aside. He set his aside untouched, but wasn't quite ready for her to crawl onto his lap, astride his legs, her arms around his neck. His arms slid around her automatically, holding her as close as he could, ignoring the pain as she rubbed against his skin. His pain was nothing compared to hers at the moment. He could stand it, for her.

"What was it you called me? Cara?" she whispered close to his ear.

"I won't if you don't like it," he said, not wanting to admit it had slipped out inadvertently. He'd had some private thoughts where he'd addressed her that way. It had seemed natural. "It means 'dear one' in Italian."

She nodded. "I know." She hugged him tighter. "No one's ever called me that. I like it."

"Good."

Ophelia had settled in before the fire, but the two Ridgebacks hadn't figured out the iguana yet. They circled that table where Caryn had placed her pet's cage, only retreating when the iguana bared its teeth with a spine-chilling hiss.

He gave Caryn one last squeeze, then set her gently aside. "Let me feed them. Maybe it will distract them from Niabi. I'm not sure they'd understand the significance—and honor—of being baptized." He winked and got up, snapping his fingers for the dogs, who bounded after him.

It was nearly midnight by the time he'd set out the food mix and fresh water for all three dogs, and he was about ready to crash. He wrestled with some excuse that didn't sound either like he was bailing on Caryn or waiting to jump her bones. Could they just go to bed for shared comfort? Was there an easy way to ask her?

Rehearsing what he thought was a diplomatic suggestion, he returned to the den to find her asleep on the loveseat. Traces of drying tears glistened on her cheeks. He debated waking her to go upstairs, but decided she was better off undisturbed. The dogs would let him know if anything untoward happened. A green afghan his mother had crocheted hung on the back of a nearby chair, and he laid it over Caryn, thinking she looked beautiful in the firelight.

I won't let anything happen to her. No matter who I have to take down. This is finished.

He stood there, watching, until his knees threatened to give in, and then he left Caryn, Niabi and the sleeping dogs in peace. Tomorrow would be time enough to plot their next move.

Chapter Eighteen

The faint gray light of dawn trailed dark shadows across the den, revealing just enough for a disoriented Caryn to recognize the unaccustomed surroundings. She held perfectly still, listening to her own breathing, and Niabi's fidgets in her cage.

And then she remembered.

The loss of her sister seemed heavier today, more real. It crushed her chest until she could scarcely breathe. Such a stupid thing, telling Trescha to stay in the motor home.

Logic was an illusion. Certainly Caryn hadn't taken the shot, or forced Trescha to be homeless. A horrible succession of decisions had led to the final outcome, most of them out of her control. But the guilt gnawed at her soul.

Thankfully, she hadn't dreamed much, but had slept like a blank page in a closed book. If she'd had to relive that bloody scene overnight, she might have gone mad. Now that she was awake, burning questions began rotating through her head like an accusing conveyor belt.

She dismissed the pagan group and the Native Americans both. The first was a different kind of crazy, and the second didn't function that way. Gunnar was still a possibility, but if Trescha's claims were right, he wanted her out. Once she was gone, that should have been the end of it. He didn't seem like a vicious type, just stupid.

But I can't say the same for Levi's team.

The recent history of the ecotagers, now infiltrated by the militia, was both violent and unpredictable. If Levi's revelations of his loss of control over the group was true, that even lent more credence to the likelihood that one of them might have taken action, irate that Levi had attached himself to an agent of the BLM.

Irate enough to kill?

That she didn't know. But it seemed possible.

He was no fool. The same idea must have occurred to him. But he hadn't brought it up. Why not? Was he still interested in protecting his people, even after what they'd done to him? After they'd likely killed Trescha? A murder charge would reflect badly on his group, even splintered as it was. But he couldn't put their welfare over justice for her sister. Surely he wouldn't.

Something sharp twisted inside her. She wished everything was different. If she'd met Levi ten years before at the University, they could have been working on the same side, not the opposite one. She wouldn't have to depend on him to provide her with housing and shelter. She coped with crisis better when she was alone, when she had peace and quiet to sort out what was going on. *When I could just stand on my own feet and act without having to deal with anyone else...*

She pushed herself up to a sitting position, tugging the blanket close around her. A cool draft came from the hall, giving her a chill. Niabi clawed at the cage, eyeing her with a cocked head and displeasure showing in her open jaw.

"All right, all right. I'll get you something."

Pets didn't have to wrestle with all the emotional minutiae of a family member's loss. They still had a routine. They depended on that food and water, the daily walk, whatever they were used to. The mundane task actually lifted Caryn's spirits—a hint of normal on a day when nothing else would be.

She padded into the kitchen on bare feet, filling the coffeepot to brew before tossing some fruit and vegetable chunks into a bowl for Niabi. She poured a glass of water, then carried what she'd prepared to the den.

"I can't let you out, love. Not until you and the dogs have decided who's in charge," she said softly, refilling the water dish.

The dogs.

The reminder brought her to a still pose. Even though she'd been up and certainly not silent, the dogs hadn't made a peep or come to investigate. Why not?

She tiptoed to the bottom of the steps, then stopped, listening. Nothing.

Was Levi all right? It was so quiet.

A thought flitted through her head that his recovery from his own ordeal had hardly been complete before she'd thrust him into her own. Maybe he'd relapsed… She took the stairs two at a time, heart pounding.

His bedroom door stood half-open, and she barreled through like she was doing a drug bust. It slammed against the wall, but disturbed no one. The bed was empty. The bathroom, too.

She crossed to the sliding glass door that led to the deck, peering out over the yard. She saw no sign of them, not even as far as the lake. The truck was where he'd parked it, just along the edge of the yard by the garage.

Well, what the heck.

He was a grown man. If he chose to push his health boundaries, that wasn't within her control. Like most everything else. With a sigh, she went back downstairs. Niabi had sorted through her breakfast, shifting aside what she'd found less than appealing. She glared at Caryn.

"Out of my control," Caryn repeated, and took a cup of coffee out onto the stone patio, settling—upright—into one of the Adirondack chairs. She had no plans to fall asleep today. Her cell buzzed in her jeans pocket. Half-hoping, half-dreading it was news about her sister, she tugged it out. The number belonged to Sam Evans.

Damn. This might be even worse.

She cleared her throat, wiped her hand over her face and answered it.

"Orlane."

"Caryn." Her boss was hesitant, sounding awkward using her first name, and for once, in a tone that wasn't like some big-city news editor yelling for the nearest copy girl. "How are you?"

She shrugged, then realized he couldn't see her.

"All right, I guess. Anything new on what happened to my sister??"

"We're not really in the loop on the inquiry, if that's what you're asking." He coughed.

Of course. That would be a county matter, not federal. *Come on, Caryn. Get your brain working.* "Right, right."

Sam cleared his throat. "Is there anything you need? Everyone's been asking what they can do, but I haven't heard from you."

"No, I know you haven't." Guilt bubbled up in her, even as she tried to dismiss it. *I don't owe them updates on my personal life. Especially when my personal life is a tangled up mess like it is now.* "I should have c-called."

A non-committal grunt. "We—I mean your co-workers and I—we're here if you...if you need something."

Sam was stumbling, unusual for him. Was this display of sympathy too much for the brusque supervisor? Or was there something more to it?

Caryn resisted the urge to hang up. "That—that's kind of you, Sam. Thank you."

Dead air hung for the next several seconds, then Sam cleared his throat.

"Caryn, can you come in to the office today?"

The question set off a tremble that ran through her body as if it were a California fault line. "I don't know, Sam. I'd rather not. I'd counted on a couple days to deal with Tresch... I mean, I haven't, you know, got things arranged yet, and—"

"That's not what I mean. I'm not calling you in to work."

She leaned back and settled into the chair and closed her eyes, suddenly understanding the real reason for his call. "Sam, I—"

His words shot out at machine-gun speed. "Look, there's no easy way to say this. You're associating with a suspect in our monkeywrenching case."

"Associating?" *That's what Sam called what she and Levi were doing?* The word struck her funny for some reason, and tension boiled up and released as an anxious giggle. She struggled to clamp a lid on her emotions. The last thing she wanted to do was give her boss more ammunition than he already had.

Sam growled, "Don't play word games with me. You're not claiming it was an accident that you and Bradshaw were on a crime scene holding hands last night? Right?"

She surrendered to the chill washing through her. The night before was a blur of pain, sorrow and desperation. She hadn't been thinking what implications Levi's support in the face of the tragedy might have. Maybe that was a mistake, but it was the truth. How could the truth be wrong?

"No. No accident."

"What in God's name are you thinking—you know, never mind," he said, cutting off his own thought. "I honestly don't want to know. Maybe we can write it off as a bad judgment in a time of significant stress." He cleared his throat again. "I would have preferred to do this in person, but I think I can trust you to carry through. Bottom line is, you're suspended. I've got no choice, Caryn. Before noon today, turn in your federal-issued firearm and your badge, pending a thorough investigation by the department."

Her heart sank. What had happened to that Sam who hugged her, who promised her support? Taking her job just tore her feet out from under her. "But—"

"That's it. And stay out of our way while we wrap up this case."

She recognized his tone. No arguments wanted. And deep inside she recognized the truth of his position. *How had she expected this to work out in the end?*

Alana Lorens

"I'll—I'll be there."

"Caryn…I'm sorry. I am."

A click in her ear cut off any further conversation.

She sat like a stone for a moment, considering what she could have said to make the situation better. But…what?

Nothing.

He was right. She'd compromised her objectivity. Compromised? Hell, she'd tossed it to the winds. Now would she become part of the case? Would they investigate her right alongside Levi?

Had someone from the BLM known even before last night?

She set her cell down slowly as implications set in. If someone from her office knew she'd slept with Levi and stood to potentially deep-six their investigation, how far would they go to stop her? Would it run to attempted assassination?

She considered Robert and Jessalyn and Sam and the others. Her friends. Her few friends. People she worked with day in and out. People with whom she trusted her life.

Was that trust misplaced?

The scrambling of dog claws on stone grabbed her attention, and she turned to find Levi and the crew coming toward her, Levi with a handful of pink shooting stars. "Flowers for you," he said with a smile.

It was the sweetest thing someone had done for her in days, so naturally, she burst into tears.

With the dogs scrambling all around them, agitated by her emotional display, the scene degenerated into chaos. Levi held back, his expression unsure, and she tried in vain to get control of herself. She nearly had it

226

before remembering Sam's terse words provided the frosting on her cake of despair, and she lost it again.

She mopped her face with the back of her hand and imagined her ugly grimace of sorrow, silently castigating herself for falling apart. Here she was, demonstrating all those qualities that men had told her for years should disqualify her from doing the job she wanted. But she could no more change her path than fly to Venus.

"Enough!" Levi shouted. She twitched, but his admonition was directed at the dogs. "Go inside." He held the sliding door open for them. Belatedly, he asked, "The iguana's not out, right?"

She shook her head and focused on the flowers again. She'd have to go to town later to see Sam and make arrangements for Trescha. No old homestead at which to bury her; better to have a quick cremation and scatter the ashes in the wild. *Hell, maybe that useless Cynthia person could have a ceremony bonding Tresch to the trees or something...*

The absurdity of that image helped her escape the panic and pain, returning to some semblance of self-control.

"Thanks for the flowers," she whispered. "Very thoughtful."

"Are you sure?" He still looked a little stunned at her outburst.

"Yeah, I'm sure." She forced a smile. "Thank you. Where were you all?"

He walked to the edge of the porch. "We took a long walk along the perimeter. I felt a little stronger this morning, and I especially didn't want the dogs to wake you." He turned back to study her. "You needed the rest."

She nodded. "I suppose. Although it looks like I'll have plenty of time for that."

"What do you mean?"

"Sam called." She wrestled with strong feelings that threatened to bring the tears again.

"News about the militia?"

His prompting didn't help. "No. I'm officially suspended."

He studied her face. "Because he saw us together last night."

She nodded. "So I've got plenty of down time."

His jaw tightened, pulling his mouth into a frown. "I'm sorry, Caryn. That's my fau—"

Boiling frustration brought her to her feet. "No. No more 'fault' stuff. This isn't your fault and it isn't my fault, but by God it's someone's fault, and we've got to find out who!"

"We will," he assured her.

His eyes were warm, and his arms were inviting, but she couldn't find comfort there, not yet. *That's what got you in trouble, Caryn Lyn.*

She blinked, a cold chill running through her, even in the bright morning sunshine. Where had her father's voice come from?

He might not have openly condemned her, but she didn't need much imagination to visualize his blue eyes, pale with disappointment, his lips set tight against each other, his hands shoved deep into his pockets. She'd taken the career she'd fought so hard for and tossed it away on a chance at this relationship.

But it wasn't gone—

Maybe not. But it was certainly tarnished. Now she

was on the outside of the investigation looking in. She'd lost her contacts and her badge. She could rant all she wanted about finding a culprit, but how in heaven's name would she ever make that happen now?

****

Nearly three days passed before the coroner released Caryn's sister's body, and Levi devoted that time trying to be as close to Caryn as she'd allow.

They'd never spent so much time together, and the span was educational for him. He'd seen Caryn's brash spirit many times since the day they'd met at gunpoint. She'd never been afraid of anything. Until now.

Not of the criminals who'd taken her sister's life, of course. That, she was livid about. Alternate bursts of rage and grief propelled her across his floor, pacing so powerfully he expected to see ruts in the rug.

"When they're brought to justice, we'll make sure it's real justice! No worming out of the charges on a technicality, no. We'll do it right, make sure all the evidence is locked up tight until trial and then we'll crucify them like the murderers they are!"

She'd pause at the far end of the room, lost in thought for a moment, then turn and walk the other way, starting again on a litany of perpetrators and why they were or weren't likely to be the killers.

It disturbed him that she'd added her own police unit to the possible suspects. He'd always assumed that the BLM agents weren't any more criminal than the usual paper pushers, mostly a nuisance for the common man, perhaps more so for the uncommon one who nailed trees to keep the forests safe. He'd never considered they would strike out at one of their own. How could he possibly keep so many potential attackers at bay?

While she was awake, Caryn was angry and vengeful.

But each night she slept in his arms, letting him shield her when nightmares left her shivering and terrified.

Levi had bad dreams of his own, though he mostly kept them to himself. Hardly a week since the Ranning brothers' stunt had sent him, burnt like a barbecue pig, to the hospital. He'd been on a roller coaster ever since. Once only a fantasy, his relationship with Caryn had gone from an occasional teasing glimpse to a full-time journey of discovery. Her unexpected intrusion had sidetracked his own life, though her tragedy understandably took center stage. But it wasn't the only mystery.

What the hell had happened to Alex Sullivan?

Stealing a few minutes while Caryn slept, Levi scrutinized the online bulletin boards, the semi-secret forums where the militia group left each other vague messages in code. He'd learned enough of their baffle-speak to get the gist of the conversations. The unit had big plans, if he interpreted correctly. The loss of Ron and the others hadn't slowed them a bit.

But there was nothing about Caryn's sister. And nothing about Alex.

****

When Caryn got the call from Columbia Mortuary the next afternoon, she stopped pacing. She silently left the room, then returned dressed in somber black slacks and jacket. Pausing at the doorway to the kitchen, she glanced at him, then away.

He'd been expecting the call, since the sheriff had

called to tell Caryn the night before that the body would be released. Imagining the existence of multiple threats 'out there,' he was ready to go. "I'll drive," he said, starting toward her.

"No."

He missed a step and grabbed the counter for balance. "All right, you can drive."

She studied him, then shook her head. "I'm going alone."

"But—"

He cut himself off. No sense in making her day more difficult by provoking an argument. All he wanted was to be by her side, to protect her, to smooth her way in any manner he could. But she was a big girl.

Frozen in the doorway, she waited for his response.

"All right." He forced an encouraging smile. "You know I'm available if you change your mind. If you need anything. Really, just call me."

Her lips curved slightly, and he couldn't help remembering how soft they were against his skin.

"You're hardly recovered from your accident. Please take it easy today. Rest."

He nodded, his thoughts in turmoil. He wanted to insist that she was wrong, that she needed him. Although, time to himself would allow him a serious opportunity to dig into his own puzzles, out of her sight and earshot. "Sure, no problem. Remember, if you want—"

"I'll call," she whispered. Tears shadowed her voice. Her staccato footsteps echoed in the foyer as she left the house.

He followed to the door, watching through the beveled side windows as she drove away. A cold nose touched his hand. He grinned down at Ophelia, and scratched her behind the ears.

"Don't you worry, girl. She'll be all right. We'll make sure of it, won't we?"

Walking to the den, tension flowed out of him with each step. Caryn's dark grief hung around her like a cloud, and, as much he loved her, a short respite was welcome. The heavy woods of the room looked black in the half-light of the den. Ophelia followed on his heels, then joined the other dogs, flopped on the rug in front of the cold fireplace, where Rosie was snoring. Levi slid into the leather chair, then activated his computer.

Should have brought coffee in. Oh well.

When his screen brightened, he signed into the TOR software that would let him proceed with the expectation of anonymity, hiding his internet address with a proxy. *Code name Conall.* The magic word let him in, and he went to work.

He quickly scanned the board, finding nothing of interest. Now that he knew he wouldn't be interrupted, he entered a search for Raff B, Alex's code name. *It had been kind of him, like a brother, to take a name meaning Beta Wolf. He'd been part of our pack who acknowledged my orders.*

"Until I let him bring in the damned militia," he growled aloud.

Guildy's head lifted and eyes opened, curious mahogany eyes inspecting the room for threat before he snorted and laid his head down again.

Levi traced threads of conversation where Alex had been involved as Raff, everything from their basic monkeywrenching plans to enigmatic exchanges with the Rannells about the state capital. They all stopped on

June 28, a week after the incident at Martin City, where the firefighter had died.

"What happened to you, Alex?" he murmured.

If his friend had been in trouble, he could have called. Surely he knew Levi would have helped him at any cost, no matter what he'd done, or what had been done to him.

At least at that time. Now Caryn would come first.

The realization dribbled into his consciousness like the ooze of warm huckleberry jam.

He really did love her. He leaned back in his chair, hands slipping from the keyboard into his lap. As they'd grown up, Alex became his second in command, someone Levi trusted with no reservations, up to and including his life. While Zane had made it clear he wanted no part of this unsophisticated country life, Alex had stuck by Levi's side. Levi owed him a great debt.

He couldn't possibly ignore the very real chance that Alex had met with foul play. In the right hands, Alex's computer probably held information that could take down the militia. But it was missing.

And what it would reveal probably incriminated Alex, and Levi himself.

Damn.

Caryn isn't the only one with torn loyalties.

With a sigh, Levi checked the dates again. Alex had vanished from sight weeks before Trescha was killed. Were the two related? If so, that would narrow Caryn's list of suspects considerably.

Who am I kidding? There's only one list of suspects, and I know very well who it is. Someone in the militia wants both Caryn and myself neutralized. Alex must have tried to stop the Rannells from coming after me, and paid the price, whether he's dead or on the run for his life.

It's still my fault.

Ironic that he and Caryn held the same futile guilt for what had happened to someone dear to them. In the next few minutes, he formulated a cryptic message for Alex. With a finger tap, he posted it in the ether, hoping against hope that it provoked some sort of response, something just strong enough to reassure Levi that Alex was still alive out there, somewhere.

He nearly held his breath, hoping for an immediate response. As the minutes ticked by, it became apparent that wouldn't happen. More waiting.

"That's all right. Plenty to do," he muttered.

He rummaged through the piles on the desk next to the computer and found the materials for his fundraiser for Friends of the Trees. The event was set for this coming Friday night—three days away. He'd done nothing to prepare other than send out fifty invitations.

Fifty.

Fifty people would be at his home in three days, expecting to be wined and dined and solicited for cash.

What in the hell was he going to do?

Before he could enter full-blown panic mode, his cell phone rang. He grabbed for it on the corner of the desk, praying it was Caryn and she needed something so he had a good excuse to run away from home.

It was his brother Zane. "What in blazes do you think you're doing there, trying to get the house seized under RICO?"

The angry surprise onslaught stunned Levi, and he had to scramble to respond.

"Who's Rico? What are you talking about? Try, 'Hi, Levi, what's going on?'"

"I know what's going on. I've had my eye on the news on that corner of Montana for a while now. Bombs, monkeywrenching, red flags from the Feds? Mom didn't give you that house just so you can lose it in a forfeiture action…"

As his brother continued, Levi sucked back his ready retort, finally recognizing Zane in lawyer mode. He was a power litigator worthy of the usual comparison to a shark. Zane lashed out at his opponents like a desperate man clutching his way up a drowning friend's body to get some air. No holds barred, ever. *The only way to win was not to play.*

He took a long, deep breath as Zane ranted on, accusations dropping like grenades. When Zane paused for effect, Levi said, "Are you finished yet?"

"Don't you have something to say for yourself?"

"Sure. I'm feeling much better now that I'm home from the hospital. No permanent damage. Thank you for asking."

A shocked silence. "Haven't you heard a damned thing I've said?"

Irritation threatened to rattle Levi's intended calm. He tried levity. "Some of it."

"That spread, the lands, the forests, are worth a lot of money, and I'm not going to let you just throw them away!"

"I'm not 'throwing them away'. I'm done with the militia. I'm taking care of myself."

Levi could almost hear the gears in his older brother's head ticking as he regrouped. "I'm coming back there. Someone's got to—"

"Someone *is.* Everything's under control. Just keep on with the benign neglect, huh? I don't need your 'protection' anymore."

"Damn it—"

Levi clicked his phone, hanging up. What did Zane care anyway? When it had become clear Levi would be staying in the old homestead after his parents' death, Zane had blown out of here like a rocket ablaze. He'd sent nothing to help out, not so much as a Christmas card, despite his successful practice, paid no taxes. In fact, he'd never mentioned much about the place at all, except to criticize Levi's failure to finish the house on his infrequent visits.

The dogs stirred, then got up, stretching, tails wagging. Rosie gave a little whine with a pointed look toward the front door.

Levi shoved himself out of the chair. "You're right. Better walk it off before the next twist of fate dumps a load of manure on me, huh, boy?"

Now fully enthusiastic, the ridgebacks howled in unison, and Levi rounded up the other two before they went to take a walk down to the lake, forgetting all about his promise to Caryn that he'd rest. Only action would help his frustrations fade—that, and the beauty of his Montana home.

Chapter Nineteen

Caryn found Cynthia Fallingstar and the pagan group much more sympathetic and helpful than she'd expected in arranging a memorial service that Trescha would have found meaningful. They set a date for two days hence, which would be the new moon, just after dark.

Levi drove her there, on her lap, a hand-quilted tote packed with several framed photographs of Trescha and some other prized possessions rescued from the motor home. She appreciated his attempts at conversation but found herself without much to say. Her gaze kept being drawn, like a magnet, to the box at her feet that contained Trescha's ashes.

Cynthia met her on the trail to the open space in the woods where the ritual would take place. She made a show about embracing Caryn, welcoming her to their sacred space. "I promise, this has nothing to do with the tribe's claimed area. We're above board here."

Brightly garbed in a multicolored flowing robe, Cynthia directed her devotees in setting candles and propane lanterns around the forest glade where the Earthenkrafte group usually met. She paused to examine the pictures of Trescha.

"Such a sweet girl."

Caryn read the unspoken corollary—*unlike her sister*—in Cynthia's wry grin, but she was too numb to flare up about it.

Trescha's former boyfriend Gunnar was there, too, slinking around on the farthest edges of the group, warned by Caryn's glare not to approach too closely. His expression was drawn. Caryn even spied an occasional tear on his cheek. Perhaps she'd misjudged his feelings for her sister. Perhaps he actually cared. Trescha could have strained his nerves and he just needed a break.

It didn't matter now.

Caryn carried Trescha's tote to the makeshift altar created from two broad stumps and a flat log in the center of the glade. A lavender cloth had been spread lengthwise on the top. The bench was decorated with flowers, pinecones and branches, a small metal dagger with a carved white handle, and other mysterious items. She arranged Trescha's photos and items she'd brought.

After she'd finished, others added their tokens in remembrance. She perused the items with a sense of discovery, curious how a quartz rock or blue jay feather might have invoked a memory of the younger sister she thought she'd known. Clearly others had experienced another side to Trescha she'd never uncovered.

Levi waited for her at the edge of the clearing, and she returned to join him. He met her with a gentle caress to the back of her waist, supporting her as she faced the altar.

"Are you sure you don't want to be one of the acolytes?" he whispered.

She shook her head, watching the others congregate in a wide circle around the altar. "I never honored this while she was alive. I'd be a hypocrite."

"I understand. I think she'd be pleased you were

here for her."

When Cynthia beckoned, he and Caryn stepped forward to close the circle.

Cynthia stood at the head of the table, a solid lump of granite in her hand. She raised it in front of her. "This rock is of the earth, the ground that holds us. Blessings from the North to all those gathered here."

A slight brunette took the place to Cynthia's left, a large black feather in her hand. She held it in front of her, then raised it as Cynthia had the rock. "This feather is of the air, the wind that lifts us. Blessings from the East to all those gathered here."

Gunnar joined them, standing to the right of the altar. The sharp strike of match to flint was followed by a hint of sandalwood scent in the air when he lit a long stick of incense. The burning tip glowed red in the near-darkness.

"This flame is of the fire, that warms and keeps us in the cold season. Blessings from the South to all those gathered here."

He risked a look at Caryn, a faint smile struggling with his lips.

Damn him, he was trying. Why couldn't he just let me hate him?

She inclined her head in acknowledgement. The young man visibly relaxed, the incense trembling in his hand.

Another woman stepped up, holding a goblet. "This water is of the rivers and lakes that sustain us. Blessings from the West to all those gathered here."

Cynthia intoned an invitation to the spirits of the four directions to join the group and be watchful over them as they sent to rest their sister Trescha Orlane.

Caryn's throat choked up. The next section was a blur as she silently fought an internal battle against letting her sister go. Words implored the elements to walk with the departed to the lands beyond, and prayers were made to protect her until she crossed to the other side.

Levi's elbow poked her in the ribs, bringing her to a more focused state as Cynthia Fallingstar approached, the blade in her hand. Apprehension zinged through Caryn as she eyed the point of the dagger, extended toward her. What was she expected to do? Fall on it? Take responsibility for the death of her sister? She swirled in a sea of loss.

"Give me your hand," Cynthia said softly.

After all the confrontations she'd had with this woman, she hardly trusted her with a knife and her own hand. Caryn's jaw set, but with the eyes of all the group on her, their breaths held, waiting, she surrendered.

She held out her hand, and Cynthia turned it palm up. The pagan leader laid the blade flat against Caryn's open palm and closed her eyes.

"Blood of my blood, bone of my bone, flesh of my flesh. Keep my soul alive, and I will live on within your hearts. I am not afraid where I am going but await the next adventure. Remember me."

She smiled at Caryn in that uber-priestessy way she had, then moved on to the person to Caryn's right, repeating the same ritual words. When she'd made the circuit of the thirteen mourners, she laid the dagger on the altar once again and turned to Caryn, gesturing toward the outskirts of the glade.

"You may now scatter the earthly remains of our friend and sister."

Her feet felt frozen to the ground, the box heavy in the tote she held. Somehow Levi got her moving, and she made the complete ring, dumping a small amount out of the box at each tall pine tree that made up the border. While she walked this trail of death, the group sang a song in a language Caryn didn't recognize, a tune that started out melancholy, but changed key partway through and became something celebratory.

Levi's arm around her, she returned to her place in the circle, then set down the empty tote. She was now without family in this world. Tears burned her eyes and ran down her cheeks as the song concluded.

"I invite any who would like to speak to come forward," Cynthia said. "I shall begin with a brief recollection of my work with Trescha. She was always willing to do what was asked of her, so dedicated to protecting nature and the ancient ways. I shall miss her dearly."

She stepped away from the head of the table and another woman took her place. Caryn listened with growing pride and love as each speaker added a piece of the puzzle that was Trescha's life and inspiration, sharing some personal connection that had fulfilled them. After all had come forward who wanted to, Cynthia asked if Caryn had anything to add.

"I—I can't." She smiled through her tears. "Thank you. Thank you all for this. I promise…" Pain, sorrow and fury bubbled up inside her at the thought of such a gentle soul being lost to thoughtless violence.

"I p-promise…" She took a deep breath and forced the words out. "I p-promise I'll get whoever did this. They won't go un-p-punished."

Cynthia's eyebrow raised, but she didn't miss a

beat. "Thank you. I shall bring our ceremony to a close with the words from the holy book."

She raised her empty hands and spoke again in a language Caryn didn't understand. When she finished, those in the circle broke into small groups, exchanging hugs and wiping tears from each other's cheeks. Many came up to Caryn, taking time to embrace her firmly, whispering words of encouragement. She tried to remember to thank them, belatedly glad that her sister had this small group of people who loved and understood her, even if Caryn hadn't always been very attentive.

Once the farewells were said, they quickly cleared the altar and packed it away. Caryn retrieved what she had brought and thanked Cynthia again. Levi went to the truck to wait for her.

Movement in the trees caught her eye. At first she couldn't tell if it was a person or an animal. Then, in the last lantern's light, she identified two sets of eyes, definitely human. Fleshing out her view, she determined both were male, dressed in native American tradition, a buckskin tunic over dark pants, with a beaded headdress and many-tiered shell necklaces. She froze. Why were the Kootenai spying on them? Cynthia had promised this was not forbidden land.

A small voice of logic prodded her with the reminder she was not on duty—indeed, not with the department, even. But it didn't make her feel any better.

Especially when the man on the left, eyes glittering with malice, raised his arm in her direction, his finger pointing at her in silent accusation.

"Do you see that?" she murmured to anyone who was nearby. "Cynthia?"

"See what?" Cynthia answered, coming over to join her.

"There—" She'd only taken her eyes off them for a split second, but it was too long. The men had vanished.

"See what?" Cynthia repeated. Her brow furrowed, and her lips pressed together in a pouty frown.

"Kootenai," Caryn replied, now beginning to doubt herself.

"Here?" Cynthia laughed, a warm, rollicking belly laugh. "They've got better things to do than to follow us around. Go on home now and raise a glass to your sister's spirit." She gave Caryn a little push toward the parking area.

"I—okay." Stealing several glances over her shoulder as she walked away, Caryn searched for any other sign of that malevolent specter that had frightened her. She found none.

Wishing she'd brought a gun with her, she hurried the last stretch to the truck, and jumped in quickly, slamming the door.

Levi studied her curiously. "Someone after you? That nice pagan witch?"

She debated telling him, knowing if she did, he'd probably run back into the woods and spend hours searching for the threatening offenders. As her adrenaline drained away, all she wanted to do was go home and curl up with a warm body. She didn't care if it was man or dog, she was just looking for comfort. That drink didn't sound like a bad idea.

"No. I'm just…it's been a lot today. Let's go back to your place."

He smiled at her. "Your wish is my command."

Chapter Twenty

The next day, Levi presented her with the plans for the fundraiser.

"I invited you," he said, a small sheepish smile on his face. "Under the circumstances at that point, you probably wouldn't have been ethically allowed to attend. But now…"

"Now I'm practically unemployed. Yes. Thanks for rubbing it in."

He frowned. "You know that's not what I meant."

She read genuine rebuke in his eyes. Of course he hadn't meant it. Her sense of loss and betrayal spurred her to strike out even when it wasn't warranted. "I do," she said. She caressed his cheek. "I'm sorry. It's just—"

He nodded and laid a finger on her lips, silencing her. "No explanation needed."

They looked into each other's eyes for a long moment, then she broke away with a shudder of emotion. "So. Fundraiser."

"Right."

He led the way into the kitchen, and they sat on tall stools at the center island reviewing the plans he'd begun but never completed. Party planning was not her forte; Caryn had always played with the boys instead of the girls. The thought of ordering flowers and catered food trays set her guts spinning. He handed her a contract, which purported to be with a well-known caterer in Kalispell. The bottom line was an outrageous figure she couldn't believe.

"Did you pay this much?" she asked after sorting through the file of disparate notes.

"I—I don't remember. You know, I think I never did. Things got too hectic."

She tried not to roll her eyes. "Right. Well, I'm sure we could manage for half that."

"At the time I was doing the best I could. I was bus—"

"Busy?" A wave of irritation ran through her. If Levi had spent less time playing in the woods with his lowlife Oathkeeper wacko friends and more time tending to his own business, this party would be ready to go, and he wouldn't have gotten blown up, and her sister would still be alive, and…

Her throat closed with tears, and she felt wetness on her cheeks. Control slipped away from her faster than a mudslide. She'd lost her sister, she'd lost her career, she'd lost everything…what was left?

Before she could disappear into an abyss of grief, strong arms slipped around her. She was gathered up by Levi, warm whispers in her ear, held close and comforted.

"I want to make things right, love," Levi said. "Please let me help you. Anything."

One thing I haven't lost. This man.

She clung to him, her thoughts in turmoil.

I've pushed through my life on overdrive, keeping my eyes on a goal, being strong for myself. How can it be right that all I want to do right now is surrender…to allow him to help me, take care of me? It feels like heaven and betrayal all at the same time…

Levi smoothed her hair, pressing her against him for support. "You don't give up anything by letting me in, Cara. We're all allowed to be vulnerable once in a while. God knows, you're entitled after what's happened."

She struggled to find her way out of the confusion that surrounded her like an invisible cage. "B-But I don't know how."

He laughed softly. "Honey, you don't have to know. You just *do*."

He held her apart from him, just enough he could look into her eyes. "Trust me, when I woke up in the hospital, I felt the same way. The last thing I wanted was to acknowledge that I wasn't in control of my own life."

"But it's not my way. I've got to…got to…" She couldn't find the words to insist what she wanted to say.

He squeezed her shoulders with his warm hands and leaned back. "You've got to figure out what to feed fifty people."

"R-right."

Of course it made more sense to focus on something concrete rather than keep muddling through cloudy emotions. Caryn gratefully turned her attention in the new direction. "I'll run into Kalispell and see what I can find."

"Good." He nodded, giving her a smile. "I'll line up out printouts, propaganda, and large donation envelopes."

She plodded for the door, grabbing her wallet and phone on the way. It was a distraction, but perhaps taking a break from such intense focus on the investigation and Trescha's death would give her mind some breathing room to begin fresh.

Hardly hearing his goodbyes, she climbed into her truck and headed out to Highway 93.

****

Caryn came out of the Dollar store, arms loaded with bags full of paper plates, napkins and other stuff she'd found that was "woodsy." This was her last stop. She'd already been to the grocery and ordered vegetable trays, a fruit platter and trays of cold cuts. It probably wasn't politically correct, no more than the foam cups she'd gotten for coffee. But by heaven, the shopping was done. *And for a whole lot less.*

She balanced the bags on her knee as she fumbled in her pocket for the car keys.

"Caryn?"

She froze at first, but then caught sight of Jessalyn Brown from the corner of her eye. Fashionably slim in denim, Jess wasn't in uniform, so she must be off duty. Caryn shoved the bags in her front seat, then turned around to greet her former co-worker, taking a long look around to make sure no one else from the office could see them.

"What's up, Jess?"

"Nothing. I just hadn't seen you since...well, since..." She trailed off. "I'm so sorry about your sister."

Caryn's jaw tightened. She swallowed hard. "Thanks."

An awkward silence stretched between them. Caryn had a hundred questions and she imagined Jessalyn did, too. Finally, she cleared her throat.

"So, what's up with the investigation? Did you

track down who started the fire at Martin City?"

Jessalyn's green eyes widened. "You know I can't talk to you about that."

Caryn laughed, a bitter tang to the sound. "No, I don't suppose so. Just because I might be able to help..."

Jessalyn surveyed the street around them. "Come on." She grabbed Caryn's arm.

The unceremonious yank served to get them both running toward The Rainbow, a local bar of low repute that, nevertheless, seemed to pack customers in on the weekends. They slipped inside, stumbling in the dim light, after the bright sun outside.

Jessalyn's determination and energy propelled them into a booth in the back. Several of those at the bar hesitated long enough to scope out the newcomers. Caryn hoped her fierce glare would ward them off.

Her eyes blazing with curiosity, Jess leaned forward. "Is it true you're *living* with Levi Bradshaw?"

Caryn shrugged. "Not like I could stay in the camper, not after what happened."

"Oh, my God. What were you thinking? Of all the people—you could have stayed with me. Heck, Sam has a cottage somewhere. I know he would have let you stay there."

She studied Caryn intently. "But it wouldn't have mattered, would it? There's a lot more to it than convenience."

Caryn looked down at the table, not wanting to confess her feelings, not now, and certainly not to Jess.

"You gals gonna order something?" called the middle-aged woman behind the bar.

"Stay here," Jess said. She slipped out of the booth

and walked up to the counter, returning a few minutes later with something for each of them, tall and pink in a glass with a pineapple slice on it.

Caryn eyed the concoction suspiciously. "This is a beer and shots joint. What's this?"

"I happen to know Gertie loves making froofy drinks. Don't complain." She grinned and stuck a straw in her drink, taking a long sip. "Ummmm."

No sense in fighting the tide. Not like I can't use a good strong drink, hmm?

She sipped repeatedly, letting about a third of the frozen beverage trickle down her throat. Perhaps if she let the alcohol work on Jess, she'd be able to pry some information out of her about the investigation or at least something of value.

Sure enough, after they'd enjoyed some companionable silence, punctuated by occasional pleasurable sighs as they drank more, Jess said quietly, "You know, I agree with you about Levi. I don't think he's the one behind all this destruction."

"The others. They are out of control."

"Exactly. Sam's got us all tracking them. Honestly, he's not even looking at Levi right now. There's someone outside the area they're looking at."

"Outside? Where?"

Jessalyn shook her head. "Robert's been on it. He and Sam are all hush-hush. I think they got some intel after the group ended up in the hospital, that explosion that sidelined your man."

Caryn nodded, not wanting to spook Jess into realizing what she'd let slip.

Jess went on, "I mean, why would they try to kill one of their own men? Seems to me that they must have some serious divisions in the group."

Quiet confirmation seemed the right approach. "So they did try to kill him. That's what Levi thought."

Jess nodded. "I don't know why he's broken off, but clearly the other group has a more violent agenda."

"Clearly."

"I mean, not that monkeywrenching is all right in and of itself. Still causes injuries."

"And it's illegal," Caryn agreed.

"Exactly." Jess took another long sip of her drink, her gaze wandering out over the bar's few patrons. Most were self-absorbed. The long-haired guy in the cowboy boots and the worn T-shirt that showed every rippling muscle in his back glanced over his shoulder at the two women.

Men. Always looking for an opportunity.

Caryn's patience, already strained, reached its limit. "And someone's outside the group? Orchestrating things?"

As if she suddenly realized her error, Jess froze. "Now you can't go running back to Levi and tell him all this," she gasped.

"No, I won't," Caryn said. "I promise. But you know I'm still thinking about this all the time. It's my nature. If I have information to work with, I may be able to help you if something comes together in my thoughts. Something maybe you can't see because you're too close to it."

Jess chewed her lip, looking away.

Caryn knew she was at least considering helping her out. She pinched herself under the table to keep focused on saying nothing more.

Finally, her companion nodded.

"If anything else comes up, I will. They don't know much now."

Jess checked her watch and finished her drink. "I'd better go. I've still got errands and my future mother-in-law coming to dinner."

Frustrated at knowing just enough to drive her curiosity up the roller coaster hill, but not enough to send it over the top, Caryn took another sip, staying where she was. "You go ahead. We probably shouldn't be seen together."

"Good thinking." Jess started to leave, but came back to stand close, her voice dropping into a soft range.

"You know, Care, if these wackos are trying to kill your friend, you might want to consider how safe you are staying there. That's not even factoring in what happened to your sister." Her voice had coiled wire inside, but her eyes were soft with sympathy. "If they were determined to get you, and they figure out where you both are…"

Jess trailed off.

Had she really been that blind? Or just too distracted?

She'd let Levi talk her into this, and she'd been so thrown for a loop she'd just agreed.

"Caryn? You okay?" Jess asked.

Her mind awhirl, Caryn nodded. "Yeah. Fine. You go. I'll talk to you soon."

The other woman hesitated only a second, then was gone. Caryn was left with her misgivings, and more to worry about than she'd had when she came in. Who was involved with the monkeywrenchers from outside? Could it be the mysteriously absent Alex Sullivan?

And what was she going to do to protect herself now that she and Levi had practically painted targets on their backs?

Chapter Twenty-One

"Are you sure the dogs will be all right upstairs?" Caryn asked for the third time.

Levi rolled his eyes at her.

"They'll be fine. The TV puts out enough white noise, they won't be jumping at every little sound." He straightened his bolo tie, centering the turquoise brooch, then checked his reflection in the mirror.

She admired the navy-blue suit, the polished boots...the whole package, really. Levi Bradshaw was a lot of things, including a handsome, desirable man. "You look great," she said wistfully.

"Hard to tell I was blown up and almost died a month ago, hmm?" He eyed his fading cheek scars in the mirror.

She reached out and lightly touched the scars. "You know how it is. Gray hair and a rakish scar make a man look more dashing. It's women who can't pull off that look."

He smiled, and she looked away, her cheeks flushing.

At least my scars are on the inside. With any luck, I can keep them there tonight.

In reviewing the guest list, Caryn had identified a handful of potential donors who might be an issue for her in terms of local politics, especially since she'd been suspended from work. She might have chosen to remain upstairs with the dogs, but Levi had pooh-poohed any chance of confrontation at such a social event. Besides, he needed all hands on deck. She intended to stay in the background as much as possible, making sure the food and drink were amply available, but not interacting with the community leaders and guests.

"Cara, I love you, wounds and all," he said. He winked at her and headed out the door. His footsteps echoed on the polished wooden stairs.

Touched at his ability to read through her defenses once again, she blew out her breath on one long exhale, using the next 'in' breath to summon courage for the evening. Then she followed him down to finish setting up.

****

Fully apprised of the guest list, which included a heaping handful of local residents with deep pockets and courtesy invitations to the Kootenai and governmental agency heads, Caryn's priority was to make the layout as self-sufficient as possible. That way she could set it up once, then just make quick passes through to refill trays or ice. No point in rubbing in her association with someone suspected in the bombings.

So you're ashamed of him.

No.

The question nagged at her as she divided the food from the vegetable trays onto smaller dishes she could set around the kitchen, living room and den. Levi got a small fire going, not because it was cold, but just because it made the den look cozy. The two of them worked side by side in silence setting out wine glasses and bottles. Just when she thought she was in the clear, he caught her hand and pulled her to him, embracing her.

"Are you sure you're okay with this?" he whispered close to her ear. "I promise I'm not going to introduce you as my lover."

Finding it unnerving that he had read her mind once again, she kissed his cheek and pulled back. "I'll do you the same favor," she said, more lightly than she felt. "I'll let you play host, all right? I'd prefer to stay in the background."

"I know." The stricken look on his face let her know he felt guilty for her discomfort. "No problem." He gave her a quick peck and turned back to setting up the bar.

Battling her own anxiety, she slipped out to set some potted plants from the deck onto the steps, to discourage anyone from going upstairs uninvited.

They'd get through this. It was only one evening.

What else did she have to do while she waited to hear about Trescha's murder and her own reinstatement? Not a whole lot. If she couldn't do her job out on the trails of the Bitterroot forests, at least she could help Levi raise money to preserve them.

It was a great plan.

****

The pantry where they'd stored Niabi for the party was down a side hall from the kitchen, far enough away that the noise of the gathered locals shouldn't disturb her much. It was warmer than the bedrooms, and certainly contained less dogs.

Caryn slid open the louvered doors, grateful for an excuse to slip away from the party. Her plastic smile had become painfully tight. Thank God Sam Evans wasn't in attendance, but he'd delegated Robert to keep an eye on things. Not openly, of course. Robert carefully socialized with the other guests, but his curious gaze fell on Caryn and Levi too often for her comfort. She'd narrowly avoided a couple of close calls where he was intent on accosting her face to face. What would she say? She didn't even know.

The roughly seven-foot square space of the pantry made it awkward to get around the iguana's cage, set on a stool in the middle of the room. She pushed aside some boxes of prepared food mixes to gain access to a flat space, then cut an apple and carrot into pieces.

Only another two hours, then I can go back to my own life, such as it is...

"What do you think, Niabi? It's not so bad here, right?"

She glanced over her shoulder to find the green lizard eyeing her hands, its tongue sensing the air. Implications and complications didn't matter to Niabi. Just food.

"Right, as long as we have something yummy to eat, we're good. Nice to have a simple outlook."

A shadow fell across the shelves in front of her. The folks at the party must be out of something yummy to eat, too.

"What do you need, Levi?"

"It's not Levi."

She recognized the voice just before she turned to see who'd left the festivities. The tall state trooper turned slightly, his handsome profile sharp against the overhead lamp, his broad shoulders blocking the light, and his body blocking her escape. Mike Thompson hadn't been among those on the guest list, she was sure of it. What was he doing here?

"Mike? What a...surprise to see you."

"I wrangled an invite from a friend in the community," he said, lazily lounging against the door frame. "This I had to see for myself. I heard you'd shacked up with Bradshaw, but I couldn't really believe it."

He shifted in the doorway, and the room grew more shadowed. "Yet here you are."

She couldn't see the smirk on his face, but she heard it. It revolted her. She fidgeted with the food on the shelf, wishing like hell he'd just go away.

"So, tell me, Caryn, was this going on two months ago when you came out here to 'interview' him?"

Before she could answer, he went on, "Is that why you wanted to come without backup? Did I interrupt a roll in the proverbial hay?"

The accusation shocked her into frozen silence. Her jaw actually dropped, she felt it, but she couldn't help it. Her breath choked. Her fingers grabbed at the nearest support, which happened to be Niabi's cage. The iguana flipped her tail, banging her empty fruit dish into the metal bars. Niabi hissed and nipped hard at Caryn's fingers, the sudden pain freeing Caryn from her horrified paralysis.

She took a step toward Mike, cradling her bloody hand.

"Where do you get off with such a load of crap?" she demanded. "Where I stay is none of your damned bus—"

Mike's hands came up in front of him in surrender. "Hey! Simmer down, girl. I'm just wondering what you're really getting, sleeping with the enemy." His voice dropped to a near-whisper "You're working undercover, right? All this suspension garbage is a ruse to fool the wackos?"

She was close enough to see the salacious glitter of his eyes.

What an ass.

But he had a point. This could work for her. At least as far as the rest of the law enforcement community was concerned. Didn't matter that Sam would probably deny it. What else would he do, right? Even if it were true.

Blood now trickled down her wrist. "Damn it."

She surveyed the shelves and found some paper towels, then tore open the pack. She wrapped several layers around her hand while she concocted a reply.

"You know I couldn't confirm or deny something like that."

She added just enough of a frown to sell the lie.

He chuckled. "Woman, you've got balls, I'll give you that." He stepped back, letting light through the doorway again. "I'm not sure that federal paycheck would be enough for me to…"

He trailed off, and she was glad. No polite way to end that sentence. Just no good way.

She held up her hand in its makeshift bandage. "I need to get some disinfectant on this. Iguanas carry Gram negative bacteria. I just hope I can avoid the ER."

"Really? Damn, Caryn, I'm sorry. I didn't—"

He backed out the door. The light shone on Niabi's dinner. She'd have to get it in the cage somehow, or Niabi would continue to work herself up.

"Mike, can you help me out here? Grab this fruit and kale on the shelf and toss it in the cage when I open the latch?"

His brow furrowed. "It won't chew on me, will it?"

Only if I'm not lucky.

Please, God, don't let me say that out loud.

"Not if you're quick."

She used the bandaged hand to grasp the cage door, and the operation took place in a few seconds. Food in, cage latched again. Done. With a sigh of relief, she gestured toward the door. "I really have to go now."

"Sure, sure." He stepped aside and she headed out for the back hall to the stairs. His gaze burned into her back all the way.

She left her shoes at the foot of the stairs to avoid setting off the dogs, slipping between the plants. Tiptoeing the short distance between the top of the stairs and the bathroom, she reached her goal and closed the door, her knees suddenly weak. The door propped her up for a moment, then she transferred her weight to the sink, leaning on the cool marble of the cabinet top.

Why did I let him get to me like that?

I'm not doing anything wrong. Levi loves me. I love him.

But the guilt of letting her love trump her duty continued to sap her strength.

For days before tonight, she hadn't seen anyone else from her other world except Jessalyn. No one from the office, no one from tribal law enforcement. Not even the sheriff with updates on the murder of her sister. Mike was the only one she'd come across. And his first impression of her was one of betrayal.

Heart pounding, her attention turned to the paper-towel wrapped hand, now soaked with blood. Niabi had gotten her right at the joint of her left index finger. The iguana's sharp teeth could shred skin. Even flinching could make the bite much worse. This one wasn't great, but mostly surface damage.

At least the iguana had let go. The bars of the cage had probably saved Caryn from even worse. More than once, Niabi had been so worked up that her bite had to be unlatched by putting a drop of tequila in her mouth. That was usually enough to shock the lizard into release.

The wound became her new focus. Better than the bigger picture of her life. Certainly more solvable. Peel off the paper towel and throw it away. Wash with warm water, then disinfectant. Try not to groan with the pain. Damn Mike and his superior attitude. Rinse away the blood again. Had Levi even noticed she'd left the party? Would he mind if she stayed up here with the animals?

Forcing her attention back to the blood, she blotted it with a thick handful of tissues. Better. No trip to the hospital this time. She sighed and rummaged through the medicine cabinet. Levi had an outstanding selection of antibiotics in cream, spray and oral forms, along with just about anything she might have wanted in the way of first aid supplies. She smiled, surmising he probably treated his own wounds for the most part, being a woodsy boy and all.

You wouldn't want to alert the hospital to any kind of monkeywrenching injuries, huh? That'd call the law down on you.

She shoved that thought away and finished treating her own gashes, awkward without the use of half her left hand. When she was satisfied that at least she wouldn't bleed all over herself and anyone else, she took a long look at herself in the mirror.

The dark circles she'd had under her eyes since Trescha's death were finally fading. Her face felt pale, and thin, but she felt more human. Levi, for all his human errors, was the main cause of her improvement. So Mike and the rest of the judgmental Others could just...leave her the hell alone.

The crowd had begun to thin by the time she came back downstairs. Mike and Robert, at least, were both gone, which put her more at ease. A full basket of envelopes sat on the kitchen counter. Levi and a couple of local politicians were dug in around the kitchen island, waving celery sticks as they argued points. She smiled as she passed through, stopping only to pour herself a glass of wine, which she raised in their direction when they stopped talking to acknowledge her presence. Levi frowned when he saw her hand.

She shook her head.

"It's fine. You go right ahead," she said softly and continued around to find an escape onto the patio, where she sat until the stars came out, hoping their cold beauty in the night sky would erase her worries and fears.

The heat of the day had faded quickly, with a cool breeze floating up the yard from the lake. She laid her head back on the soft cushion of the deck chair and sipped her wine, idly listening to the crickets and the muted buzz of the remaining guests' chatter wafting through the windows. Her stretched nerves gradually came back under control, and she was able to put Mike's implications out of her mind. She had enough on her plate at the moment. Being off work gave her more time to sort through all the rest of the craziness that was her life. Besides, spending time with Levi made her happy.

Any excuse will do, right?

The slightly tangy silent jab stung her. Was she avoiding things?

Another sip of wine reassured her that she was all right. She swirled the rest of the red fluid slowly in her glass. Maybe by the time she finished, she would quit worrying.

She took a long drink, hearing the door to the front yard open, and the bellow of wild male laughter move away from the house. Levi's voice rose over the others, bidding them good night, thanking his guests for coming. Car doors slammed, motors started, then silence set in. She took several deep breaths, letting her relief at the departures sink in.

A few moments later, a faint light shone from inside as the door opened, and the scratching of nails on the stones of the deck announced the arrival of the dogs, freed from their temporary prison in the bedroom. They rubbed up against Caryn as they passed by her, tails beating her legs before they dashed out into the darkness of the lawn beyond, barking and yipping.

"May I join you?" Levi asked. "I brought some wine. Thought you might need a refill by now."

He walked up from behind, setting down the bottle he held, then pulling a chair close beside hers. He sat down, then picked up the bottle and held it out. "Ready?"

She held her glass. "You bet."

He caught her hand with his empty one, eyeing the bandage. "What's this about? You looked like you'd had a battle."

"Niabi." She sighed.

He let go, then poured her glass half full. "Was that all?"

She didn't look him in the eye. He knew her well enough to read her mind half the time, she didn't want him to see the hurt Mike's interrogation had caused. "She was rattled by the noise, I think. But she got fed."

"Mm-hmm."

He sat back in his chair, staring off toward the horizon, the faint glow of lights from the town below. She couldn't tell whether he believed her. Maybe he'd been in the hallway and overheard. It didn't matter. She'd handled Mike. Would Levi believe she was working undercover? She couldn't see how he could. She wasn't that good an actress.

The silence stretched out like a taut rubber band. Before it could snap, she asked, "Did you collect a lot of donations?"

"I didn't bother to count yet." He sipped his wine, his face hidden in shadows. "At least some people must believe they're not funding monkeywrenching."

The words brought Caryn up short. She hadn't even considered that. Talk about hiding those donations in plain sight. She peered into the growing darkness, wishing she could read him through the gloom of twilight.

"Levi." She swallowed hard, her mouth suddenly dry. "You're…you're done with that, right? Not just the group, but all of it?"

He didn't answer.

Were his eyes open? Maybe he'd fallen asleep. She whistled low for the dogs, and they came back, having made whatever survey they'd felt necessary of the lower yard. Enthusiastically wagging their tails, they crowded between the two of them, and Levi stood up. Caryn caught his face in full light from the windows in the house. His jaw was set, and his eyes guarded.

"I don't know if I'm done," he said. "I still believe in saving the forests. I'll do it legitimately if I can. But I want to always be honest with you, Cara. I'm not making promises."

He walked over to the door and opened it, the dogs bounding after him and shoving through all at once in a chaotic rush. Drawn to follow him, she got to her feet. She didn't know exactly what to say in response to his confession. Of course she hoped to get back to work in the future, but his continued pursuit of this goal would mean they'd always be separated by the law.

Holding the door open for her, he finally added, "I'm not getting into anything more until I help you get the current mess cleaned up. Ron and his crew have to be stopped."

Fair enough. That would have to do. For now.

"Deal," she said. She went inside, and they began the long process of after-party clean-up.

Chapter Twenty-Two

A few days later, Caryn stood at the front door, waiting for the dogs to return from a run around the yard, when the strident summons of a car horn came from beyond the closed gates. A familiar Flathead County Sheriff's office white SUV was parked just outside.

Had Mike come to follow up on his accusations from the night of the party?

Dread slithering up her spine, she walked slowly across the yard, her boots crunching on the gravel of the driveway. She had half an argument formulated in her head before she finally caught sight of the occupant of the driver's seat. It wasn't Mike. It was John Folden, the sheriff.

Something about Trescha? Her steps picked up speed, and she threw the gate open wide. The dogs bayed in the distance. John drove in and parked his vehicle in the open, twenty yards from the house, taking a look around before he got out.

"Don't worry about the dogs," Caryn said, as they appeared over the hill. "They're friendly."

John grunted. "They all are, until they decide to take a bite out of your leg."

Caryn tried to corral the ridgebacks, knowing they were the more likely to bristle at strangers, but they just seemed curious, not worried. Ophelia actually licked

John's hand.

The sheriff waited by the SUV, until the dogs had finished reassuring themselves that he wasn't a predator. "Bradshaw around?" he asked, with a glance at the door.

Caryn shook her head. "He went to town this morning for some supplies." She cleared her throat, both anxious and terrified to hear what Folden had to say about the case. "Are you looking for him? Or for me? Do you want to come in?"

"Only if you've got some fresh coffee," he said, with half a smile, and his eyes crinkling at the corners. "It's been a long morning already."

"It always is in your business."

She led the way into the kitchen. Did his social attitude mean he didn't have news for her? Or that it wasn't as bad as she'd expected? He certainly wasn't approaching this cop to cop. *But then he probably doesn't think of me that way anyway.*

She poured John a big mug of coffee and gestured him to sit at the kitchen island. He sat his well-worn body onto the stool like it was a branch that he expected to snap at any moment.

She studied him, thinking he looked larger than life in this kitchen. Or just that he was too real-life for her in the fantasy escape she'd found.

"I know they have coffee closer to town than this. You must have come for a reason." She stood across from him, the counter between them, and steeled herself.

He took a deep breath and sighed. "It's about your sister. We've followed every trail of evidence we had, Caryn. Best we can figure, it was an AK-47 that was used. That's from the bullets we found. Could have been in semi-auto or auto mode. The spray into the door shows a series of close shots. The shattered window didn't leave us any traces. The, um—" He coughed and took a sip of coffee. "I'm sorry, Caryn. No kind way to say this. The wounds on the corpse would tend to discount auto."

A glimpse of Trescha's bloodied body popped into Caryn's mind, unbidden. Recalling what she'd seen, she would agree. Not enough damage done for the kind of rapid fire that weapon would have generated. Plus, the noise of a series of automatic shots would have attracted far too much attention, even if the neighbors weren't very close. She tried to file that vision back into the shadows. "Yes. I guess I'd say so, too."

"Nothing was stolen, as far as we can tell. No witnesses. Nothing on her computer indicated any overt threat. We've got a lot of nothing, actually."

"Did you check out the tribe? I know they're not a menace, as a rule. But Cynthia Fallingstar and her people can be pretty…irritating." Even as she heard the words, she realized they were ridiculous, and the look on his face reflected that.

"This isn't the Wild West, Caryn. Native Americans are not out scalping people and killing them over a piece of land. I hear they've got Landry in town whipping up one hell of a lawsuit, though."

"And not Tresch's boyfriend? Ex-boyfriend?"

John snorted. "That boy is beside himself. He says it's all his fault because he asked her to move out."

Yeah, no joke. Idiot. He wasn't worthy of Trescha. Not one bit.

"You have any other ideas?" John said.

Caryn debated sharing her concerns that someone in her own office had come after her, knowing about her illicit alliance with Levi. But holding that up to the light of day would produce the same gut reaction that suggesting the Kootenai had. It wouldn't have been worth the risk for any of them.

Caryn shook her head and asked, "So what do you have then? Who do you think did it? Just some random gunfire?"

He eyed her. "You know what I think about who did it." He looked around the kitchen and back into the den. "And yet here you are, right in the middle of it."

She frowned. "It wasn't Levi. He's not with those…those…militia types. I mean, come on, John. They tried to blow him up not a month ago!"

"Yeah, that's true. But he surely hasn't come forward to testify against any of those men, now has he?"

The sheriff's suspicious look set her nerves on edge.

"Damn it, do you think I'd stay here if I thought for one minute he had anything to do with what happened to Trescha? Those anarchistic fools are dangerous, and someone's got to do something about them."

"Exactly. *Someone* does."

He finished his coffee and set the empty cup on the counter.

"We haven't closed the investigation yet. Believe me, if we could get anything on those yahoos, we'd be getting warrants before they could load up any more of those fireworks. Tell your boyfriend, huh?"

He clambered off the stool, his foot catching on a rung, then glared at it. She could almost hear him thinking about "uppity" people without real chairs for guest seating but did her best to pretend not to notice.

"I'll walk you out," she said.

Their stroll to the SUV was silent. Now that she'd heard what the sheriff had to say, disregarding the inevitable exchange of jabs over Levi, she experienced a true wave of disappointment. Law enforcement solved cases; that's what they did. Trescha deserved the best that justice had to offer.

"Nothing" was unacceptable.

The sheriff hoisted himself into the SUV with a grunt. "Damned arthritis. Used to only haunt me in the winter. Now it's coming all year." He closed the door, leaning on the windowsill, and looked her in the eye.

"I don't mean to sound so harsh, Caryn. We're all sorry for your loss, and we wish we had something hard and fast to go on. As long as you're here, you should keep your eyes and ears open. Some information might come across the threshold, even by accident."

He quirked an eyebrow, as if to say an 'accident' wasn't what he expected.

"The whole department respects you. No matter why you're here."

His hesitation made Caryn wonder whether Mike had shared his undercover theory with the rest of them. *Still couldn't hurt.*

"Thanks, John. I appreciate it. I'll let you know if anything else comes to mind. I promise. But you do the same, all right?"

"You've got it. Take care of yourself."

She waved as he pulled out of the driveway and disappeared on the road down toward town. She closed the gate, then checked on the dogs, who were sunning themselves in the side yard. Maybe she'd join them.

Filling my days with useful pursuits, that's me.

****

Caryn walked along the path to the lake, the dogs bouncing alongside her. The sun beat down on her shoulders, bared by the skinny tank top she wore. Five weeks now she'd stayed up at the Candy Cane house, leaving her destroyed camper parked back in Hungry Horse. Even after the police were done, it was clear the thing was a total loss. Caryn wouldn't be able to sleep there again.

I've got to get it towed away. But not today. I'm just not ready yet.

Sam had promised to keep her in the loop if he heard anything further in Trescha's case, but he hadn't called more than twice, and even then, he didn't have much to say. It looked like the shooter was military-trained from the accuracy of the shots, but she didn't know much else.

Folden had to be right. The prime candidates had to be some of Levi's more radical folk. They saw her as a threat to their whole movement. Pillow talk? Ha! *Levi and I have better things to discuss when we're alone. Not like I've got any official plan to interfere in his monkeywrenching, since I'm on indefinite leave from BLM.*

She ran a hand through the front of her hair, pulling the thick strands back away from her face. She had no need to keep it in the bun or the tieback she often wore on duty, so she let it fly loose in the wind. She had hardly a care in the world, as long as she looked through the window of her life with a narrow screen, only allowing a certain amount of light in.

Like her time with these dogs. She broke into a run, calling them to follow her. "Come on Rose, Guildy...Pete?" She didn't see Ophelia anywhere, but she could always come out the dog door if she wanted to join them. "Everyone, let's roll!"

Caryn let loose, feeling each point of contact her foot had with the ground, swinging her arms to increase her speed, taking in deep breaths that invigorated her. The downhill slope added momentum as well. By the time she reached the stretch of grass at the bottom of the hill, she was traveling so fast that when Rosie cut in front of her, she had no way to avoid her. She tripped over the dog, taking a jarring landing face down on the ground, her breath knocked out of her, and her arm and side burned.

The dogs came over to her, sniffing at her and licking her face, encouraging her to get up. Ribs aching, she caught the glimpse of blood pooling on her forearm. She must have scraped herself...no.

Studying the wound, she realized that it was not a scrape of any sort, and there was no object lying near her that might have caused a vicious cut. What the hell?

A flash of light near the top of the hill in the trees caught her eye. At second glance, she recognized it as the sun reflecting off the long barrel of a rifle. The shooter aimed, fired, and some turf four feet in front of her tore off as the shot echoed in the mountain air. Her stomach went askew. *They're shooting at me? Shot me?*

Anger bubbled up inside her and it was all she could do not to launch herself from the ground and take off up the hill after him. Or her. But the shooter had the advantage here. She was in an open field at this point, and a clear target. What could she do?

She froze, knowing she made herself vulnerable by not moving, but hoping the shooter thought his job was done. "Rosie!" she whispered. "Come here!"

The dog obediently came over to her.

"Look, boy. Up there."

Caryn was able to get the dog's attention focused on the shooter, who had left the safety of the trees, standing in the open, probably trying to assess the situation. It didn't take long after that. Rosie took off in that direction, baying loudly, his brother on his heels. Pete hung around her spot on the ground, seemingly concerned when she didn't get up.

Caryn "played dead" for several long moments, waiting to see if the dogs took the guy down, but he vanished back into cover as soon as the dogs launched themselves.

Her arm still bled into the grass. She didn't even have a sleeve to tear off to wrap it with. She'd have to get back up to the house before long. *It better be safe...*

She pushed herself upright, hesitating and listening another moment. The dogs still barked as they pursued their quarry deeper into the forest. *Now or never.* Holding her wrist against her stomach, pressing it inward with the other hand to try to stanch the bleeding, she ran back up the hill, not making it a straight line, but weaving side to side, just in case someone else thought they'd try to finish the job.

Stumbling as she reached the outer edge of the parking area in the side yard, she paused when she saw movement. Someone was coming around the corner of the house. Levi's truck was still gone, so she knew it wasn't him. As the person came into clear sight, Caryn was startled to realize they wore traditional Native

American gear, right down to the beaded headband. She made a stumbling dash for the deck, and the man saw her. He started for her, but Pete headed straight for the man. Caryn took the final step and leaped up onto the deck, and the person stopped just short of actually following her.

In a frozen moment when they were less than ten feet apart, they stared at each other. The intruder wasn't a man at all, but a woman wearing a men's costume, with a black wig of braided hair, and the most startling blue eyes. The incongruent detail stole Caryn's attention and fixed in her memory before she grabbed the handle of the sliding glass door and the woman bolted for the gate, dog on her heels.

Her blood-slippery fingers slid the glass door open, then closed, tapping the lock home. She yanked the curtains closed and headed for the bathroom. Halfway there she heard her phone ringing and ringing, but she didn't stop to answer it.

Instead she ducked in the room, digging in the closet for first aid supplies. She didn't close the bathroom door—yet—so she could hear if anyone tried to break in or if the dogs had returned. Her little tank top was drenched in blood. The sight of it made her dizzy, but she slapped her other hand into the wall, the sting helping to get herself focused once again.

After a quick rinse under the faucet, she laid several thick gauze pads over the wound with her right hand, dropping them on carefully, before she wrapped them tight with a single roll of gauze tape around and around her arm, pulling the end tight with her teeth.

A quick glance around the room revealed few potential weapons short of hand-held razor blades. *Not exactly my weapon of choice.* Her handgun was just around the corner in the bedroom, however. No reason she couldn't snatch that up as long as she was alone in the house.

She kicked off her shoes and stood close to the door, listening. Nothing. She couldn't even hear the dogs barking anymore. Perhaps they'd chased the shooter up into the resorts above. *Damn. Then he'll blend in with the tourists and we'll never find him.*

Silently counting to three, on the third number she launched herself around the corner for the bedroom, where she pulled her gun from the bureau drawer, checking its ammunition, wincing as her movement pulled at her makeshift bandage. Just having it in her hand made her feel better. She inched back out into the hall, her back against the wall as she made her way out to the living room, her gun pointed forward, checking to make sure as she went that no one got past her.

No one was in the kitchen or the living room. She glanced up the staircase, pain making her reluctant to climb up there to see if someone was hiding. *But that's the only way you'll know for sure.*

She made sure the front door was locked before she made the trip. At the foot of the steps, she had her foot on the first one when she detected movement upstairs. Lowering herself into a crouch to make a smaller target, she took one more step, then the next, before she heard the tap-tapping of dogs' claws on a wooden floor. Ophelia came into sight, a small bark escaping when she first spotted Caryn on the stairs, but then the pointer dissolved into a full-scale welcoming wiggle, complete with tail.

"Hey, girl," Caryn said softly, giving the dog a

quick scratch. Now that she knew Ophelia was up and around, there was no question that if a stranger had been in any of the second-floor spaces, she would have made a fuss long before. So maybe they were okay.

She sank down on the step, giving herself permission to catch her breath, at least for a moment. A faint tinge of pink leaked through the gauze. She'd have to make another wrapping soon if—

The front door latch rattled, then a key dug into the lock. A moment later, the tumblers rolled and the door opened. Caryn still held her gun, but her gut told her it was fine.

Levi burst through the open door. "What the hell is going on here? I've been calling for twenty minutes." He took a look around, then his gaze fell on her bloody shirt and arm. "What's that?" He knelt down on the steps next to her, taking her wrist gently in hand. "Who did this?"

"Good question."

"Let me see it."

"I took care of it already."

"Dr. Levi will determine whether you've done a good job or not. Come on."

He led her down to the bathroom again, muttering at the blood spattered all over. "I'll deal with this in a minute. Tell me what happened."

He got a washcloth with warm water and her scented soap. She would have taken it from him, but he insisted on washing the blood from her body himself. While he used his two good hands to place butterfly bandages to pull the sides of the wound together and then re-wrap her injury, she explained her walk and subsequent attack.

"I came in and locked everything up. I don't know where the boys went. Last I saw them, they were heading up into the copse of trees by the triangle rock. Pete went after the woman."

"Stay here. I'm going to check the doors."

He was gone for several minutes, during which she fussed with the bandage, trying to pull it into a place she felt more comfortable. The shirt was ruined, as was the carefree attitude she'd had before she'd taken the dogs out. Before she'd tripped over Rosie and...

What would have happened if I hadn't tripped?

The thought chilled her.

She replayed the fall in her head, remembering her half-turn, her arm reaching out for the ground? The dog? It had been up in the air. The rest was a little fuzzy. But the shooter could have been aiming to kill her.

First Trescha, now her?

Or maybe it was always me.

He returned, out of breath. "Didn't see anything. No Indians. No dogs. No anything." He frowned, studying her. "Let's get you out of that."

He maneuvered the tank top off of her arm with great care, then pulled it off over her head.

"Just throw it away," she said.

He tossed it in the wastebasket without question. "I'm sorry I wasn't here, Cara. I would have done anything to protect you."

For the first time, the shock of what happened faded a little and her eyes teared up. "It's not your fault," she whispered, her throat choked.

He quickly finished cleaning her up, then took her in his arms. "It's not yours, either."

"When's it going to stop? Not until they get me, right? Until they get both of us?"

He pulled back, holding her shoulders, looking in her eyes. "They won't get us. I promise you that. I *promise* you, Cara."

She rested her head on his shoulder, aware of her bare skin next to him. "I don't know what's stopping them. The woman on the deck wasn't the shooter, I'm sure of it. But her costume wasn't right for Kootenai. So there's something else going on here, a concerted effort to mislead. Do you really think we'll be able to avoid them all?"

In a split second, his voice changed from its soothing tone to the crack of a whip. "Come on, now. This doesn't sound like you. You're no defeatist." He stood and pulled her to her feet. "We've let *them* run this campaign long enough. Now we're going on the offensive."

"Who's this 'we' you're so brave about all of a sudden? You? And me? Against your buddies, this militia that's armed with bombs and all kinds of other weaponry?"

Her challenge lay between them, hanging in the air like stale wood smoke. She thought it would choke her, especially with the stricken expression on his face. He turned away from her, and she hesitated, wanting to reach out to him, but afraid to.

He cleared his throat. "Well, we do have the Hamlet crew."

"We—we what?"

As if in response to his statement, the two Ridgebacks skittered in through the dog door, snuffling about till they located Levi. He checked them over, but then let them go, satisfied they weren't hurt. Pete wriggled in shortly after.

"They may not be the Second Cavalry, but they're loyal. Which is more than you can say for the militia types."

Caryn was more interested in the security breach that the doggie door presented. "We have to seal that up."

He turned to see what she was talking about. "We can do that."

Realizing belatedly that she was half-naked, she headed for the bedroom Levi had given her for her own work. The first thing she did was pull the shades down. *Damn it. I don't feel safe. Anywhere.*

The thought disconcerted her deep inside. One of the most precious gifts of all her law enforcement training had been the knowledge that she could take care of herself. And now these bastards had even taken that away from her.

We're going on the offensive, he'd said.

It was a great sentiment.

Totally impractical.

Favoring her wounded arm, she found a plain black t-shirt and wiggled herself into it with only a couple of painful movements. She studied herself in the mirror, finding some grass in her hair that must have been there since she landed on the ground, and some dampness on her cheeks that she would swear was not tears.

Levi's voice came from the door. "We're not alone, you know."

She swiped at her cheeks quickly, and used her good hand to brush her hair, using a little more force than she usually did, just trying to do something for herself. "Oh? Do you have a secret army that I don't know about?"

"Army, no." He stayed outside the door, and she knew he was making a show of respecting her personal space. "But we have allies we can call on. Everyone would benefit from taking the militia down a notch."

"I'd thought the Kootenai had my back, in the beginning, but…" She thought again about the woman she'd seen. "So strange."

"What?"

She sat on the edge of the bed and patted the mattress next to her. "You might as well come in if we're having a serious discussion."

He smiled and joined her. "Now what's strange?"

"The woman in the costume. I know I've seen those eyes before."

"You said they were bright blue. No one in the tribe that you know?"

She shook her head. "Not with those eyes." Puzzling through a visual list of her acquaintances, she couldn't come up with a name. "In the Earthenkrafte group?"

Levi leaned back, his expression one of consideration.

"Frankly there aren't that many women. I think I'd remember blue eyes like that." His own eyes twinkled a bit, trying to tease her back into a state of comfort. She appreciated the effort but being shot just didn't lend itself to any flavor of jolly she could think of.

"It's not BLM, or any of the environmental agencies…or the local police…or…" She went through the staff at her hairdressers, considered the clerks at the grocery stores she frequented. The surroundings that came to her memory was her office lobby. A temp, maybe, who'd spent a week with the BLM? Who could it be?

"It'll come to you. I know your mind—it's as sharp as a razor edge." He rubbed her back gently. "What do you want to do about this on a more immediate basis? Want to go to the hospital? I may be a great field medic, but I'm no professional."

She grimaced. "Reporting bullet wounds not earned in the line of duty always generates too many questions. Honestly, I didn't think it looked that bad. Did you?"

"Bullet's not in the wound, for sure. I think you could probably use a couple of stitches, but the butterflies may work just as well. And I've got plenty of antibiotics left in the cabinet. I think we can stave off an amputation."

"Agreed."

"We could call the sheriff's office. They'd at least try to keep an extra eye out for patrols." He shrugged. "They've got a lot of territory to cover up here, but they've known my family for years."

She didn't even try to keep the sarcasm from her voice. "Yes, I'm sure they're proud of all your law-abiding terrorist acts."

A little smile crossed his lips. "You might be surprised."

His implication set in and she stared in stunned surprise. "No way. You've got sheriff's men on your team?"

"Now you know I can't say that."

"Who is it? Ira? He seems like the type to go out on a limb."

She pictured the chief sheriff's deputy. Close cut light brown hair, a dimple in his cheek, well-built in the way he filled out his uniform. She'd half-entertained a little crush on him ever since she'd arrived in Kalispell, but he'd never seemed interested. *Maybe he played for the other team...*

But thinking about him jogged her memory. She suddenly remembered when she'd seen the woman with the blue eyes. It had been that same day in the lobby of the BLM building, along with the rest of the pagan group. Ira had been called in to help keep a lid on things. Cynthia, Gunnar and Trescha were all there, too, on that day, when they'd been brought in for disturbing the peace. The woman had blonde hair, cut short and feathery, probably a hundred-dollar haircut and bleach job. Her jeans came from the Gap, not the Goodwill. Trescha had introduced them, but she couldn't remember the name.

She was a friend of Trescha's. How could she be working with the people who'd killed her?

"What is it? You've got that look."

"She's one of the Earthenkrafters. I remember seeing her with Trescha and the others."

"Wait. So one of the pagans showed up here at the same time as you were shot, but dressed as a Native American. It's not the first time, either." She told him what she'd seen after Trescha's funeral, the two men in native garb.

"Are they trying to throw suspicion on each other? And how does that play with the militia people?"

"No clue." She sighed. "Clearly this a much bigger mess than we've thought it was. The real question will be who's pulling the ultimate strings?"

Alana Lorens

And what will we do when we find them?

Chapter Twenty-Three

"You know what? Let's get out of here today."
Levi stood by the sliding door to the deck, looking out
over the lake. "We can go up to Glacier and hike at
John's Lake."

It wasn't a bad idea. Caryn realized she'd been
moping around the place for days since the intruder
shot her. She hadn't gone outside much. Fresh air
would do her good.

"Sure. Let me get changed."

"What's wrong with what you're wearing?" Levi
leered in her direction, ogling the thin peach camisole
top she wore over cut- off denim shorts, her feet bare
and comfortable.

She gave him a dirty look. "Right. Because
climbing over a bunch of heavy rocks is so much better
when you can scrape most of the skin off your body."

She pushed herself out of the chair she'd been in
for at least an hour longer than she should, then hurried
down the hall to her room. A few short minutes later,
she was more properly dressed for a summer hike, in
jeans and a University of Montana T-shirt, socks and
her hiking boots. She grabbed her sunglasses off the
table and her purse as well. "Let's go."

He hesitated. "Maybe we should take the long way
around. We want to avoid any chance that the militia
groups will be staking us out."

"If they're smart, they're hiding out. Or maybe they've left the state. That might be far enough away." She chewed her lip. "Sam's people have kept the heat on, so they may have gone to ground."

He came over to her and slipped his arm around her shoulders, giving her a squeeze. "They better not touch you again. Ever."

"Believe me, they won't." She forced a smile. "Are we ready? My feet are itching to go."

He studied her face a moment, then leaned in to kiss her. "Then let's get walking."

They went out, and he opened the truck door for her, then climbed in the driver's side. Rosie followed them to the truck, but Levi shook his head. "You stay here, boy. Guard the house, all right? Last time we went up to Glacier, you took off and it took me an hour to find you again."

The dog kept wagging his tail, clearly convinced he should come along anyway. As they pulled away, Caryn watched him in the side mirror, his enthusiasm gradually fading, and when they left the driveway, he just sat inside the gate, disappointment written in his very posture.

She couldn't help alternately scouting the sides of the road for potential assassins and scolding herself for being a paranoid fool. *You're only paranoid if they're not out to get you, right?* She pinched her leg, trying to get her focus on the escape Levi was trying to provide. *Let go, Caryn. Just be yourself.*

She laid her head back on the seat and looked out the truck window, admiring the mountainous backdrop to the vistas around her. The sky was robin's egg blue today, the white clouds lined with a narrow silver-gray undercoat that seemed to indicate there might be a shower by the end of the day. None of the mountains down here had snow on their tops any longer; she knew that probably wouldn't be the case once they got up the road. She and Levi both kept a jersey hoodie in the truck for occasions just like this, because even if it was seventy-five and beautiful down here, up on a mountain it might easily be twenty or even forty degrees colder. One of the first day trips she'd taken this summer had been a chair lift ride to the top of Big Mountain, where she stood atop the Rockies, able to see for fifty miles in any direction.

Funny how I didn't even know that if I looked down the hill I would have seen Levi's house. Maybe I saw it and didn't even notice. And now I can't imagine being without it...

"You're doing it again," he said, pulling onto Highway 2.

"Doing what?"

"Brooding."

A faint curve of amusement tickled her lips. "Why, yes, I am. But it's good brooding." She told him what she'd been thinking about.

"Ah- ha." He grinned. "And if I'd looked up, I would have seen an angel descending from heaven..."

She grimaced. "Oh, brother. Get yourself some new lines."

That made him laugh, and her relax a little. "I like the lines I have, thanks. They seem to work on you."

"So you think I'm easy, huh?"

He was about to answer when her phone rang. She glanced at the small screen and saw an unfamiliar number. She nearly didn't answer it, but then she thought perhaps it could be someone with information about her sister's death. "Hello?"

"Caryn Orlane?"

A male voice, one that she didn't recognize.

"Yes. Who's this?"

"Your pagan friends are about to make a big mistake, out here by Hungry Horse Dam. The tribe won't stand for it."

"Who *is* this?" she demanded.

Levi watched her, his brow furrowed. "Cara?"

"Unless you want to see them die, you'd better come warn them to go home." Before she could ask anything else, the caller hung up, leaving a silent line.

"What the…" She growled and hit recall, but couldn't get a response.

"What is it?"

"Some man warning me that Earthenkrafte is about to be attacked out by the dam." Nervous fingers tapped the front of her phone. "I don't put anything past that Cynthia. She probably is treading on spiritual turf, but why would someone call me on this line?"

"It wasn't one of your tribal connections?"

"No. One of the rangers would have identified themselves. I mean they've complained before, but they've always been real up front about it."

"You should call that in to the police. Or Sam." He pulled the car to a stop at a red light, still watching her, his face somber.

"Why? Because the police have done so much to help me? Hell, they'd probably be just as glad to have someone take all the pagans off their plate, not only Trescha!"

She stared at the blank screen of her phone. Why

had she said that? She had no reason to think that the cops were purposely botching the investigation. *I'm just frustrated. And when I'm frustrated, the best thing I need is action.*

"Turn here," she said.

"We're not going out there."

"Turn here," she said again. "Or let me out and I'll go back and get my truck." She eyed him, setting her face to serious mode.

"Damn stubborn woman." The light changed to green. He hesitated for a long moment, then turned down the eastern road, toward the dam.

She dialed down through her phone's contact list to see if she had any of the pagans' contact information on it. The least she could do was call them and give them a heads up. She'd hoped she had at least Gunnar's number, in the event that Tresch had given it to her as an alternate contact point at one time or other, but she didn't have it. She'd had Cynthia's at one time, but she'd erased it like it was a virus.

Well, we'll just have to go out there and F2F it.

They pulled into the parking lot, which was nearly full of cars. "Jeez, they must be calling the sun god home or something," Levi said. He found a place to park near the path that led to the foot of the dam, and they both bailed out.

She took her gun from her purse and tucked it in her hoodie pocket. He paused to dig his out from under the front seat. "Just in case," he said.

Doubt there will be any 'in case' about it. Trouble, trouble, trouble. That's all there was with this group. For a band of hippie tree huggers who claimed they wanted love and peace, they certainly generated their share of disruption.

She took off down the path, the breeze carrying some sort of music up from the river ahead. The path split into two, and she gestured that Levi should take the one on the left. "Be careful," she said, pausing just long enough for a quick kiss for luck.

"I don't think we should separate. Let's both go this way, and we'll come back up the other path."

About to argue with him that she was perfectly capable of taking care of herself, she surrendered in the interest of time. "All right, whatever. Let's just hurry."

He winked and took off running down the path. She followed him, hand on her gun in her pocket. While he seemed bent on following the dirt trail, she wanted to follow the music, which she could hear now had developed into chanting.

Yeah, that was them.

The farther they continued, though, down the quarter-mile trail, past picnic tables and little natural cul-de-sacs, the music seemed to fade. She slowed down to listen a moment, to determine from which direction it came from now.

The crack of a gun going off just behind her deafened her for a moment, but she didn't feel any pain. Startled, she went to turn around, but someone grabbed her from behind, and a cold, wet cloth reeking of chloroform was held to her face. She tried to fight off the person holding her, but he was thicker than she was, and muscular. Another gunshot went off behind her. If they weren't shooting at her, who were they after?

Levi.

Did they get him?

Was he already hit? Left there bleeding? Or could

he be dead?

She struggled wildly, but it was no use. Her limbs got all loopy, her eyelids got heavy and her consciousness sank into a deep pool of nothing.

****

When she woke up, she found herself on a bed, wrists tied together. Her thoughts seemed to move through thick gelatin, but she forced herself through a quick, step-by-step assessment of her status. Someone had removed her hoodie, but otherwise she remained dressed. Nothing particularly hurt, so she guessed she hadn't been shot, but—*Levi!*

The burst of adrenaline that ran through her as she remembered the moments before she was taken helped clear the fog quickly. If they'd hurt Levi, they were obviously not averse to killing her, either.

So why hadn't they done it?

She ventured a second peek, this time more aware of her surroundings and alert for potential dangers. The walls were paneled in rough wood, some stuffed animal heads hung at odd intervals for display. Male voices came from beyond her feet, and she quickly closed her eyes and concentrated on holding still.

"So what do we do now, Alex? We got the woman, right? That's what you wanted."

"That's what I wanted."

The smug satisfaction in his tenor voice chilled her. Was this the mysterious Alex who had disappeared? Levi's dear friend? What did he want with her?

Alex continued, "Now we wait to hear from Levi. Let's hope he's smart enough to follow directions."

What? Follow directions? So he wasn't dead. Intentionally so.

A third voice, deeper, more polished. "How can you say that, Alex? You're talking about my dear brother. He's brilliant. Just ask him."

Zane? Levi's brother, involved with the militia?

The dark laughter that followed was frightening. His comment was obviously facetious—did he want Levi dead? Did Levi know? A sick feeling washed across her midsection.

Alex spoke. "The only reason I left her alive, Zane, was so we could drag Bradshaw in close enough to finish him—financially, for you, and then permanently, for the pack." A chair scraped on the floor, and something glass clinked hard against other glass. "I'd hoped going after her would be enough to discourage Levi from interfering. But you screwed that up, Randy, at the motor home. And whoever botched the attempt at the house."

"Alex, I—"

The sound of a soft slap on skin. "Don't worry, Randy boy. When you finally get him, we may have some fun with her before we sink her in the lake."

Belatedly Caryn realized the pagan call had been a set up.

I should have phoned it in to the police, just like Levi said. Gods, my instincts must be severely fried after what's happened in the last few weeks. Had the pagan group even been in the woods? The chanting could have been recorded. No wonder the sound had come and gone, moved around...*I'm such an idiot!*

She had to cling to the news that Levi wasn't dead. They expected him to come for her. Zane wanted something financial from him. The most likely choice was the Candy Cane house, and the land around it. Levi had said, though, that Zane left the area to go to school and had never come home to live. He'd never cared to.

But that didn't mean that he wasn't jealous that Levi had gotten the inheritance perhaps Zane had expected.

Footsteps approached her. She concentrated mightily on appearing unconscious.

Alex grunted. "This bitch ruined the good thing we had going, by screwing with Levi's mind. I thought he was a stronger man than that, leader of our pack. We would have shown him the way, if he'd only listened. But instead he got Ron killed, then he turned on us. He shoulda shot her that very first day. Would have saved us one hell of a lot of trouble. Now we're established here, people have houses and families here in the Valley, but we can't do our best work—the work that really needs done—under the cover of his pantywaist organization."

He spit on the floor. "Putting nails in trees. Like that's gonna do anything to take down the government that wants to oppress its people."

Damn.

The believers were always the most dangerous. Their cause meant everything, more than themselves, more than a random human life. Levi's information hadn't done enough to take them down. Not nearly enough.

And in my opinion, that jerk doesn't deserve a dog like Pete. When we finally take him down, I'm getting someone to cite him personally for animal abuse.

"How long has it been?" Zane asked.

"Two hours."

"You should have left his truck there. He could

have gotten back to the house faster."

Alex cleared his throat. "Yeah, maybe. I was more concerned about leaving traces. That's why I brought it here."

"If what you said is true, time is of the essence. The sooner I get my name on that property, the sooner we both start making money."

"It'll be fine. The logging company is waiting on the final permits. We have time."

A brief silence followed. Then the sounds of them moving away, more clinking of glass, running water in a sink. Their voices blurred under the additional sounds, and she lost track of what they said.

Caryn took the respite to test the cord around her wrists. *Humanely tied—surprising. Not loose enough to slip out of, but perhaps with a little work...* She shifted slightly, away from the sounds the men made, hoping to hide any effort with her body.

So, they expected Levi to go home before he took whatever steps they'd instructed him to do. *That's where I need to be, then.* She took another peek, confirming they were in a cabin. Her gaze slid across the nearest wall and revealed a mirror that reflected the location of both the three men and the door. She recognized Randy from the hospital, though she didn't know why he wore native garb. *More fake Natives? They had to be trying to pin the actions on the tribe.*

Bastards.

Alex and Zane were both tall and well-built, Zane's coloring and facial structure so like Levi's, she identified him immediately. Dressed in nearly-identical jeans and flannel shirts, the men had lost interest in her for the moment, now leaning over a table, studying a computer screen.

Alex's missing computer.

She watched them, seeing no gun on the table or obviously worn on their persons. *Where is my gun? Not with me or anywhere useful, clearly. So if I'm going to escape this, I've got to make it past them and out the door. That's about a fifteen-foot space to clear to get outside.*

Then what?

Doesn't matter if I don't get that far.

She slowly tested her legs, assuring she had full strength and that they were not hobbled in any way, watching the men in the mirror to make sure they were still occupied. Randy seemed agitated, which irritated Zane. Alex put an arm around Randy's shoulders and led him out of Caryn's view.

Now or never.

She rolled off the bed on the side closest to the door, using her bound hands to push herself upright. Zane, seated at the computer, rose to his feet, but that's all she took time to see. She sprinted for the door, then yanked it open. Before her lay a graveled driveway with four pickup trucks—one of them Levi's. Yelling behind her spurred her on, and she dashed for his truck, weaving a little across the short grass of the lawn to make herself a less viable target.

Bullets flew past her, the echo of the ricochet coming back at her from the pine forest that surrounded the small cabin. She fumbled with the driver's door of Levi's pickup, but managed to get it open. A bullet shattered the driver's side window, spraying her face with bits of glass. She pulled herself up into the driver's seat, finding the keys in the ignition. Thanking any gods she'd ever heard of—up to and including Trescha's pagan deities—she kept her head down and awkwardly turned the key.

The engine roared to life and she floored the gas pedal. The truck jumped forward, slamming the driver's side door closed, and she skidded in the gravel before she got control of the wheel. But luck was on her side as bullets pinged on the car, never quite managing to hit her. She drove like a madwoman down the driveway, ramming straight through the wooden gate at the main road.

A glance in the rear-view mirror showed her own face bloodied, but no vehicles yet in pursuit. Good enough. The first stoplight she came to was surrounded by an open, sloping valley. She glanced from one side to the other and finally chose right. She sped off along the road, no phone, no gun, still tied up, and not sure where she was. But she knew where she needed to be.

At the Candy Cane house. With Levi.

Chapter Twenty-Four

Levi woke up sweating. The sun burned down on him, and he lay in grass that tickled his nose. He rubbed his face, then pushed himself up to a sitting position. He was alone, and dizzy as hell. No dogs, no truck—no Caryn.

What the…?

"Caryn?"

He stood, surveying the road behind him. "Caryn?" he called again. *Where had she gone?*

His thoughts coming together at last, adrenaline firing the neurons, he remembered the sound of gunfire…several men in native garb…they'd…

They'd grabbed Caryn!

Had she been right all along, and this was something to do with the Kootenai? He found it hard to believe that was the case, even if the call diverting them here had allegedly been about Earthenkrafte.

He looked himself over, expecting to find bullet wounds or some indication of why he was still here. No injuries, but he came across a small dart in his upper left arm, the kind rangers used to take down predatory wolves.

"What the—?"

He pulled it out, hurt and then furious. They'd taken Caryn. They'd left him here. Alive. He had no idea where to begin. Who were "they"? What did they want? Why the hell—

His phone rang.

The ringtone was the one he'd assigned to his brother Zane, an old country song finding it "Hard to Be Humble." Zane had played it incessantly as a young teen, always thinking himself too good for the life his family led.

Figures Zane would call at one of my worst moments, ever.

Not wanting to get into a discussion of his current circumstances, Levi left his phone in his jeans pocket and marched back along the path toward the parking lot where he'd left his truck. His thoughts remained a bit foggy from the sedative, and he knew walking would help clear his head.

A beep came, indicating a voicemail had been left.

Fine. At least I'll have some entertainment while I'm walking.

He queued up his voicemail and put the message on speaker.

"Still dreaming, Sleeping Beauty? You're wasting time."

Levi went still as the speaker took a deep breath.

"I'm done playing games, brother of mine. We've got to keep that property in the family, and on the right side of the law. I've sent a messenger to the house to leave you some documents to sign—a deed, assignment of mortgage, all the usual. Once you have signed them all, you can contact me. I can make arrangements to give you your, ah, 'payment'. I'm sure you know what I'm talking about. Don't wait too long—you might push past her expiration date."

The subtle threats registered, one by one. Some of

what Zane had said rang true. If he really meant he was worried that the property would be seized by the government...

That's not what he meant.

You know it.

Son of a bitch.

The rush of adrenaline mixed with rage. Zane had walked away from the home place and washed his hands of it in search of his legal career. Or so Levi had thought. Perhaps there had been a lot more resentment. Enough to kill for.

He began to run, headed down the path for the parking lot. He'd jump in the truck and head home straight away and—

The truck wasn't where he'd left it.

"What the hell?" he muttered. He walked up and down the row, making sure his racing thoughts hadn't made him miss it. No, it was gone.

Whoever had taken Caryn must have taken the truck as well. How was he supposed to get home to do Zane's bidding—even if he had intended to?

At least he had his phone. But who to call? Alex was missing, the rest of the group untrustworthy, and the BLM would just as soon arrest him as look for their disgraced officer.

I can't leave Caryn at their mercy.

Although it had been implied that Levi should do this on his own, Zane could hardly blame Levi for reaching out, since he'd had the truck spirited away. He dialed the sheriff's office and asked for John Folden, who'd been so kind to Caryn at the scene of her sister's death. The gruff old man had known Levi since he was a boy—even despite his current "untouchable" status, surely he'd help Levi under these desperate circumstances.

"Folden," barked the voice at the other end of the connection.

"Sheriff, good to hear your voice. This is Levi Bradshaw. I've got a bit of a problem, and I thought you could help."

Levi explained that his truck had been stolen, along with his girlfriend, and some of the circumstances surrounding the attack.

"This related to what happened to Caryn's sister?"

"It may be."

Folden hemmed a moment, then cleared his throat. "Think I'll handle this myself. Where are you again?"

Levi told him, then settled in on a broken pine stump to wait for a ride.

Zane's audacity burned him. Zane hadn't been the one sitting by each of their parents' side, wiping their worn faces, feeding them soup. He hadn't contributed to a damn thing. The more Levi brooded about it, the more it seemed to him that this was an out and out power grab. Zane, with his usual lawyerly detachment, perceived an opportunity to have Levi's cake and steal it too. *Poor little brother, who can't manage his own life worth a damn...*

After what seemed like hours, Folden pulled up in his battered county SUV, then rolled down the passenger window. "You know I should charge Uber rates," he drawled. "C'mon, let's go."

Levi climbed into the passenger side and fastened his seat belt. He'd heard legendary, frightening tales of the sheriff's driving skills, which bordered on the extreme.

"Thanks. I appreciate—"

"Cut to the chase, son. Are you all right? Who the hell knows what they shot you up with. Do you need to go to the hospital?"

"I don't think so. Zane made it clear he wanted me to do some things for him. He wouldn't want me impaired." Levi sighed. "I never thought he'd hook up with the militia, just on principle. I mean, those people are violent, and—"

Folden gave a dry laugh. "You mean he'd have to get his hands dirty? Yeah, I remember your brother. Mr. Prissypants. Always thought he was better than all of us who were invested in the land." He took the road out of the lot heading toward Whitefish. "Besides, you can't paint the militia with a single brush. It's made up of all kinds, Libertarians, right-wing, left-wing, both wings, professors and professional trail guides."

He frowned. "As long as they were meeting out there on their own and making plans, I didn't have a beef with them. Just like you and your people."

Levi shot him a sidewise glance.

"Don't you think I know about your pinning the trees before the corporate cuts?" the sheriff asked.

"You never said anything."

"No." His gaze on the road, Folden shifted uncomfortably in his seat. "Can't say I'm unsympathetic. Seems to me we're losing more of nature's beauty every year, sacrificing it to the almighty dollar. I'm in a place where I can claim lack of manpower or even lack of jurisdiction. Once you came to the attention of the BLM, that's over my head." He smirked. "And you walked right into it, didn't you?"

Levi shrugged. "Whatever I may have started out

doing, my priorities are different now."

"As they should be." Folden took the next turn north, much too fast, and cleared his throat again. "So, Caryn. You said they've got her?"

"She was gone when I woke up. And Zane's message…here, let me play it for you."

He put the phone on speaker and replayed the voicemail.

"Zane's smart enough not to say the words, damn him. But I think it's clear."

Folden nodded. "Sounds reasonable. Any idea where they might have her?"

"Hell, it could be one of a hundred places. Depends who took her, exactly. Zane doesn't have another place out here as far as I know, so it's got to be one of the other guys."

"But they're planning on meeting you back at your place."

"They're planning on me being there anyway. With "documents," whatever that means."

"Did you call anyone at the BLM?"

Levi snorted derisively. "After they put her on suspension for associating with me, I'm sure they'd just write it off as she got what she deserved. Lying down with dogs, or whatever."

A vision crossed his mind of her wrestling with the dogs in front of the fireplace, and a ghost of a smile came to him. *There were worse things than being with his dogs…*

"She's a good officer, Levi. I'm sure it killed Sam Evans to pull her badge. Can't blame him, of course, as long as you're still wrapped up with the militia. But…I'd hire her in a minute. Even after this. Because I know her. And I know you."

Levi scowled. "Doesn't make me feel better for the way they treated her. Right now, all I want to do is get my hands on my brother."

"Let's hope you get your chance."

Folden chuckled and continued back to Whitefish, picking up his radio mic halfway there to order a full complement of whoever was available in the department to join them at Levi's place.

"There may be snipers out there, Nan," he told the dispatcher. "Tell the boys to be careful."

She agreed to pass on the message, and Folden turned to Levi.

"I take it you don't want to sign over the property."

"What? Why would I—?"

The sheriff raised a hand. "Just asking. I didn't think you would. So, we've got to lure Zane in close enough to pick him up, with as many of the other miscreants as possible."

Levi nodded.

"And then we have to meet him somewhere with the paperwork, is that right?"

"That's what he said."

Levi's insides still burned with fury that Zane would dare—would *dare*—to threaten Caryn just to get to Levi. Zane had no right to this land. He was just taking advantage of Levi's conscientious choice to stand up for the old forests. *But it was a long way from causing a little mischief for tree harvesters to kidnapping and murder.*

They arrived at the house. Levi jumped out and opened the gate long enough for the sheriff to drive his vehicle inside. He closed it behind them to contain the dogs, who came running, barking wildly at the strange truck. Levi called them aside, trying to calm them so he could get in the house. He took the dogs in, and Folden waited outside.

Sure enough, on his kitchen table was a thick packet of papers in a manila envelope that bore his name. Levi opened the packet carefully, thinking that would just be a perfect Rannell trick, since they were so in love with explosives at the moment, to wire an explosive to Zane's documents.

But what was inside was much more straightforward: a deed transferring title of the property and a notice to quit the premises within ten days after signature.

You've picked the wrong patsy, Zane.

The dogs barked again, and Levi heard the crunch of tires in the driveway. A peek out the window revealed two more sheriff's cars, one of them driven by that guy Mike who always had his eyes on Caryn. Since it seemed like things would be getting exciting, Levi took all four dogs into the den and closed the door. No need for anyone to get bit in the heat of the moment.

Wondering for a moment whether Zane had eyes on him, either by a nannycam—though he hadn't noticed an obvious camera anywhere—or through binoculars, Levi made a big show of reading over the papers, writing "Go to hell" on the lines where he was supposed to sign. He shoved them back into the envelope and called Zane's number.

He didn't wait for Zane to speak when the line opened.

"What's this really about, big brother? Just what it seems? You want a land grab? After you walked away from our parents in their hour of need?"

Zane laughed, that cool, unperturbed sarcastic laugh that had always burned Levi as a child. "Poor Levi. You still think the world is fair."

Levi growled. "The world is what you make it."

A snort. "Do you have my papers? I'd really like to get them recorded as soon as possible. "

"Where's Caryn?"

"She's safe." Some muffled voices behind him, male. "Watch out!" A squeal of tires.

What was Zane up to? Clearly something was not in line with his calm statements. Levi listened closely, trying to catch other clues. "Where the hell are you? She'd better be untouched, you—"

"Meet me at Montana Coffee Traders. Alone." Zane's voice had tightened. "Half an hour, Levi. You've got half an hour."

"Yeah, I'll be there."

Levi tapped the phone screen, frustrated he hadn't learned much other than what he already knew. What was the big rush to make this happen? Sure, Levi had left himself open to blackmail or prosecution with the monkeywrenching, but he'd been doing that for several years. Something must have changed.

Regardless, he had half an hour. *Better get moving.*

He grabbed the envelope and stalked out to the porch.

"You set up the meet?" Folden asked. Four men waited with him, two in full uniform and two apparently called in from home.

"Yeah. Outside the Coffee Traders. I'm supposed to come alone." He gave a dry laugh. "Not sure how I'm supposed to do that. Ride my lawn tractor into town?"

"Got you covered." The sheriff gestured to his blond second-in-command. "Ira volunteered to come after he picked up his kids from school. He's got the silver Jimmy there." He turned to Mike. "You don't mind riding with me, do you, son?"

Mike made a face and the other deputies chuckled.

"Whatever," he said. "Let's nail these sons of bitches."

"Damn straight."

Levi's mind still clicked through possibilities. "What if he's trying to get me away from the house, so he can…I don't know. Do something here?"

Ira shrugged. "Wouldn't they have been just as well to come while they knew you were unconscious and couldn't stop them?"

"I guess. But—" He couldn't let go of it, though.

"I'll leave one of my guys. Ira?" Folden gestured to him. "Pull Mike's car out of sight somewhere and keep watch."

A hint of a scowl passed over Ira's face, but he straightened and nodded. "Sure thing."

"Anything else?" Folden asked.

"No, that's it." Levi held out his hand for Ira's keys, then they all loaded up for the hunt.

Chapter Twenty-Five

Certain that the militia men would follow her as soon as they recovered, Caryn barreled down the highway, looking for some identifying sign. *With any luck, I'm still in the Kalispell area. Though as far as that goes, I could even be in Canada. Never asked a Mountie for help. That could be an interesting experience.*

The mental picture of a cartoon Dudley Do-Right zipped through her thoughts, but she didn't smile in response. Things were deadly serious. If their plans involved dumping her in the lake, they wouldn't hesitate to put a bullet in her when they caught up. She kept taking anxious glances in the rear-view mirror, wishing she'd taken better note of what kind of vehicles had been parked in the cabin's drive.

Without her phone, it was impossible to get a GPS location. Levi's truck didn't have one built in. She scanned the sky to see if she could get a reading from the sun's location. They'd left Levi's house about ten in the morning, then had driven half an hour or so north toward Glacier National Park. She had no idea how long she'd been unconscious, but she guessed it hadn't been overnight. The sun was at a forty-five-degree angle, to the right of the road, so she was headed south.

It felt right.

She finally spied a sign for the Cripple Creek

Horse Ranch that indicated she had two miles to go. Relief flooded over her. The Ranch was just outside Trego, which bordered Dickey Lake, which ran along Highway 93. *Christ, we were nearly to Canada! Okay, okay, don't panic. The highway will get me to Whitefish, but not for at least forty minutes. Thirty if I really haul ass. Which I intend to do.*

Her mirror reflected trucks behind her in the distance. She didn't know if they belonged to Zane, Alex, the younger Rannell brother or oblivious, happy tourists. It didn't matter. She couldn't let them catch up.

Her tires squealed around the corner at Trego Road, and she floored the gas pedal, hoping to make the highway as quickly as possible. A lot more people drove on 93, the main road in the county, and she had to believe those chasing her wouldn't cause an incident out in the open. If she got caught speeding, at least she'd have a law enforcement officer at hand.

How far up 93 was the lake again? She tried to picture a map in her mind. Had to be at least twenty miles. The most important objective was getting to Levi's place before he did whatever it was Zane wanted him to.

Her driving slipped into something like autopilot as she rounded the curves, then found the on ramp to the highway. Fairly heavy traffic, including logging trucks and other semis—should be easy to lose them for now.

She was more focused on reconstructing the conversation she'd overheard. She'd never met Zane or Alex, so it was hard for her to interpret any hidden meanings in their tones, but they had clearly discussed the potential to make money from the property. Selling it could—

She swerved to pull in from of a semi, making it harder for someone driving behind to spot her. Studying the truck in front of her, stacked with thick cut logs, she remembered.

The logging company is waiting on the final permits.

That's what Alex had said.

Zane intended to log the family property. That would destroy Levi, after all he'd done to protect the old forests all around the county. Surely he'd refuse, unless he felt he had no other choice.

And now he could refuse, because I'm safe. As long as I get there in time.

She thought back to the conversation again, this time what Alex and Randy had exchanged. Randy being militia, and the brother of the now-dead Ron, who'd blown himself up the day they tried to get Levi, had definitely seemed like low man on the totem pole. Alex had castigated him for what? Botching previous attacks. The first one he'd mentioned was...

The motor home.

As the punch of his meaning caught up with her in real time, her foot slipped off the gas pedal and she tensed up.

Randy Rannell had killed Trescha.

A car beeped behind her, and she pulled herself together, speeding up to blend with the flow of traffic again.

Randy killed my sister.

The realization couldn't be a surprise; it was what they had suspected all along, that it was a militia hit. But just hearing it from them in their own words was hard, and brought that pain crashing in again.

My sister asked me for a little help, and I got her killed.

The confession had removed her last excuse, her last chance to leave that guilt on someone else's doorstep. It hadn't been random, and it hadn't been because of anything involved with Trescha.

It should have been me.

This isn't the time. I've got to focus.

But as soon as I can stop, I'm going after him.

Trying to set this revelation aside, she concentrated on getting to Levi's as quickly as she could. Gradually, she worked the rope free, twisting her wrists back and forth until it loosened enough to get a finger inside the loops. At last, she was unbound.

She maneuvered around the larger vehicles, always checking her rear-view mirror when she crossed into another lane. After her panicked dash, she'd remembered that at least one of the trucks had been red, another, tan. She couldn't picture the third. It could be next to her. No way to know.

She saw vehicles of similar color, but so far behind she couldn't identify the drivers. She just had to drive on.

Just outside Olney, she came up on a Montana State patrol car and inserted her vehicle into traffic just behind it. *Even if they catch up with me now, they won't try anything. Surely they're not that foolish.*

Feeling a little relieved, she followed the officer all the way to the Whitefish turn-off, then she sped through town toward Big Mountain, only slowing when she approached Levi's gate.

The gate was closed, but no one was there. She paused, engine idling, trying to decide her next steps.

No Levi, no dogs...*am I too late?*

If he'd been here, maybe he'd left her a message.

With a sigh, she put the truck in park and got out to open the gate. Still no dogs. *Strange.* She drove in and locked the gate behind her, saving one long, anxious glance down the road for pursuers.

She pulled the truck around to the far side of the garage, where it would be less likely to be seen from the road, then got out slowly, listening. *There.* The dogs were barking, inside the house. Since they hadn't come out the dog door onto the deck, they must be closed in somewhere. Who would have done that? Why?

Feeling naked without her gun, she inched along the back side of the garage, scanning the yard for intruders. She saw no one. Adrenaline firing her effort, she sprinted for the kitchen door. Surprised that the handle turned in her hand, she yanked it open and ducked inside, locking it. The kitchen echoed with the dogs' woofing and growling. She turned toward the den to check on them and encountered a man with a gun in the hallway, Caryn right in his sights.

She lunged for a kitchen chair, lifting and swinging it at him in a single move, only realizing he was calling her name when it was already in mid-air.

"Orlane! It's me! Ooooofff" The chair hit him square across the thighs and knocked him from his feet, and he dropped the gun.

Her eyes narrowed and she studied the face, belatedly recognizing him.

"Ira? Damn, I'm sorry. What are you doing here? Where's Levi?"

She walked over and gave him a hand up, regretting the limp he now displayed.

"He went downtown to meet his brother. Something about paperwork." Ira winced and tested his injured knee.

"No, he can't do that! Zane wants to sell the place to loggers. He can't give him the deed."

"He what? What a bastard. Hang on."

Ira picked up his gun and put it on the counter, then took out his phone and dialed.

"Chief? Ira here. Look, Orlane just showed up here at the house. She's alone. She says Levi shouldn't give his brother the papers. Something about logging on the property—yeah, I don't know. But she's here, and she's safe. So… Right. Gotcha."

He tucked the phone back in his pocket. "The chief's going to get Levi and the rest of the deputies back here." He studied her a long moment. "You are all right, aren't you? Sorry I didn't ask."

She allowed a smile, still trying to catch up with the program. "Yeah, I'm fine. Thanks."

"Good." Ira looked around, his gaze going to the door of the den, where the yipping had gotten more intense, along with the heavy scratch of claws trying to get through the wood. "Should we let them out? Levi stuck them in there."

"He must have had a reason." Caryn paced, thinking. "I imagine Levi will come back here. Who's with him?"

Ira brought her up to date on what had happened. So she did her best to return the favor and briefly shared what she knew about Zane and Alex's plan. "I suppose they'll be along, too, then, if they want the paperwork. Alex said they had to conclude the transactions quickly."

."Holy…" Ira shook his head.

"That's not all. They confessed to killing my sister."

"Which one did?"

"Well, Alex Sullivan said Randy had done it. Randy was apologetic, the bastard. Not to *me*. To Alex, for killing the wrong woman."

Caryn couldn't believe she could say the words so calmly, as if she were talking about some stranger, not her own death. But there was no time now to deal with her anger and desire for justice and revenge.

The time would come.

"Damn it, Caryn, I'm sorry. I didn't know her well, but your sister seemed nice enough."

Caryn nodded slowly.

"Let's just do this right, okay? We need a good, solid bust in order to set all these charges against the guilty parties."

"You got it." He took a deep breath and surveyed the room. "Sounds like it could get interesting here pretty fast. Do we have any other weapons?"

Caryn had a few ideas, and she hoped they had enough time. "Let's see what we can find."

Chapter Twenty-Six

Levi sat in Ira's truck at the south end of the restaurant parking lot, shoulders slouched and head spinning. He'd much rather have done this at home, on his own ground, but Zane, for the moment, had the stronger hand.

If Zane had hurt Caryn...

Then he remembered the commotion he'd overheard in their brief phone conversation. Perhaps it wasn't Caryn he needed to worry about.

That thought was worth a little smile. *I can only hope.*

He wasn't sure where the men from the sheriff's office waited. Somewhere out of view of the north side of the lot, presumably.

Waiting, waiting, waiting.

Tired of feeling defeated, he called Zane. He had an answer on the second ring.

"Ready to do this, Conall?" Zane drawled.

That brought Levi up short. Conall was his secret name, known to only the monkeywrenchers who accessed their online bulletin board. How did Zane know it? Either someone had been talking when they shouldn't have, or he'd been lurking all along. *A betrayal either way.*

"Let's get it over with."

Levi grabbed the envelope and jumped out of the

truck. He studied the vehicles at the far end and spotted a hand waving to him out of the passenger window of a red pickup. Alex Sullivan's red pickup. His forward progress stopped.

What was Zane doing with Alex?

Where had Alex been?

What the hell was going on?

"Alex?" he asked, unable to help himself.

"Oh, you mean my new business partner?" Zane was unbearably smug. "Seems that Alex has been making some connections around and about your little criminal venture. Come on over and we'll tell you all about them."

Stunned, Levi stumbled through the parking lot, unable to grasp what he was hearing. He wanted answers. He wanted them now. Here, he'd been so worried about Alex's disappearance, sure something bad had happened to him, and yet...now he was Zane's 'business partner'? He eyed the truck, seeing only two people in it. If Zane and Alex were here, where was Caryn?

A mud-covered Jeep skidded to a stop in front of Levi, so suddenly he actually ran into it. He looked up, shocked, through the open passenger window at John Folden. The sheriff barked orders dismissing his team into a handheld walkie talkie, then turned to Levi. "Get in."

"But, Zane—"

He gestured feebly with the envelope.

"Orlane's up at your house. She's safe. C'mon, son, let's get out of here."

"She's...what? Safe?" Moving like he was in a dream, Levi opened the door slowly and climbed in.

Folden hit the gas as soon as Levi's butt hit the seat. He had to grab for the door and pull it closed before he fell out. They spun gravel in a wide circle as the Jeep left the lot for the main road.

He realized belatedly he still held the phone and that Zane was screaming obscenities after them.

"That's it, little brother! Your woman's dead, you hear me! She's dead, you son of a bitch!"

Levi just stared at the screen, listening. "You're sure she's all right?" he asked the sheriff, desperately fastening his seat belt as Folden laid on the horn.

"Ira's got her there," he said. "I expect they've dug in for a fight."

Zane went on. "I need those papers and I need them today! Come back here and do this like a man!"

Levi stared another moment, then hung up on him. "He'll have to come get them. And me."

Folden chuckled. "Don't worry, son. He's not going to get you. Or her. But from a public safety point of view, I'd rather have a confrontation contained at your place rather than here in town. We're leading them straight there."

The consequences of a potential gun battle at his home alarmed him for a second, but his mental protest slipped sideways. *Caryn was safe. That's all that mattered now.*

Levi grabbed the overhead handle as Folden slid across the road, nearly sideswiping a passing vehicle. "I'm more worried about your driving! It won't matter if we get there dead!"

Folden just laughed and headed up the road toward the Candy Cane house.

Levi pulled down the visor, checking the mirror to

see if they were being followed. They were. His thoughts spilled over from one scenario to another, wondering if they'd make it back to his house safely, whether Ira and Caryn were ready for what was coming, and of course, the nagging betrayal of Alex Sullivan. What did Zane mean that he was partners with Alex? What was it they wanted to do? Clearly it had something to do with the property…and more than just some inflated worry over a RICO action by the government.

What was going on?

But Caryn was safe.

"Can I radio the house?" Levi asked.

"Sure. We'll be there in ten minutes."

Levi picked up the mic and pressed the button. "Ira? It's Levi. Come in? Over."

Folden snickered at Levi's technique but didn't correct him.

"This is Ira."

"Can you put Caryn on?"

"Ah, sure. Hang on." A moment later, Caryn's voice came on the radio, scratchy and stressed out, but clearly her.

"Levi?"

He sighed with relief. "So you're really there. You're safe."

"Yeah, but I expect we'll have trouble here any time. Where are you?"

"We're on the way. We should be there in ten minutes, the sheriff says. Zane's on our heels."

Caryn growled. "Look, Levi, I know he's your brother, but that man's a son of a bitch. You know what he wants? He's going to log your place. He and your buddy Alex are in bed with the militia, just hoping to make a buck here. I don't know if they're going to turn the proceeds over to the group or what, but—"

Levi's heart sank. He knew very well Zane wasn't in it for the politics. "No. He'll keep the cash. They just want rid of me."

"They were willing to kill me to achieve their objective. So screw 'em all." Her voice was bitter.

"I'm with you. Be there soon."

He hung the mic back on the unit and sighed.

"That's hard luck, son," Folden said. "The BLM and their associates are ready to take the militia down. They'll meet us up there."

That stunned Levi. "What? At my place? How did they know?"

"I called them while you were waiting in the parking lot. They're the ones with more sweeping jurisdiction, and Sam Evans already had warrants prepared, waiting for the right opportunity."

Somehow the thought of Evans with warrants didn't sit well with Levi, but he couldn't worry about that yet. A battle was about to break out. He meant for he and Caryn to survive it.

Somehow he survived Folden's driving up the hill to his driveway, where Ira had the gate open and waiting for him. Almost before Folden came to a stop, Levi slid out of the passenger seat and hit the ground running. He headed straight for the front porch, where Caryn met him at the door.

He embraced Caryn quickly, then held her back from him, looking her over. "You sure you're all right?"

"I'll get over it. No time to brood on it now. How

close were they?" She peered anxiously toward the gate. Inside the house, the dogs barked furiously

"Not far behind. But Ira said the sheriff's men got the first call, so they should have a jump ahead of them. Come on."

He pushed past her, stopping when he saw the array of firearms laid out on the kitchen table. "I guess you found everything."

She laughed, without humor. "Honestly, I'm not really down for a shootout here."

"It may not happen. Folden said he'd called BLM. They're on their way."

Her brow furrowed. "Wait, what? Why?"

He checked over the pile of ammunition while he explained Folden's thinking. "Is that bad?"

She bit her lip. "I guess we'll see."

He studied her face, admiring every treasured curve. "Whatever happens, we'll get through it, Cara."

She managed a faint smile, but he could still see every bit of dignity and confidence this experience had taken from her. She would heal with time, and so would he. They would fight for that time, for their life together, for just as long and as hard as it took.

Several cars roared into the driveway, and he snatched up a rifle. Taking a spot in the doorway, he held the weapon at his side, not wanting to make himself a target until he saw who was there. As he'd suspected, it was the rest of the sheriff's department. They drove onto the lawn and joined their boss, several hiding their vehicles out of sight, leaving plenty of space for someone to follow them.

"Well, that's it, then. All that remains is to see if Zane has the guts to come here and face me."

He turned back to her, finding her ready with her service weapon in hand. The look in her eye held no sympathy.

"They did kill Trescha," Caryn said.

Shock sucked his breath away. "W-what? For sure?"

Her jaw tightened and she looked away. Her voice lost all emotion. "Alex said so. He said they'd been trying to get rid of me to keep me from distracting you. Then he said that Randy Rannell had screwed up the first time, and the second time. That's why they did it together the third, apparently."

"So he shot you from the mountain, too?"

A red-hot flow of fury burned through Levi's body. His face flushed and his hands clenched tight. His thoughts buzzed, and it was hard to get hold of them, pull them under control. *After all I've done for them— for my friends?!—this is how they repay me? I could have lost Caryn before I ever had the chance to really know her. If I could blow them all up with their damned rocket...*

He reached for Caryn, meaning to comfort her, but she stiffened and pulled away as there came another set of crunches on the gravel of the driveway.

"They're here," she said. She marched outside.

"Caryn, wait!" Imagining a spray of gunfire heading to her or from her, he ran out after her.

Four vehicles sat between the house and the open gate: one Alex's silver pickup, a red truck Levi knew had belonged to Ron Rannell, and two other SUVs he'd seen before at monkeywrenching events.

Zane got out of the passenger side of Alex's truck, his empty hands held up. "I don't want this to get ugly,

Leev. Just give me the papers and we'll be on our way."

"Right. To go to the courthouse so you can screw me and the rest of the neighborhood over by selling the place to loggers!" Levi growled, his anger ready to burst out like plasma tongues from the sun's surface. "You've got some big brass ones, I'll have to give you that."

Caryn stepped to the edge of the porch, gun in hand at her side.

"Like hell he does. He's a damned coward. He hires all these minions to do his dirty work. He's too good to get filth on his own hands."

Zane glared at her, in a way that brought back memories from Levi's childhood. That was always the look that preceded Zane's striking out to hurt whoever had frustrated him, whoever got in the way of what he wanted. Levi had to get her out of a potential line of fire.

"You want the papers, Zane, come get them!"

Levi waited to make sure his brother had heard, then he grabbed Caryn's gun arm and dragged her back inside the house. She fought him, ready to face those who had brought them harm, but Levi preferred to control the situation his own way.

"Let me go!"

"Come on. We can get strategically positioned inside. Let them come in. We'll see what happens."

She turned to glare at him. "I'll shoot them down right in your yard. I don't care!"

"I know. I know." He looked her straight in the eye. "But we've got observers, remember? Let's give them what they need to see."

She rolled her eyes. For a moment, he thought she

would run back outside in spite of his plea, but she stood her ground, watching the door.

Heavy footsteps sounded on the porch, then the door opened slowly. Zane stepped inside, hands still raised and empty. He looked at Caryn, then at Levi, a slow and tentative smile appearing on his face.

As if I'd forget all that's gone before this? I'm not five years old any more. I've got an attention span now. And I certainly don't have the same hero worship I had then. You're no one's hero at all.

"All I want are the papers, Levi. Any other trouble is between you and the troops. I can try to negotiate a truce—for Miss Orlane's sake."

He gestured broadly, then scanned the room for the envelope, which sat behind Levi on the kitchen bar.

"I can negotiate with your buddies myself," Caryn snapped. She raised her gun and pointed it right at Zane. "I could start with you."

Levi stepped forward, one hand out to do…he didn't know what. Stop her? It was the last thing he wanted. But it didn't matter. When the gun barrel came up, the door burst open. Alex and several others burst in, guns in hand.

"Drop it!" Alex yelled.

"You drop it, cowboy," Caryn said. Her barrel swung left and right, including all those who had just entered.

Levi's heart pounded in his ears. The room was overcrowded now. If bullets started flying, it was likely they'd all be hit, one way or another. The dogs continued to bark in the den. That gave him his next step. If he wanted Caryn out of their line of fire, then he'd have to give them something better to shoot at. He snatched the envelope from the table and ran for the den. He threw the door open and ducked inside.

The Ridgebacks barreled out past him into the kitchen, their claws digging into the floor in a frantic attempt to protect their humans. Each launched himself at a militia member, planting their paws on the men's chests, knocking them to the floor. Several shots rang out, making Levi sick to his stomach as he wondered whether someone had shot his beloved animals. He'd started on this course now, he had to see it through. He retreated further into the den, hoping to draw Zane and Alex in after him. The others would be expecting orders—without their bosses handy, their reactions might be slower.

Why didn't the sheriff and his men come in, now that shots had been fired?

He backed up and tripped over Niabi's cage, which lay sideways on the floor, its small gate open. The cage was empty. He looked around desperately, hoping like hell that the dogs hadn't devoured Caryn's pet in their frenzy. He caught a couple of quick movements at the base of the bookshelves, but that was Ophelia, cowering behind a chair, frightened by the noise and chaos. Pete ran out into the kitchen, barking, after the Ridgebacks.

Would Pete remember his loving owner? Would he let Alex off the hook based on past affection?

Caryn yelled, followed by a loud crash. Several more shots were fired.

Damn it, why didn't Zane come for what he wanted?

As if in answer, Zane popped through the door, closing it quickly behind him.

"You always did have to do things the hard way,

little brother. Now give me the damned papers."

"I don't think so." Levi threw the envelope into the fireplace, scrabbling in his pocket for a lighter to set the wood ablaze.

"Don't!" Zane dove for the envelope, getting his hands on it before Levi could produce a flame on the excited shaking of the lighter. A split second later, he let out a scream that chilled Levi's blood.

"Get it off, get it off!"

The envelope fell from his fingers and Levi saw Niabi attached by her teeth to the inside of Zane's wrist, blood flowing freely. Zane continued to scream in pain. He stumbled backward, the iguana clearly furious, swinging its tail left and right until it clipped Zane in the face. Levi had been the recipient of one of those tail whips, and he could verify it hurt like hell. The injuries didn't split Zane's skin open, but his cheek turned an angry red.

Zane tried to grab the iguana's body, but it wriggled and twisted out of his grip. "Do something!" he screamed.

"I'm not getting anywhere near that thing," Levi muttered.

Zane then snapped his arm away from his body, intending to fling the reptile away from him. She went, but she took with her a mouthful of flesh from Zane's hand. He yelped and clutched his bleeding hand to his chest, picking up a fireplace log with the other hand, which he waved in Levi's direction.

A burst of noise, men shouting mostly, came from the kitchen. *At least the shooting has stopped.* Levi took advantage of Zane's distraction to cross the few feet between them and plant a solid fist against Zane's jaw.

Zane, never much of a physical fighter, went down with a grunt. Careful not to bend down or get his hands close to the floor for fear Niabi was still on the attack, Levi inched around his fallen brother and reached for the door handle.

As his hand hit the metal, the door swung open, Sam Evans taking up the majority of the doorway. Sam took in the scene before him, with Zane on the floor in a pool of blood and crossed his arms.

"Levi Bradshaw, you are under arrest."

Chapter Twenty-Seven

Caryn was shocked twice when Levi left the room to go to the den—the first time that he'd abandoned her in the midst of these hostile men, and the second that she didn't feel strong enough to take them on. The past few weeks had sapped her self-confidence, despite her earlier bravado. Fortunately, when he released the frantic dogs, they commandeered the action.

The Ridgebacks took down two of the militia members Caryn didn't know, their guns going off as they fell, the rest of them ducking to avoid the ricochets around the crowded kitchen. The shots echoed in the enclosed space, making Caryn's ears ring.

Randy took off through the kitchen door, leaving it open. Caryn caught a glimpse of the sheriff's men taking him into custody. Ira glanced inside and gave her a nod before he led the militia man off.

Zane disappeared after Levi, which made sense after the fact. *That must have been his intention from the beginning. Okay. That leaves me with Alex.*

The gun in Alex's hand swung wide as his attention came around to her. She was prepared to take him down if she had to, but it was hard to grasp who was where as the Ridgebacks continued to protect their humans with teeth and claws. Two of the others managed to crawl outside, the Ridgebacks on their heels, and were quickly taken up by the sheriffs.

"You should go." She gestured to the door.

Alex laughed darkly. "You're the one who's expendable here, lady." He raised the gun.

Pete came loping out of the den, first barking, then sniffing, then leaping up to greet his master.

"Leave me alone, you moron!" Alex reacted by slamming his weapon into the dog's head, knocking him sideways. Pete yelped and stumbled into the kitchen island, whimpering.

That's it.

Caryn aimed and shot Alex in the shoulder, then moved so the island was between them. Pete lurched over behind her and laid on the floor. Alex dropped the gun with a string of curses, and started for Caryn.

"Hold it!" came the booming voice of Sam Evans from the doorway. Caryn looked up, startled to see Sam's gun pointed at her attacker, but Alex didn't stop. He came for her, grabbing her by the shoulders, his hands working up to her neck.

"You've ruined everything, bitch. You're going to pay—"

Choking as he squeezed tight, Caryn brought her gun up and cocked it.

"Drop it, Orlane. Now!"

Sam's order snapped like a whip. She let her trust in him carry her, and the gun slipped from her hand to the floor. Black spots appeared in front of her eyes, but she heard more footsteps enter the kitchen.

"Get away from her, you asshole!"

Was that quiet little Jessalyn? Caryn had to be hallucinating. Were they all here? Just as things started to fade, Robert Novio appeared in front of her, grabbing Alex by the shoulder and shoving him into the refrigerator with a heavy thud. Jessalyn came to hold Caryn's arm, leading her to a chair to sit down.

"We're going to need an ambulance," she yelled out the door.

Caryn came back to the room, nearly herself again. Sam had disappeared. "Levi?" she asked. Her throat hurt and her voice surprised her with its hoarse tone.

"I haven't seen him," Jessalyn said. "Are you okay?"

Caryn coughed. "I think so."

Novio got handcuffs on Alex, ignoring the trail of blood he left as he dragged the man outside. "Nice to see you, Orlane," he drawled on the way past.

"Yeah," was all she could manage. Her head spun a little, and she felt nauseous. "The dog?" she asked.

"Dog?" Jessalyn said. "Let me see."

She slowly released her grip on Caryn, making sure she wouldn't topple over, then knelt down beside Pete.

"Mmmm," she said. "This looks bad. Definitely needs to go to the vet."

"Okay. I'll tell Levi. Where is he?"

She looked up just as Sam came out of the den, Levi in front of him in handcuffs.

"Wait—what's going on here?" Caryn tried to get to her feet, but had to clutch the island for support. Jessalyn came quickly to her side and held her up. "This wasn't Levi's fault! His brother and Alex Sullivan engineered these attacks. Rannell killed my sister. Why are you arresting Levi?"

"Caryn, don't worry—" Levi said.

The BLM chief scowled. "He's broken the law with his monkeywrenching, and you know it. His warrant was in the stack the judge had signed. He'll have to take it up with the court."

Sam went on, his voice softening. "Besides, if he's arrested with the others, it may save him some face. Now as for you, we'll get you some medical treatment as soon as the ambulance gets here from town." To Jessalyn, he said, "There's a man down in the den. Get cuffs on him before he wakes up. Watch the blood."

"Blood? What happened?" Caryn gave Levi a quick once over, just seeing a spatter of blood across his shirt. "Did you—"

"Niabi," Levi said. "The dogs must have knocked her cage over, and she was loose. She was pretty angry. Zane won't mess with a lizard ever again." To Jessalyn, he said, "Niabi's a green iguana; keep a watch out for her."

The Ridgebacks came running back inside, sniffing and looking for bad guys. They stopped in front of Levi, waiting for him to pet and praise them for good work, but of course he couldn't. So they came around to Caryn, who idly petted them. Then they went to check out Pete, comforting him in the way of canines.

Sam handed Levi out to one of the sheriff's men. "Put him in one of your cars, not our van. Likely to be some fireworks otherwise."

Jessalyn left the room and went into the den, coming back with a handcuffed Zane, who looked quite different from the urbane, polished man Caryn had first seen at the cabin. He stared at Caryn a moment, then walked out with Jessalyn without saying a word.

Sam remained, coming over to inspect Caryn himself. He gently turned her head this way and that, frowning at the deepening bruises.

"The sheriff told me what happened today. Doesn't

surprise me, considering the kind of people we're dealing with here. You should definitely go to the hospital and get checked out."

"I've got to take the dog to the vet," she rasped.

"I'll do that, if it's okay," John Folden said from the door. "Seems like the scene's secure here." A siren sounded in the distance. "That'll be Three Rivers heading in. You need to go with them, Caryn."

"I—um, yeah, I guess." She looked at Sam. "I should go with Levi, though. In case you have questions."

Sam half-laughed. "My girl, I have plenty of questions, and I'll have them for days to come. Don't worry, you'll get your chance. Hospital. Now." He patted her on the shoulder.

"You're not my boss anymore, remember?" she asked, unable to keep the bitter note from her voice. The reality of Levi being taken from her, just when they were about to be safe from the militia, was tearing open her heart.

"I've been thinking about that. We'll talk. Next week." He shook hands with the sheriff. "John, you make sure she gets there, will you?"

"You bet."

Folden waited for Sam to leave. He and Caryn watched as all the police vehicles pulled out and down the driveway, heading into town with their prisoners. "We got them all, Caryn. You helped us get them all."

She sniffed, not feeling like much of a hero. "I've got to put away Niabi," she said.

"What?"

"My iguana. She's loose in the house."

She shuffled into the den, scanning about for a

likely hiding place. Rosie followed her in, sniffing along the floor, then suddenly froze. Sure enough, he'd located the iguana, under the couch. Caryn let the dog startle Niabi out of hiding, then she took the afghan from the back of the sofa and dropped it over the agitated iguana, making sure its head was covered to protect her from its teeth. She quickly picked it up by the midsection and shoved her back into the cage, then closed the gate.

The paramedics came into the kitchen through the door that was still open. "You got any injured in here, Sheriff?"

"Just one." He quietly explained what had transpired, and they got Caryn seated and started their routine.

She answered their questions dully, feeling herself floating on automatic pilot. She knew she should care more, that she'd had a rough time, that she'd been through some serious trauma. Tears streamed down her cheeks, but they weren't for her. All she could think about was that Levi was gone, and she didn't know if she'd ever see him again.

Epilogue

Caryn bundled up in her thick Sheriff's Department uniform jacket and her furry boots before she opened the door to the mostly-shoveled patio. The dogs bounded out into the eighteen-inch snow in the yard, crystal spray flying in their wakes, sparkling in the bright morning sun.

Her cup of coffee steamed; her breaths did, too. She made her way to the sole Adirondack chair she'd left out, and brushed the snow off onto the shoveled stones. The sky was a brilliant blue, just a few flakes blowing down from the roof, looking like diamonds glinting. It was a beautiful day, in more ways than one.

Today Levi was coming home.

He'd served six months of a two-year sentence for tree-spiking, to which he'd freely confessed. Because of his group's involvement in the death of the paramedic that had happened at Martin City, he could have faced up to ten years, but his alibi held up, and his frank discussion with federal agents had led to the convictions of Zane, Alex, Randy and several others of the militia. The federal judge had agreed to the short sentence.

Because of his unique situation, and the likelihood of his coming in contact with jailed militia members or those working for them, Levi had been able to opt into a private prison north of Butte which housed some federal prisoners. The location had at least allowed Caryn to have some visits, though the three-hour drive through the mountains had certainly become more difficult once the snow began to fall. It helped her peace of mind to know that Zane, Alex, and Randy were locked away, facing charges of kidnapping, extortion and attempted murder for what they had done to her and Levi. Randy was properly tied to Trescha's murder and got life imprisonment for it. The others were charged with the death of the man at Martin's Lake, destruction of property, and pretty much anything else the Feds and locals could hang on them. The local militia was considerably silenced.

She sipped her coffee, eyes narrowing against the glare of the bright sun on the snow. After staying alone in the Candy Cane house for the past six months, Caryn had achieved some measure of serenity. It had taken awhile to distance herself from the trauma, and she hadn't really begun until Levi left in July to serve his time. It was the time alone that had really allowed the pieces to fall into place. Some had hurt like hell; others she was just grateful to let go.

The motor home had been the last vestige of her former life to leave. She'd shoved it into the back of her mind as long as she could, but she hadn't stayed there since the shooting, though she'd continued to pay her lot rent. The park eventually sent her a letter asking her to remove the empty hulk. She went to clear out the last few things before the towing service took it away. Watching it disappear down the drive, she had to wipe away tears. It may not have been a sumptuous castle, but she and Niabi had enjoyed an interesting, independent life there.

Part of that life, of course, had been her position at the Bureau of Land Management. Sam had called her into the office, as he'd promised, to debrief her and have his questions answered. She'd been as forthcoming as she could, hoping that anything she said might help out Levi.

He'd bonded out of jail, of course, and stayed with her at home before his plea date, but he was preoccupied with the upcoming consequences. Not wanting to leave Caryn unprotected, he'd installed the cameras and other home security measures he'd been planning for months. He signed legal papers to let Caryn handle decisions about the home and property while he was away.

That, Sam told her, was the final piece of information that chose his course of action regarding Caryn's continuing at the agency.

It had been an awkward meeting. Sam cleared his throat, actually fidgeting in his big old leather chair behind his desk.

"Orlane—" He coughed and cleared his throat again. "Caryn. You've been a real asset to this office. I can't fault the work you did, prior to all this mess."

Caryn sat still, clutching her cooling coffee in her favorite office mug. She hadn't been hopeful she'd be reinstated to begin with, but Sam's leaving the door open had given her a lifeline.

"Thank you," she said quietly.

Sam patted the stack of papers on his desk. "I mean it, sincerely. But the last several weeks, you understand, they've really muddied your performance."

She set her cup on the desk. "So you're firing me."

Sam pursed his lips. "You know I could. It's been a

classic example of conflict of interest. Frankly, the people in DC have been calling for your termination since the beginning."

He paused, mostly for dramatic effect, she thought. There still seemed to be a "but" hanging in the air. She waited for the other shoe to drop. After all, if Sam really wanted to come down on her, he might have filed charges against her, part of the conspiracy net that had caught so many of the militia. She hadn't done anything to further the crimes, but she knew in her heart that her involvement with Levi during the investigation could have repercussions.

"But, sweet Jesus, Caryn. You've been through hell, kid." He sighed. "It hardly seems fair to heap punishment on top of all you've already lost."

What did that mean?

She wanted to burst out with questions and explanations, but managed to control her tongue before she ruined whatever was left for her to salvage.

Sam coughed again, then leaned forward, forearms on the desk, looking her in the eye.

"Here's what I've decided. It's the best offer I think you'll get. I'm going to extend you a three-month paid leave, because of the death of your sister, starting a week after it happened. Post-trauma stress, whatever you want to call it. That gives you another six or seven weeks, right? After that, I recommend you resign, no reason given. Considering that you're intending to pursue your relationship with Bradshaw, it seems the appropriate course of action."

The proposal stunned Caryn. He really didn't owe her anything, so this generous move made her grateful. Sam's safety net was a good outcome. She accepted on the spot, acknowledging in her heart that she'd now lost everything she'd started with—and within a week or two, she'd lose Levi as well.

But he'll be back.

Just when the money was about to run out, in a way that could hardly be coincidence, John Folden reached out to her with an offer to join the sheriff's department.

"You still have the contacts, and you know the lay of the land. It would be stupid of me to waste that," he explained. "We're finished investigating the militia, and your sister's death, so I can't see a conflict at this point."

He grinned, and his blue eyes twinkled. "At least it'll keep you close to home."

And so it had. She found the work fulfilling and it kept her busy. Sure, it still wasn't the FBI, but she felt respected and appreciated, here in this perfect winter.

She checked her watch. The man she loved would be waiting to be picked up downtown. It was time to go.

Before she could get to her truck, the dogs burst past her, barking as they ran for the gate.

Caryn stiffened, her now-usual response to potential threat since the militia incidents. A look over her shoulder revealed a man, alone, walking up the mountain road. His head was covered by the navy-blue hoodie he wore, and he carried a backpack over one shoulder.

Not wanting innocent passersby to be frightened by the dogs, she called out, "Come on, you guys, leave the poor fellow alone!"

Her gaze was drawn to the man. Something about

him… She couldn't see his face well, but it was the dogs' response that solidified her recognition.

Levi opened the gate, the dogs leaping joyfully and barking to greet him. He tried to pet them all, laughing at their enthusiasm.

When he looked up at her, though, she could see his attention was all on her. She ran down the driveway to take him in her arms. The way his arms wrapped around her and pulled her close started to make up for all the time they'd missed.

Minutes passed there, cuddled in each other's arms, as they breathed in synch, together, kissed softly, and thoroughly reconnected as quarter-sized snowflakes drifted down around them.

When they finally pulled away, the dogs demanded their own greetings, which were promptly given.

"I was on my way down to pick you up," she said, her eyes still drinking him in. *So hard to believe he was really here…*

"Can we go inside? This isn't much of a winter coat." Levi smiled, his cheeks red with cold, but his expression was weary.

"Sure." She took his hand, and they went inside, trying not to trip over the ecstatic animals. He paused just inside the threshold, taking it in.

"Glad to have you here," she said.

"Not as glad as I am to be here."

He strolled through the kitchen into the den. "Where's Niabi?"

"I moved her to a spare room upstairs—the one with the southern exposure windows. Want to see?"

"Soon." He stared into the fireplace, which was stacked with wood, ready to light.

Caryn studied him. He seemed out of his element somehow. This wasn't surprising, considering his last six months. Even in a place like the Shelby prison, the experience of being confined there had to be unsettling to the core. "Take your time," she said. "No hurry to get re-assimilated. We've got forever, now."

He didn't turn around. "I know."

Minutes passed in silence. She felt awkward, unsure what to do to help him. "Do you...need some time?"

He shrugged and shuffled his feet.

"I—ah, I have to run in to the office to do some paperwork, though," she lied. "Will you be okay by yourself?"

He did turn around then, looking a little relieved. "I hate to—I mean, I've dreamed of this moment for weeks. I just..." His face settled into a ghost of a smile. "Maybe that's best. Want me to make dinner?"

"Or I could bring something from in town?"

"No. I think it'll be good to refamiliarize myself with the place. It hasn't been that long, I know. Not in time. But in mental space."

She embraced him and held him for several long moments. "I think I understand. I'll see you later, then."

On the drive into town, she dissected his appearance, noting the new lines in his face, the few gray hairs he hadn't had before. All she wanted to do was hold him and protect him from the world. It seemed like that was the last thing he needed.

Mike looked up, surprised, as she came into the office.

"I thought Bradshaw was out today?"

She smiled, his teasing on the subject old hat by

now. "He is. I'm just giving him some space."

He snorted. "Honeymoon's over already. Wow."

She mock glared at him and went through the basket on her desk. There wasn't much in it, but it kept her busy for a couple hours. Her mind kept drifting back to the house, wondering what Levi was doing, whether he liked the small changes she'd made. *Whether he missed me.*

Finally she ran out of excuses and headed home again.

She found him on the deck off the master bedroom, sitting bundled up in a chair, staring down the yard toward the lake. With the leaves off the trees, he could actually see a bit more of the town this time of year. Winter had fully set in—it would be Christmas soon.

"Hey," she said, leaning on the door frame.

"Hey." He turned to smile at her.

"Couldn't persuade the dogs to hang out?"

He laughed. "They preferred the spot in front of the fireplace."

"I can understand that."

"Yeah. But after so long being locked inside…" He trailed off and she didn't pursue it.

Instead, he pushed himself up out of the chair and came to slip his arms around her as he maneuvered her inside and closed the door. "It is toasty in here, though. And look, there's even a bed."

She chuckled. "Why, so there is. Do you need to get warm under the covers?"

"Only if you'll come keep me warm, too."

Sure, it was a corny line. But, damned if it didn't work. She'd waited too long for them to be together again.

She unzipped her coat and dropped it at her feet. The rest of her clothing, and his, followed quickly, and soon they were indeed warm under the blankets. They took their time getting to know each other once more, and finally lay, curled together, drowsy and grateful. Her eyes closed almost of their own accord, though she fought to stay awake, to take in every second of his touch.

"I've been thinking," he whispered in her ear. "Maybe we should get married."

"What?" she whispered back, turning to face him. "I'm a sheriff's deputy, you know? What if I find you on the wrong side of the law again? Would you make me arrest my husband?"

He kissed her. "I love a woman with principles."

"I love *you,*" she said. "Married or not."

He laughed softly. "Well, you let me know when you want to make an honest man out of me. I'll be waiting."

She smiled and snuggled closer, knowing it might be a question for another day, but there was no question what her answer would be. After all she'd lost, there was no way she was losing this man who made her whole. No way.